MW00465079

WHOEVER YOU ARE, HONEY

WHOEVER YOU ARE, HONEY

A Novel

OLIVIA GATWOOD

THE DIAL PRESS

New York

Published in the United States by The Dial Press, an imprint of Random House, a division of Penguin Random House LLC, New York.

THE DIAL PRESS is a registered trademark and the colophon is a trademark of Penguin Random House LLC.

Library of Congress Cataloging-in-Publication Data
Names: Gatwood, Olivia, author.
Title: Whoever you are, honey : a novel / Olivia Gatwood.
Description: First edition. | New York : The Dial Press, 2024.
Identifiers: LCCN 2023044550 (print) | LCCN 2023044551 (ebook) |
ISBN 9780593230442 (hardback) | ISBN 9780593230459 (ebook)
Subjects: LCGFT: Novels.
Classification: LCC PS3607.A888 W56 2024 (print) | LCC PS3607.A888 (ebook) |
DDC 811/.6—dc23/eng/20231010
LC record available at https://lccn.loc.gov/2023044550
LC ebook record available at https://lccn.loc.gov/2023044551

Printed in the United States of America on acid-free paper

randomhousebooks.com

9 8 7 6 5 4 3 2 1

First Edition

Book design by Debbie Glasserman

For my mom.

I LOVE YOU, ALIVE GIRL

—Jeff Bezos in a text to his mistress

WHOEVER YOU ARE, HONEY

n the middle of the night, the stretch of sparsely occupied beachfront properties lining Potbelly Beach Road resembles a row of gapped teeth. This is what Mitty has always imagined, at least. If a sailor offshore were awake and looking out the window of his cabin, just as he was traveling through Monterey Bay, specifically along the coast of Santa Cruz, and even more specifically New Brighton State Beach, he might notice the black pockets where the empty homes sit, broken up by the warm glow of an illuminated living room, and perhaps think of a child's gummy mouth.

Over the years, a number of these houses have been sold and converted to vacation rentals and summer stays, leaving Mitty and Bethel as the last remaining permanent residents in the neighborhood. They bemoan this change, of course. In a way, as the sole locals, this protest has become their responsibility. But still, there is a small part of Mitty that takes pleasure in the surprise of these revolving tenants. When she steps out for her nighttime walks, she's exhilarated by the inability to predict which properties will be busied, which transparent evening she'll find herself watching, which not-quite-neighbor she'll get to know without ever having spoken to them.

Outside, the eucalyptus trees whisper. The sand clenches beneath her bare feet. The houses are standing on stilts, elevated at least ten feet off the ground. As she walks, the strangers go on living above her. A middle-aged couple—she assumes they're from Berkeley, they so often are—fleeing their fog-shrouded home for a weekend on a fog-shrouded beach. The woman grates at her heel with a pumice stone while the man flips through a digital catalog of films on the flatscreen, seemingly indifferent to his wife's shedding body. In the next home, a heavy-lidded young father excuses himself from the table, while a woman slips a spoon into their toddler's mouth. He stands at the kitchen sink, looking out. It seems like he's admiring the view, soaking up this brief moment of solitude. But Mitty knows from her own home that at this hour, there is no view. All you can see is your own reflection, staring right back.

The next three homes are empty; she hurries past the gap. Not being able to see what's on the other side of those silent, sulking windows has always made her jumpy. The home she shares with Bethel is the last one on the lot, the final outpost of life before the sand disappears and erupts into jagged cliffs, making their oafish dwelling feel like a refuge. Even from afar, she can see Bethel in the window as she dries their dinner plates. Her hair is the color of oysters, eyes wide like a tree frog, frail forearms doused in sunspots that travel all the way down her lanky piano fingers. Behind her, the kitchen is baubled with apricot paisley wallpaper pinned in the center of the ceiling by a plastic chandelier.

Mitty pauses just shy of their lot and stares up at the house next door, a vast and geometric structure; so much glass that it almost appears to have no walls. She and Bethel have taken to calling it "the dollhouse," joking that it looks as though a child could reach right in and rearrange the furniture. But for the last five years, the house has remained empty. So empty, that Mitty had almost forgotten it was once like theirs, wood-paneled and lopsided. It had been owned by a pair of eccentric professors who were shipped off to a nursing home by their children. She misses watching the old couple carry their long dinner table down to the beach where graying lefties and university types would later gather around it, drinking and arguing, late into the night. She misses their persistent invitations to join, shouting up at Bethel's open windows. She misses leaving the French doors on her balcony ajar and falling asleep to the sound of their voices, the fizzy ricochet of laughter that went on till dawn.

When they left, the house was promptly bulldozed, and in its place came men in suits and hardhats, gesturing to imaginary rooms and shouting out square footage. Mitty and Bethel watched the dollhouse materialize from the front seat of their living room, cursing each new wall of glass delivered to the worksite, gawking in horror as the cement truck filled the walkway with gray batter. But this wasn't a flip like the other houses farther down the beach, some hurried renovation to be rented for five hundred a night. Whatever faceless developer was behind the dollhouse was building a full-time residence, a forever home, preparing for the coming tech exodus from San Francisco. There it had sat, empty and on the market for half a decade. A glass slipper waiting for the perfect foot. Until now.

Mitty saw the moving trucks arrive that morning as she

was getting ready to leave for work. She briefly considered hanging around to see what she could glean about her new neighbors based on their possessions. But she chose, instead, to wait and observe from the discreet bunker of this dark beach, when she knew the furniture will have already been unloaded and arranged; everything in its place. Of course, considering they have been living here for all of twelve hours, the home is still half-vacant and scattered, which leaves her unsatisfied. Heavy stacks of art books displayed temporarily on the dining table, newly unpacked trinkets from a life well-traveled—a wooden elephant from, she imagines, Namibia; a woven hat from Peru—decorating their bare pine shelves. She wonders how a person even begins to furnish a house so large, and with so little character. Maybe that's why they all remain so loyal to minimalism, based on the sheer fact that it's less of an undertaking.

When Mitty was a child, she spent Christmas wandering the wealthy neighborhoods across town, admiring their extravagant displays. Animatronic reindeer and inflated waving Santas, holiday anthems blaring over the growling generators. But really, it was the insides of the homes she was most curious about. She wondered why rich families always seemed to forgo curtains. It was bold, she thought, to build such decadent interiors and then flaunt them at every passing stranger.

Mitty studies the house's bright, empty rooms, an aura of pristine silence beaming behind the soundproof glass. She's waiting for something inside to move. But the house remains stock-still, like a showroom in a department store.

Just as she is about to lose interest, a light snaps on in an upper window. She spots a person pacing, muted into a silhouette behind a sheer curtain, disappearing to one side of the window, then turning back and crossing again. It's a woman—a small head with a sleek ponytail, a nervous pendulum—oscillating across the room. After almost a dozen laps, she walks out of sight. Mitty waits, tension clotting in her belly. But despite the woman's absence, the light in the room remains. The tide rises, and white foam swallows Mitty's ankles, thrusting her back into the world around her. She wrestles a tangle of beached kelp off her foot and begins to make her way back home.

As she walks, sporadically pausing to look back at the still-bright window, she can't help but think of the zoo she used to visit with her mother. How mesmerized she was by the massive cats that skulked from one side of their enclosure to the other, shoulder blades moving against their skin like fists stretching a disk of pizza dough. She remembers the smell of her mother's breath, soured from coffee, as she leaned down next to Mitty's ear and whispered, *They only walk like that in captivity, when they're plotting how to escape.*

I t is the second week of August, the end of a windy summer, and the paper is tiled with the mugshots of four boys, barely on the cusp of manhood, their eyes wet and black like olives. Everyone is talking about it—in the privacy of their own homes, of course, their own backyards—while they shove cauliflower and Brussels sprouts seedlings into freshly raked soil. If Mitty cared at all to be tuned into the happenings around town, she'd have already heard the rumors of the tech engineer kidnapped by four of his own scrawny interns and shot in the Santa Cruz Mountains. But instead, she is consumed by a row of stout cakes behind the glass of the pastry case in front of her, at a supermarket outside the city.

Today, she and Bethel have been housemates for ten years, nearly a third of Mitty's life. It's the first time one of their anniversaries has felt like a real milestone, a decade of living beside each other. But when she considers the fact that Bethel is seventy-nine, and that most of her time on earth took place long before Mitty was born, their years together feel so brief, so unimportant, that Mitty begins to wonder if it's worth noting at all.

She debates this with herself every year, second-guessing whether the tradition means anything to Bethel, who already has an aversion to most things sentimental. Would she even notice if Mitty bought something different, or returned empty-handed without so much as an acknowledgment? In the end, Mitty always decides that, whether or not Bethel finds meaning in these rituals, the cake—which will be carrot—is an offering, an act of gratitude.

She presses her finger against the glass. "That one."

The man lifts out the small dessert and secures it inside a box. "You don't want anything written on it?" Mitty thinks for a moment, imagining all the things she wants to say to Bethel.

Thank you for rescuing me. Fuck you for keeping me. Where do we go from here?

SHE CLIMBS INTO HER TAWNY VOLVO AND PLACES THE BOX in the passenger seat, securing it with the seatbelt. She struggles to crank down the manual window, using all of her upper-body weight, until the opening is wide enough to feel the breeze against her cheek. She drags her palms along the thighs of her jeans. Jerky and cautious, she backs out of the parking space, pulls forward, hovers at a stop sign for too long. The driver behind her punches their horn. Too humiliated to be stubborn, she sucks in a bellyful of air and pulls onto Cabrillo Highway.

She could've gone to one of the markets closer to their house, spared herself the anxiety. But their cakes are pompous and dry, bragging about all the things they aren't made with—gluten, dairy, processed seed oils—barely colorful enough to distinguish from the rows of bulk bins and cartons of nut milk. Getting the right cake is important enough to brave the wide, black tongue of the freeway, if only once a year, and feel the suffocating weight of Arizona pressing up against her. The fact that Paradise Valley is nearly a thousand miles away doesn't bring her much comfort. I-10 will always be the road she and her mother plowed down ten years ago, the back seat stuffed with lumpy duffel bags and blankets. The road where Mitty witnessed a different breed of her mother's neuroses, the kind so potent that, for the first time, she could see that her mother was trying—and failing—to hide it. Her hands trembling at the gas station while she waited for the cashier to retrieve her third pack of cigarettes. Checking and rechecking the GPS every fifteen minutes, to make sure she hadn't taken an exit that would send them back. The road where she made them eat quickly, scarfing down soggy drive-thru burgers and aloo gobi from Sikh truck stops. It was as if, no matter how long they drove, the place they were escaping never got any farther away.

They reached Bakersfield that afternoon, where Mitty spotted a motel's indigo neon sign beckoning them with HBO and a heated swimming pool. She begged, and her mother, who admittedly was too tired to drive the remaining four hours anyway, agreed they deserved one last memory together that wasn't suffused with dread. They checked in to a room with a damp carpet and two beds, waded in the foaming hot tub, allowed themselves a brief refrain from their own crippling fear to crack smiles at the misery of others on *Maury*. In the morning, her mother made a game of who could slug their lobby coffee the fastest. But despite these attempts at normalcy, it was, and would always be, the road where Mitty knew that they weren't simply driving. They were running.

"Bakersfield, Los Angeles, Palm Springs, Blythe," she whispers to herself now, when the wall of a semi-truck croons past. The chanting is a practice she's become reliant on to regulate her heartbeat, a rhythmic reminder of all the sprawling roadblocks between here and there. She says the words again as she travels beneath the Kelly-green exit signs, and again when she narrowly avoids getting stuck in the junction for a different freeway, a vein splitting off to else-where.

After twenty-six repetitions, her exit appears and she pulls off. Just as quickly as she ducks into the eucalyptus shade, her body relaxes. Down the narrow road that leads to a row of fa-miliar beachfront properties, her breath slows and the sweat on her neck begins to dissipate. She forces herself to notice all the traits she recognizes about her neighborhood—the gar-den beds packed with plump succulents and white rocks; the empty homes that still maintain the appearance of life, their patios decorated with full sets of furniture arranged to face one another as if there is about to be a conversation. And then, her and Bethel's house, with its graying wood shingles coming loose like hangnails; the faded pair of club chairs on the porch; the windows, wider than they are tall and cased in gold trim, the ones Bethel claims won her over in the first place.

She comes to a stop in the gravel driveway. She unloads the cake and holds it close to her chest as she climbs the sagging stairs to the front door, forcing it off its sticky frame. Inside, she finds relief in the stagnant smell of boiled cabbage and mold that's growing somewhere too far to reach. The air is thick with riled dust, spinning furiously in the slats of sunlight. Bethel is in the living room, sitting upright on the velour sofa, eyes closed, feet propped on a mirrored coffee table. Beyond the cocked silhouette of her bunions, Herman Munster takes his family camping to the howls of a CBS laugh track.

Mitty carries the cake to the kitchen and calls out Bethel's name. "I have a surprise."

She removes the plastic lid and places the cake on a raised tray.

"Well, maybe it's not a surprise. Unless you forgot."

No response. She keeps speaking.

"I feel like you're my wife."

Still, nothing. Before allowing herself to look into the living room, Mitty pauses. She doesn't imagine Bethel dying often, but when she does, it's like this. An abandoned cigarette and a slice of rye bread on a plate nearby. Her chest, flat as a lake, the anchovy-gray of her lips, chin succumbing to gravity, mouth pulled open. Mitty thinks of how, before even calling the paramedics, she would run to turn off the television. She knows this would be important to Bethel, who would already feel humiliated that she could hardly stay alive long enough to finish her toast. The last thing she'd want would be an audience, cackling at the cruel joke of her unremarkable exit.

Just as she begins to take a step forward, she hears the familiar sound of Bethel's gravelly sigh.

"I'm not dead." The couch springs whine beneath her as she lifts herself up. She steps into the kitchen and, when she gets a closer look at Mitty's paled face, bursts into laughter. "If I had the gall to die on our ten-year anniversary," she says, "I'd give you permission to kill me."

Mitty knows that Bethel gets touchy when her age comes into focus this way, as something fragile and bound to stop advancing at any given moment.

"Sorry," she says, forcing herself into the humor of it all. "Just residual anxiety from the drive."

At the table, Bethel dips her finger into the cake's ornament—orange icing swooped into the shape of a carrot. "Did you see the news today?" She sucks it off and slides Mitty the paper. "No criminal records, just a botched robbery." Her skin squeals as she pulls her forearms away from the floral oilcloth to sip her instant coffee. "They're kids. Messy, confused kids."

Mitty stares at the mugshot boys, their slender, hairless chins. She hadn't heard anything about it, hadn't even noticed the front page of the *Sentinel* as she left the grocery store. "What did they want from him?"

"Who knows, maybe some other tech guy put them up to it. Pawns," Bethel says. "Or maybe . . ." Her milky tongue peeks through her lips as she swallows. "Maybe they were just fed up with being broke, thought they'd skip playing the lotto. Either way, there'll be a few more murders before we all stop resisting and just let this place become Silicon Valley."

Bethel made Silicon Valley sound like an ever-expanding

Oz—a glittering behemoth, crawling outward like ivy, up and over the surrounding hills, claiming a new region for every founder who's dreamt up a machine and deployed a fleet of engineers to teach it how to remember someone's face.

The tech takeover had begun before Mitty moved in. She was used to the reality of surf spots teeming with millionaire tenderfoots, their ordinary brown hair eagerly doused with lemon juice. The way they paddled toward barreling waves in the middle of a thunderstorm, then retreated to their freshly built homes on the edges of eroding cliffs. Brazen and brilliant and believing that nothing could kill them. When Mitty arrived, she was less familiar with the time that Bethel yearned for, a previous century that Mitty, like most teenagers, associated with the stories that elderly people insisted on telling, stale and memorized. She often confused her decades, not entirely sure how the forties felt any different from the fifties beyond some vague sense that World War II and the James Dean craze didn't overlap.

But while her peers were thrust blindly toward the world of tomorrow, Mitty slowly absorbed Bethel's stacks of mid-century home and garden magazines, which promised a future that would never come. She pored through a closet of bedsheets made of fabrics and dyes that ceased to exist after chains killed off local tailors; she read every line of Bethel's handwritten ledger faithfully dating back fifty years, documenting each purchase no matter how menial, from a roll of postage stamps to a bottle of barbiturates. But it was the cheap ephemera that impressed Mitty the most—the fact that she could see the brushstrokes on the watercolor covers of Bethel's schmaltzy dime-store novels, that even something as unimportant as a jacket on a bargain book seemed to have been crafted with care, and by an artist with talent.

Mitty and Bethel did what they could to preserve the beauty of the past. As driverless cars and talking refrigerators began to spring up around Santa Cruz, they began recording episodes of their favorite TV reruns, fearing that it was only a matter of time before the strange public access station that played them would be rendered obsolete. They voted against the construction of a train line to San Francisco, as Bethel claimed the number of fatal car accidents on Highway 17— the winding umbilical cord connecting Santa Cruz to larger cities up north—was the only thing keeping the town from a full-scale invasion. She called it Blood Alley. She said she hoped they were afraid. As Mitty continued to exist inside Bethel's treasure trove of artifacts, her knowledge of and loyalty to the past didn't just grow, it materialized so vividly that sometimes it felt like a memory of her own.

UPSTAIRS, PAST THE WALLS PAPERED WITH FLAMINGO feathers and the blue-tiled bathroom with a cavernous turquoise tub, Mitty lets herself into Bethel's bedroom. It's her favorite room in the house—a king-sized bed embellished with too many throw pillows and a burly chartreuse carpet that feels best on bare feet. She likes browsing the tinctures and tubes and talcum powders Bethel keeps on a glass tray at her vanity. She likes that everything smells the same, some combination of sticky tobacco fresh out of the bag, cheap lavender perfume, and Tiger Balm. Bethel keeps it at a solid sixty-two degrees, no matter the temperature outside, and refuses to use her overhead lights, opting instead to turn on one of her many lilac-shaded lamps.

Mitty climbs up onto the mattress as Bethel ignites her collection of battery powered candles, their auburn glow imitating a wincing flame. "Make sure you call your mother," she says.

According to Bethel, all anniversaries are something to celebrate and something to grieve. *With the arrival of a new life comes the death of another.* It took them two years to begin honoring this anniversary as something positive. Before that, it was known as the day that Mitty left home against her own will.

Growing up, Mitty was only vaguely aware of Bethel as a person from her mother's past, a person her mother trusted, a recluse who'd left Los Angeles after a brief stint modeling skirts and blouses in department-store windows. When Mitty was nine, the year her father left, she and her mother drove to Santa Cruz to stay with Bethel for a week before returning to a half-empty house. Mitty remembers almost nothing from the trip. Just the woody smell of mothballs and the disappointment of a cold beach.

Years later, after moving in, she made a habit of calling her mother in tears, demanding to know when she could return. *Another month, max,* her mother would say. *Just until people move on to some other gossip.* And when Mitty argued for elsewhere—her distant uncle who ran a small dairy farm in

Vermont, the older girl cousins who lived somewhere in New Mexico—her mother explained that few people would be willing to take Mitty without questions. And even fewer would be able to handle the answer. Bethel, on the other hand, had a loner's empathy. She understood the importance of abandoning a place that no longer wants you, before it develops the gumption to drive you out.

When Bethel talks about the death of a former life, she isn't just referring to Mitty's childhood in Arizona. She is also talking about the end of that first year, as Mitty fused with the world around her, and the mourning began to dim. How Mitty's phone calls to her mother became less frequent, her pleading to come back home eventually nonexistent. Mitty knew that her own ability to adapt, a part of her no longer aching to return, was her mother's loss. And so she and Bethel agreed on another tradition, a phone call on the fifteenth of August, thanking her mother for letting her go.

"Well," Mitty says. "What should we do for the next ten years?"

Bethel flips on the radio, swiftly turning it down until it's barely audible. Just enough to lull them both to sleep.

"Maybe start building a ramp to replace those fucking stairs," she says with a grin, but Mitty knows there's a small, fearful truth buried inside the joke. She leans back into her pillows and pats the top of Mitty's hand. "We've been good company to each other."

Despite all the ways she has come to love her life with Bethel, prefer it even, it's just before Mitty gives in to sleep each year on this day that a tiny, nagging voice inside her comes awake. It isn't a voice that dreams of the past or the future, even the present, but of a time that never happened, the life she didn't have. Or the life she would've had, if it all had gone differently. Her life in college, tumbling out of her dorm room and into class, exhausted and still smelling like the sour aftermath of sex from the night before. How she would've gotten to know every tree-lined street in whatever little town she'd moved to, maybe somewhere back East with harsh winters, where she would survive on water-bagel breakfast sandwiches and buy her dishware from antiquated charity shops.

Instead, she took classes online and graduated virtually with a degree in communications. Bethel bought her a graduation cap from the dollar store and took a photo of Mitty pressing her laptop against her chest like it was a diploma. She got a job as a dishwasher at a small taco bar on the Capitola Wharf that claimed to be famous for its crab, where she found joy in the foot-pedal-powered high-pressure sink, the ignored but crucial duty of blasting plates with hot water until they shined, her apron fattening with tips as the waitresses paid her out, all while a band called Sonny and the Crab Walkers played covers of songs she only vaguely remembered as having been good.

It was this tiny, nagging voice that wondered if she liked her life now because it suited her, or because she had to like it in order to survive. She hated that she felt uncertainty at all. It seemed disrespectful to Bethel, disrespectful to herself. She tried to remind herself of what would have happened if she had stayed in Paradise Valley. How she would've woken up each morning in her childhood bedroom, walked out her front door and felt the piercing stares of her neighbors. Overheard the harsh whispers behind her in the produce aisle when she braved the outside world. Wondered what all these people thought they knew about her and, worse, if it might actually be true.

Mitty pulls the floral duvet up to her chin and turns toward the wall, allowing Bethel to rake her fingers through her hair. She notices a tuft of mushrooms springing from the ceiling. They look like shiitakes, with their rippling, fleshy sun hats. Bethel is always talking about moisture—the black mold that blooms in the walls, the fact that redwoods get most of their water from fog, manzanitas sprouting from the sides of solid rock cliffs. There's water everywhere, and so there's life everywhere, too. But this is the silent kind, the kind that goes unnoticed until it begins crawling through the floorboards and up your legs. She thinks of Arizona and the twenty-five-year drought. How, for the entirety of her childhood, the water never came. And then, the first time her mother called after Mitty left, she was talking about the sudden storm in Phoenix, six inches of rain collecting in the gutters. Everyone in the streets, barefoot and celebrating, opening their mouths toward the gushing sky. *Maybe when we left, we pulled the drain plug out with us,* her mother said. Mitty couldn't help but feel that this was actually the city just celebrating her departure.

She clenches her jaw and shuts her eyes, trying to soften the push of tears.

t's late afternoon, and a container of leftover risotto turns in the microwave. Mitty's phone buzzes against the counter. She had fallen asleep without calling her mother, despite Bethel's reminder. She curses quietly to herself and waits to answer until she's already hopping down the front steps, on her way to work.

"I would say I can't believe it's been a decade," her mother says before Mitty can greet her, "but then I look in the mirror."

"Don't talk about yourself like that." As she eases out of the driveway, Mitty pulls off the plastic lid, releasing a plume of steam into her car.

Mitty listens to her mother—Patricia is her name—on the other end. She knows the sound of shuffling cardboard, of a house key plunged into the seam of packing tape. But what she used to see as her mother's manic addiction is now just her way of being, the soundtrack playing in the background of every conversation.

"What did you win?" she asks.

"Well, the station was advertising a gift card to a smoothie place," Patricia says. "But a few days after I won, they called to say that the smoothie place had backed out of the agreement because they'd heard the station refused to allow commercials for that megachurch next to the freeway. Anyway, they sent me a few boxes of protein shakes instead." She pauses. " 'Voracious Vanilla,' " she reads aloud. "I'll sell them for half the price that the Safeway does."

Mitty makes an affirming noise. She balances the steering wheel with her knee as she sinks a spoon into the bowl of rice. There is silence for a moment; she shovels more food into her mouth while Patricia continues to unload the protein shakes into a milk crate, satisfied with how perfectly seven bottles can be slotted from one waffled side to the other.

Her mother has always lived aspirationally. When Mitty was younger, Patricia was open about the fact that what she knew she couldn't afford, she tried to replicate in her own faulty ways. Buying a silk robe from the bargain rack and staying in it well past lunchtime to mimic the romantic fatigue of wealth; scanning the display of foreign cheeses at the grocery store, proclaiming loudly that the selection is meager; using stoplights as an opportunity to put on lip gloss in the sun flap mirror of her leased car, hoping the person in the neighboring vehicle would wonder what important meeting she was late for.

But eventually, the performance of a bigger life was no longer satisfying. She wanted the real thing. She developed a talent, one that would actually earn her the things she couldn't otherwise own. Every day, she'd tune in to the radio sweepstakes—the countdown giveaways and caller-number-three competitions. She developed a system to figure out the average number of calls per second based on the position of the caller, the popularity of the radio station, and the time of day, calculating how many minutes passed before the winning call came through. Eventually, she was winning the majority of the calls she placed—earning herself matinee movie tickets, a week of free gas, microfiber cleaning towels, Moon Shoes.

Mitty was in middle school by the time Patricia started selling all the things she didn't use: a blow-up pool to the family of four with a dirt yard down the street, a sewing machine to her lonely co-worker, three sets of checkers to the auto shop with a packed waiting room. Then she moved on to boutiques, advertising the products the same way the loudmouthed men on the infomercials did, doing demos in the middle of the store for suburban housewives looking to knead away their cellulite. She attended book clubs and lied about reading the book; she just liked the captive audience, women who are always either hungry or bored. And at night, she'd go to work at the hospital, where she cleaned surgical tools and organized manila files in metal drawers, keeping herself awake by downing a few energy shots from the pack of five hundred she'd won earlier that month.

She organized her prizes by type and value in her garage. She drove to Tucson and Phoenix once she'd hit every store in Paradise Valley. She blasted Motown on her new surround-sound speakers while she deep-cleaned the kitchen with a vibrating mop. She lathered her limbs in gift-basket body lotion and gave Mitty hot-pink highlights with semi-permanent dye. No matter the product, every time a promised box arrived on their doorstep it felt like a celebration. Patricia was better than the women who bought things with the money they made at their hollow, salaried jobs. Patricia was a woman who understood strategy and statistics, a woman who got what she wanted. She was a woman who deserved it all.

"You could come back, I think," Patricia says now, her voice rustling and unsure of itself. "If you wanted. Even just for a visit."

The thought makes Mitty wince. There's no amount of time, it seems, that would justify her return to Arizona. Besides, the things Mitty misses about home are impossible to re-create. It is the mundane details she wants back, the smells they leave behind. A stick of pale spearmint gum folded into her mother's mouth after a secret cigarette; acetone lingering in the sink from her at-home manicures; the dryer belting out hot, soft breath each morning as it tumbled Patricia's purple scrubs; a rotisserie chicken sweating on the kitchen counter, waiting to be torn up and tossed with mayonnaise.

"Every time I think I'm ready, I end up panicking on the freeway." Mitty fills her mouth to avoid saying more.

"Well, have you been naming your cities?"

"Yes, but the whole point of the practice is to remind myself how far I am."

"And? Remember when you almost got to Bakersfield?"

"Will you stop?" Mitty snaps. "I'm not coming. At least not until I have to."

Patricia chuckles—she always does this when Mitty snaps at her—though it isn't from a place of condescension or arrogance; it's the way she's learned to dispel tension. But because Mitty knows this, the laugh always makes her feel guilty. She hates herself for still acting like a teenager, depositing all of her moods into the unconditional vat of her mother's heart.

"I've got to go," Mitty says. "I'm pulling up to the restaurant."

"Okay." Patricia holds on to the silence for a few seconds.

Mitty knows her mother must be racking her brain for something else to add, so before she can, Mitty says goodbye. Her mother's breath grows distant as Mitty moves the phone away from her face, and soon the line goes dead.

MITTY SECURES HER APRON AROUND HER WAIST. SHE plucks a peppermint from a small bowl next to the cash register and sucks off its stripes while she clocks in. The restaurant is mostly empty, apart from a few lonely regulars emptying fake sugar into their ice teas. The dinner rush won't start for another hour. Cat, a six-foot-tall waifish blonde, is slung over the waitress stand in the back, hair fanned between her pinched fingers, studying a collection of split ends.

"Ronnie is trying to fuck," she says, referring to the middle-aged drummer in the weekly cover band. Handsome enough, despite the fact that he has the pocked and bulbous nose of a drunk.

"Maybe if you fuck him, you can convince him to stop playing 'Hotel California,'" Mitty says.

Cat scoffs and sucks her teeth. "Someone needs to break the news to him that I'm gay." Last week, she told Mitty she had left the father of her baby for a woman from Florida whom she met online in an eating-disorder support group. She begins rolling silverware into paper napkins. "Are you going to Bianca's birthday party tonight?"

Before Mitty can answer, Cat mouths the word *No*, preemptively mocking what she already knows will be Mitty's response. But Mitty isn't offended. It's comforting, actually, knowing that no one is expecting her anywhere.

"Are you?"

"I don't know." Cat sighs at the tragedy of her own indecision. "Her family kind of freaks me out." She pauses to clean the prong of a fork with her T-shirt, though Mitty can tell the comment is leading, that she's eager to explain why. "You know her nephew was one of the interns."

"What interns?"

"Jesus, Mitty, do you just lock yourself in a dark closet when you leave here?" Behind them, the line cook smacks his bell, signaling that a plate of beef tacos has been set to incubate beneath the heat lamp. "The kids who murdered that tech guy."

"Oh," Mitty says flatly. "She told you that's her nephew?"

"No, but everyone knows it. Apparently, she's pretty torn up. Her sister's kid."

The rope of bells above the door announces the arrival of a group of beefy motorcyclists with thinning gray ponytails. Cat groans.

"Sit wherever," she yells out to them, then turns back to Mitty. She lowers her voice. "You wanna know what else I heard?" She slips a tube from her apron and squeezes a worm of lotion into her palm. The entire vicinity is swallowed by the scent of sugar, like she's polishing her knuckles with cupcake frosting. "That the tech guy had come forward about an AI project becoming *sentient*." She hugs the word in bunny-eared air quotations, having clearly just learned what it meant. "Like, *aware*," she continues. "He went to his boss and said he felt like this fucking robot he'd helped build was becoming a person. But by then he'd already seen too much. So." She shoots herself in the temple with her index finger.

One of the bikers calls Cat's name and she twirls around, securing her hay-colored hair into a bun as she skips toward their table.

MITTY SINKS HER HANDS INTO THE BASIN OF SOAPY WATER. Her fingers search for rogue forks, but her mind is occupied, the gruesome image of the shooting hazily replaying itself. The body, riddled with bullet holes, slumped against a car tire. Cat's theory, or whatever she'd heard, seemed like the plot of one of the pulpy horrors from the sixties that Mitty and Bethel watched together on weekends. Robots plotting revenge from the outposts of their flying cars. It's strange, she thinks, to be living in a time when the impossible synopsis from a film shot six decades prior can be entertained as a plausible reality. She'll tell Bethel about it later and Bethel will scoff. Say something about how they shouldn't give the techies so much credit.

"So fucking creepy." Cat's voice jolts Mitty out of her thoughts, and her finger pricks the tip of a steak knife. A shrill pain needles up her palm. "They keep asking for more ranch." Mitty removes her hand from the deep sink, a thin stream of blood trickling down toward her wrist. "Isn't that fucking creepy?" Cat says. Then she notices the wound. "What happened?"

Mitty suffocates her finger with her shirt, ignoring Cat's question. "But why would Bianca's nephew be involved? He's not in tech, is he?"

"Well, he would've been hired by someone, obviously." Cat plucks a ramekin from the dish rack and scowls as she fills it to the rim with ranch. "I mean, have you met him? He's just a baby."

"Seems like a big assignment for a baby."

Cat shrugs, clearly uninterested in debunking what she's already decided is true.

"Then where do you think the robot is?"

"Maybe it escaped." Cat looks toward the swinging kitchen doors, beyond which the restaurant floor is steadily filling with more sunburned patrons. "And now it's one of us."

IT'S SATURDAY NIGHT, AND MITTY IS EAGER TO GET HOME. She and Bethel have a tradition—each week they cram into Bethel's bed and watch a rerun of *Mystery Science Theater 3000*. They find it comforting, knowing that when the program ends at one in the morning, the channel goes off the air. Like it's just for them. During the commercials, they like to ponder what strange sentimental soul lumbered into the station every weekend and faithfully put on the old programs. Was he a nostalgian like them? A reclusive widower who also longed for some other time? Sometimes Mitty fantasized that he wasn't some balding, bespectacled boomer, but instead a mysterious fellow loner her age. Maybe there was someone else out there like her, reminiscing about a time he'd never lived through.

She stuffs a Styrofoam container with onion rings and crab cakes. By now, Capitola Village is flush with people. Drumming white transients with sad-eyed pit bulls, bow-legged skateboarders with toasted cheeks, families packing up their beach chairs and slowly moving toward the sandy row of sports bars adorned with signs made with Y2K clip art, drunken bachelorette parties floating—sometimes capsizing—on inflatable rafts along Soquel Creek. Beyond it all, the ocean is black, except for the row of glittering cargo ships lined up against the horizon.

She returns to her car, down one of the many narrow alleys lined with beach rentals, wetsuits hanging from their open windows. *Poor Man's Santa Monica*, Bethel calls it, though it isn't even that. It's less definable, less known to anyone outside this county, which is what Mitty likes about it. Here, she can blend in among all the people who have nothing in common with her or one another.

She has become an expert at avoiding the corners of the city where UCSC students land after trickling down from their classrooms on the hill. She knows to stay away from Pacific Avenue in the evenings and on weekends, when it's brimming with the girls who make her sweat. Environmental science undergrads in thrifted sundresses, licking non-

dairy ice-cream cones or dipping their upper lips into the
foam of their craft beers. The brawny farm girls lifting boxes
of heirloom tomatoes at the farmer's market. She did, of
course, once consider trying to make friends with them.
But each time she hovered in the denim aisles at Goodwill
or perched next to a statue, reading outside Bookshop, she
would catch herself staring instead. Over and over, she was
reminded that she could not trust herself to remain content
in the balmy platonic intimacy that other women seemed to
feel so comfortable living inside. So instead, she reassured
herself; even if she could befriend them, it would be point-
less. Those kinds of girls always left, every summer and soon
after, for good.

It would be easier if she could point to what happened a
decade ago as the only reason she felt so afraid of closeness.
But the truth is, even as a kid, when friendships with other
girls seemed obvious and low stakes, Mitty wasn't good at
them. Sure, there was always the bleating chorus with whom
she ate lunch on the grass in middle school, theorizing about
the myth of sex and flaunting their flexibility during a game
of Twister. But it wasn't that stage of friendship that scared
Mitty. It was the more intimate follow-up, sleepovers and
knowing each other's mothers by their first names. Then
came sharing showers, confident that neither person would
look for too long. She knew she didn't live like them—in
clean and quiet houses, with diligent and palatable mothers,
absent but reliable fathers. If she got too close to anyone, she
would eventually have to invite them over and explain away
her mother's house furnished with boxes, their revolving set

of stained futon cushions. She would have to wait patiently in the hallway while her friend showered alone, unable to trust her own wandering eye.

Mitty had studied the lives of other people for long enough to know that something about her own was off-kilter, cluttered and tense and awake at odd hours. She knew it was hopeless to try and embody whatever intrinsic ease those girls seemed to carry around so thoughtlessly with one another. It was all too foreign to her. And even if she did attempt to pinpoint exactly what it was about her life that felt wrong, she couldn't. She had been inside it for too long.

IN BETHEL'S BEDROOM, MITTY SETS THE PLASTIC BAG— heavy with kitchen leftovers, a muted yellow smiley face urging her to *Have a Great Day*—on the vanity. Bethel is at the window, waxy hair in a carefree knot at her neck's nape. She doesn't hear Mitty enter. She is transfixed as if before a television.

"They're here," she says. Across the yard, the neighbors' living room is in full view, illuminated beyond the glass. She is watching the new couple like they're a terrible rerun. Like she can smell the stink of their money through the walls, already predicting their intent on painting over the whole colorful town with the new white of the future.

"I know," Mitty says, as though it's a minor fact, something she'd heard and then forgotten.

"You met them?"

"No, I saw the woman in the window the other night."
Mitty turns away and begins to unload their food onto trays.
She can feel Bethel's eyes on her as she moves. "I wasn't
watching," she continues, before Bethel can push further. "I
just saw her briefly. Barely."

Bethel abandons whatever thought she was having. "It's
like they *want* to live in a hospital."

Mitty joins her at the window and sees, for the first time,
a three-dimensional rendition of the silhouette from the
night before. The woman, wrapped in a butter-colored silk
robe, has the kind of face women pay for. Sharp, decisive
angles. The man is shirtless, a white towel wrapped around
his waist. He isn't much taller than the woman, but he dou-
bles in size, with bulbous thighs, large enough to house a set
of organs, hamstrings pregnant with muscle.

"Wonder how long they'll stay," Mitty says.

"Until they decide to rent it out." Bethel squints to get a
better look at one of them. "I give it a month."

Mitty notices that each time the man passes by the
woman, as they shuffle around the room, tending to their
unpacking, he runs his hand across her lower back. A tiny,
gentle touch notifying her of his presence. Each time she
struggles to open a box, she hardly has to gesture for his help
before he is already there, forgoing a box cutter to rip apart
the taped seams with only his hands. She's surprised by how
comforting it is, just watching them know each other.

"We could come up with a plan to drive them out," Mitty
says.

"I'll finally get to become the Boo Radley I've always wanted to be." Bethel laughs at her own joke and turns away from the scene, lured back to bed by the rising scent of grease.

Mitty takes one last glance at the couple. The woman is now cross-legged on the rug, organizing cutlery. The man leans over to kiss her upside down, his scruffy mouth pressing against the groove beneath her bottom lip. Mitty can hardly remember what it's like to bask in the smell of another person's breath. To feel their spit on your chin and choose not to wipe it off.

■

Lena has been alone for most of the evening, trying to make the new house feel less barren. But the task is futile. No matter how many boxes she empties into their cabinets and onto their bookshelves, the rooms are sterile. Too big. Every sound parroting off the towering blank walls.

Sebastian had gone to San Francisco that morning for a few hours on his own. Something about a game of Catan with his friends. But just as she moves to the kitchen and begins to reorganize their stacks of clay dishware, she hears the front door open.

"Are you still awake, my love?" His belt buckle hits the tile as he begins to shed his clothes. She can already smell the smoke.

"Kitchen!" she shouts back.

"I have to say, being around Abigail always makes me more grateful to have you," he says, his voice growing nearer.

It's a habit of his she'd only recently begun to notice—his gratitude for her hinging on the hatred of someone else, typically another woman. Soon, he's standing in the doorway, naked and beaming.

"She can't be that bad." Lena clenches her jaw as she pries two bowls apart. He pauses to open the refrigerator and sucks at the spout of a box of almond milk. Each time he gulps, his penis bounces against his groin. The white collects at the corners of his lips. Once, in one of their few blowout arguments, she told him to *suck a fat cock,* something she hadn't even considered would be an insult until it unwillingly left her mouth. He wipes his lips with the back of his hand. She grins.

"I know you like her," he says. "But I find her exhausting."

"I don't like her." It's more a reassurance than a disagreement.

"Well, you're friends with her."

"Women don't have to like each other to be friends."

She moves to the counter and props herself up on one of the barstools. He continues rummaging through the refrigerator for nothing in particular, a mindless habit. She has always been captivated by the way he eats, how instinctual it seems for him to forage for protein like a bear digging through a campsite. She starts to count the pimple scars along the dip of his ass crack, then forces herself to stop. "What makes Abigail exhausting?"

"She doesn't know how to play," he says. "And yet, she insists on playing."

Lena was invited to one of these game nights back when

they lived in the city. Other than Abigail, who is married to the man whose turn it was to host, Lena was the only woman, which didn't make her uncomfortable until she noticed Abigail glaring at her from the kitchen. She knew she was expected to have some sense of camaraderie with Abigail, but it seemed that in order to earn it, Lena would have to forfeit her position as a player and relegate herself to some other part of the house, where they would busy themselves with a less challenging activity while commiserating about the men they've decided to love. Lena didn't want this. She wanted to play.

She won four games of poker until all the men were too dejected to agree to another round. But part of why they lost, she thought, beyond their lack of skill, was that they were too busy staring at her, studying her, to actually pay attention to the cards in their hands. On the drive home, she tried to apologize to Sebastian, explaining that she didn't mean to be good at the game, it just seemed obvious, uncomplicated. *Well, most people don't feel that way,* he said, reaching over to squeeze her knee. *But most people aren't you.*

BEFORE CONTINUING TO UNPACK, SEBASTIAN ASKS HER TO undress and shower with him. They take turns swirling soap against each other's shoulder blades. They hardly speak, switching in and out of the hot water as though choreographed. Even now, they rarely bathe apart, a tradition they've kept since they met. It had occurred to Lena that this practice might curdle their sex life, turn the other person's body into something too familiar. But they haven't struggled with maintaining desire, not once. Even though there have been periods—days, weeks—during which he was the only person Lena saw, the notion that he would ever not be a mystery was almost unfathomable. Every time Sebastian walked into the room, she felt exactly how she did the first time she ever laid eyes on him, at a party on a rooftop in SoMa.

It was January two years ago, chilly even for San Francisco that time of year, but Lena hadn't been cold in her black dress with a square neckline, the open-toed pale-green mules with straps that wrapped around her ankles. She stood at the railing, watching some poor soul work in their illuminated office in the high-rise across the street, wondering what they were doing that was so important that they needed to be there at eleven o'clock on a Saturday. That's when she heard a man's voice behind her. *What could be so important that they're doing it at eleven o'clock on a Saturday?* But when she turned around to face him, she wasn't sure if he had said it first, or if she'd just accidentally said it out loud to herself and then he'd repeated it.

He joined her in looking out at the city and began giving her an aerial tour. He told her about the forty-eight hills. That on one particularly steep hill, sometime in the 1860s, a team of horses slipped as they pulled a streetcar up Kearny Street, and how their gruesome tumble back down the hill inspired a distraught onlooker to design the cable car. He talked about how good design saves lives. Then he switched topics, rattling off a litany of myths and legends about the city—the labyrinth of ghost tunnels underneath Chinatown, the rogue hippie who kidnapped a tiger from the zoo.

He didn't ask her many questions, but he didn't talk about himself much either, which made Lena feel at ease, like he was neither consumed with trying to figure her out nor trying to make her understand him. He talked about the ever-widening class gap that had progressively managed to ruin a city that was once home to outcasts and dreamers. One of the few times he used the word *I* was when he implicated himself in that evolution, admitting that he, too, was a part of the tech industry that corrupted San Francisco, though he never quite explained whether or not he forgave himself for it.

They walked the long way back to his house in Dogpatch, past the sparkling new basketball stadium and the recently shuttered doors of what had once been the oldest Black-owned bar in San Francisco, arriving finally at his shipyard-warehouse-turned-loft. He joked about how he'd once gone to a rave here, before the steel frame windows were cleaned of their calcium fog and the once communal bathrooms on each floor had been converted to walk-in closets. When it was still an actual warehouse. Then he pointed to the corner where he'd nearly vomited on Jack Dorsey, the bike messenger.

He made her a Negroni and sprinkled orange wedges with sugar. He opened all the windows and they sat on the floor, where he grew wistful as he described how the city used to feel invigorating and chaotic and full of potential. He told her about wanting to leave for somewhere smaller, somewhere *stuck in its ways*. Somewhere without billboard ads for cryptocurrency looming over the freeway. Somewhere uncool with bad food. Lena gently suggested that there were other parts of the city that hadn't yet been overrun, but he wasn't convinced. *We're everywhere,* he said. *I wanna go where there's less of me.*

He noticed things about her that seemed trivial; then he explained why they were actually useful. The fact that her ability to taste the dash of cinnamon in her drink meant she had an advanced palate. That, based on their wrestling match on his glossy concrete floor, her strength-to-weight ratio meant she'd be a natural rock climber. Her vision was *insane*, which, among other things, would make her a fantastic bird watcher. She liked how he made her feel, like she was capable. And more than that, like she was remarkable. He was more passionate about her potential than her past. It was rare to find that in a man, she thought, someone who doesn't feel threatened by all the things you could become.

They fucked right there, against his Pendleton ottoman. Afterward, he kissed the rash on her stomach that the wool had left behind and sleepily mumbled his apologies before dozing off with his head against her chest.

She knows the fact that this is her favorite memory, out of the cluster of moments that make up her life, might be unoriginal. She assumes that other people are just lying to themselves and each other when they say that the highlight of their lives was the moment they met their partner. But for her, it feels true. Because it is one of few, if not the only one, that seems to have a beginning, a middle, and an end. Since they'd begun the moving process, this only became clearer. As she sorted through ephemera and tried her best to connect the dots of her own life, she came to realize that every other moment she could recall felt like a series of photographs that someone else took, vivid and curated snapshots that exist without context, pinned to the bulletin board of her brain. And so, in the last several weeks, she has taken to researching memories—scouring Reddit forums about how the child mind stores information, listening to audiobooks about the ways specific experiences burrow themselves into various corners of the human body, devouring memoirs by former alcoholics and cancer survivors and women who backpacked four hundred miles by themselves to heal some invisible wound. It's not that she believes something terrible happened that she can't remember. What she's trying to understand is how it can be possible that everyone but her seems to recall their lives with such chronological clarity. The fact that anyone could remember something as a story, with a clear understanding of how they came to one place and then left it for another, leaves her feeling fractured. Like all of her life she has appeared for brief moments and then disappeared, her mind going blank until she snaps back to the world in front of her.

She can hardly remember her life before Sebastian, or what it was like to exist without him as a fact of who she is. There is only one small difference between then and now that becomes clear whenever she lets herself fold into the past, something that has since gone away. The morning after that first night together, when she stepped out of Sebastian's front door, she was perfectly content to leave. She had re-adjusted her dress, her underwear stuffed into her purse, and, on the bus back home, basked in how excited she was to just go off and miss him. Now there is no time to miss him. That day was the last time she remembered being at any sort of monumental crossroads. She had so many choices then. These days, it seems, there is only one direction to go.

THEY RETURN TO THE LIVING ROOM AFTER SHOWERING, their bodies damp and smelling of eucalyptus beneath their robes. Sebastian is sorting records, recounting the origin story of each as he slips them out of the box.

"Seattle, 2011," he says, holding up a Lesley Gore album, a gauzy portrait of the singer—her downturned nose, icy eyes beneath a bounce of pin curls. "An estate sale on Whid-bey Island."

She feels warm, thinking of Sebastian out in the world during some past she wasn't a part of, taking the ferry across Puget Sound just to rummage through a dead woman's crates. He has so many stories from before she'd come along—a motorcycle trip along the Silk Road, his brief stint as a bassist in a garage rock band with a couple guys from Berkeley, a fractured wrist that still clicks after a bar fight in Nashville. In some ways, she thinks, it's like he's lived enough life for the two of them.

He begins making a pile of records he doesn't want, gifts from people who didn't know anything about his taste in music other than the fact that he prefers it on vinyl.

"*The Dark Side of the Moon*," he says, scoffing and putting it to the side. "You think the neighbors would be interested in some hand-me-downs?" They both look toward the neighboring house, which is dark except for an upstairs bedroom. "Something tells me they absolutely have a record player."

Lena chuckles and walks to the window. "I think a box of old records would make a nice gift," she says. She studies the tired home, or at least what she can make of it in the dark. On the roof, a weather vane spins. Faster and faster and faster.

■

Bethel rips an onion ring in half and fishes out its slippery innards. On the television, the Mystery Science troupe watches a sixties spy spoof called *Dr. Goldfoot and the Bikini Machine*. Frankie Avalon twists and turns his red getaway car down and around San Francisco's Lombard Street.

"I think I'd like to learn to drive again," Bethel says.

"You know how to drive."

She takes a swig of her Bud Light. "I forgot."

Mitty nudges her shoulder. "You can't forget how to drive."

"When you've lived as long as I have, you can forget anything."

"Then I'll teach you," Mitty says. "Again."

Bethel's eyes are trained on the television, but she's inside herself somewhere. Chewing aimlessly.

"I can't believe I sold the Woodie," she says.

The car Bethel drove from Los Angeles in 1965 was a wood-paneled Ford Galaxie with a teal interior. On their refrigerator, Bethel had pinned a photo she'd taken of it, parked at a vista point somewhere in the Central Valley. It was on that same trip that Bethel detoured to the Madonna Inn in San Luis Obispo, where she was inspired by pattern-clashing and textural collage, a design style that would later be called maximalism. It was an approach she'd heard described as the most personal form of interior decor. *It's a reflection of humanity and all of our many contradictions,* a tour guide explained as he gestured to the watermelon booths in the dining hall. *Proof that when we lean into what we love and let go of meticulous organization, things often fall perfectly into place.* Continuing north, she came across a pamphlet at a gas station in Cambria, advertising Santa Cruz as *California's favorite beach and mountain playground,* where it was *always sunny,* and there was *always something to do.*

Mitty has always struggled to imagine Bethel as the kind of person who could be wooed by the outdoors and entertainment. But then again, Bethel was almost seventy when they began living together. Who knows who she had been long before that. Mitty hardly even knows what she looked like in her twenties and thirties; she refuses to keep photos of herself around the house. Once, when Mitty asked why, Bethel told her there was no use in being reminded.

The Bethel that Mitty knows is the Bethel who smokes

inside, stretched out in her recliner, and rarely changes out of her mint-green bathrobe. The Bethel who used to like floating in the water on hotter days until Mitty showed her drone videos of long-distance swimmers blissfully unaware of great white sharks lurking toward them. Now, Bethel always jokes as she peers out toward the ocean, every small wake or seagull looks like a fin. She falls asleep most nights to re-broadcasts of San Francisco Giants baseball games because she believes Jon Miller's voice cures nightmares. She stirs leftover wine into her coffee each morning, sucks on sugar cubes while she reads, and prefers her eggs snotty, under-cooked. She has few needs and even fewer complaints. If not for Mitty, she'd be alone. But somehow, Mitty thinks, she would never be lonely.

"I hate thinking that car is sitting in some garage or dis-membered at the dump," Bethel says.

The Supremes belt the movie's theme song while a ma-niacal Vincent Price proudly surveys a conveyor belt serving up women's limbs. *There once was a man with a machine, when-ever he needed a girl on the scene—*

"Oh, come on," Mitty says. "It's probably still running. Driving down the 1 right now, all of its windows open."

Bethel grins. "No need for the radio because the engine sounds so good."

He pushed a button, and just like nothin, a girl would appear.

"And where will you go when you remember how to drive?"

"Small distances first. I'll come have dinner with you at the restaurant. I'll take myself to the dentist."

"And then?"

Bethel thinks about this for a moment. Then she turns to look at Mitty, her face suddenly humorless.

"I'd like to go to Big Sur. To the Henry Miller Library." Her eyes wander into the past. "The house had just been built when I was driving up the coast. I remember reading about it in the paper. I've always wanted to walk around in there, see a jazz concert on the lawn."

Mitty admires Bethel's face. The small folds in her cheeks where she smiles, the deep parallel lines between her tattooed eyebrows, now faded to the color of eggplant.

"We could do that even if you don't learn to drive."

"But half the fun is getting there." Bethel returns her attention to the movie. "And I want to be the one to take us."

Whoever you are, honey, the television blares, *I could love you to pieces.*

ena has always felt fluent with the ocean. Never once has she experienced nightmares of looming tsunamis, sinking ships, plunging canyons in the deepest parts of the Atlantic. Of course she understands the fear. But it seems unproductive to be afraid of something so infinite, something that couldn't be aware of your presence, that would never even target you, but instead simply overwhelm you without any sense you'd ever stood in its way. But maybe that's what people are really afraid of—being irrelevant—and maybe that's the feeling Lena doesn't mind. She quite likes it, actually. Being in the ocean is the only time she doesn't feel like she is being watched.

She has grown used to the ways Sebastian is protective, has come to see it as a form of love. While other women complain about the fact that their boyfriends seem entirely unconcerned with their whereabouts, or the threat of another lover, hers is always checking to make sure she is safe, healthy, has had a full night's sleep. She knows better than to take Sebastian's scrutiny for granted. Which is why she feels guilty when he is paddling behind her at dawn and she catches herself reveling in the fact that there's a great expanse of water diluting the way he looks at her. His pupils shrinking to pinpricks as she gets farther away. She likes focusing on the horizon while she pushes against the current on her surfboard, gunning past the white water. And then when she gets far enough, she looks back at the eroding coastline and wonders how much time everyone has left until it finally decides to give up and resign itself to mud.

A cross-breeze travels through the bedroom. An indigo scrub jay screeches furiously just beyond the window. Mitty is yanked awake. It's dawn. In her dream, she was being pulled down an icy river by a rope, feeling the smooth rocks brush against the underside of her bare thighs. When she opens her eyes, she sees that the French door to the balcony is wide open. The wall thermometer reads fifty degrees.

She crawls out of bed, taking the comforter with her, and steps outside. She only notices the next-door neighbors once they are at the edge of the water, heaving out of the tide in their wetsuits, slick as seals. Each of them drags a ten-foot-long surfboard, leaving a slender line in the sand behind them.

When they reach the dollhouse, the man lifts their boards onto a rack in the yard, while the woman stares at the ocean. Mitty feels gluttonous, getting to look at her without restraint. Her posture, pulled tight. The way she gathers her hair to twist it up and away from her neck in one seamless motion, as quick as a string trick.

Mitty's mother used to say that blaming beauty on genetics is just an excuse to quit. *Beauty is about what you distract from by way of what you accentuate,* she'd say, conjuring a waistline with a belt. *Once you figure out what you don't want a person to notice about you, you can make everything else louder.*

What strikes Mitty about her neighbor is that it seems she is doing neither—accentuating nor distracting. The wetsuit seems obedient to the curves of her body—calves sloping to a fragile ankle, the bight of her lower back. Nothing about her is flattened by neoprene.

Before Mitty can make a list of all the ways she herself falls short in comparison, the man approaches and starts to help the woman peel off her wetsuit, tugging it down past the lip of her shoulder. They both work to deliver themselves, pulling their feet through the impossibly small neck hole. Mitty feels her blood soar up through her face at the sight of the woman, naked. It isn't uncommon to see nude people on the beach in Santa Cruz, but they are usually leathered men playing badminton, their genitals tossing around with each clumsy serve. The only thing this woman has in common with them is that it looks as though she's never worn clothes for long enough to earn a tan line. Mitty stares at her belly, hilly and fertile. Her nipples, erect as missiles. She's hairless everywhere. Mitty feels a sudden mourning for the loss of what must be thick body hair in favor of something more infantile. She wants to see the woman with her armpits grown out, a bush like those disco Playmates.

The man drapes the suits, still echoing the shape of the couple's bodies, onto the fence like animal hides in a butcher shop. When they walk inside, Mitty's own disappointment only proves how badly she'd wanted it all to continue. She felt she was owed it, somehow. As though the couple's ease with being naked meant she had permission to look, that there shouldn't be a limit to how much she could take in.

But then, only a few minutes later, the woman reemerges onto the balcony, still nude, now gripping a mug. Mitty leans forward to look more closely, doubly exhilarated that she's returned alone. The woman settles onto an outdoor couch and props her legs up on the coffee table. Her labia pudges out from between her thighs. She strangles the ends of her hair, letting the saltwater crawl down her chest and stomach. She watches it collect in her belly button for a moment, then leans back and parts her legs, gradually sliding her hand in between. Mitty can see that she's not using her fingers. Instead, she's kneading herself with the mound of her palm, moving faster with each push, the whites of her eyes peeking through her half-open lids, clouds of mist erupting from her mouth. But just as Mitty anticipates that the woman might let out an audible moan, she lifts her head, her face blooming into an impish grin.

Mitty had been so focused on the woman that she hadn't noticed the man, standing several yards away, watching the same scene unfold. He nods at the woman to keep going, the two now making eye contact with each other, touching themselves at opposite ends of the glaring white balcony. His sudden presence feels disruptive. Mitty is almost repulsed by the woman for smiling at his arrival, for inviting him at all. He walks toward her, his erect penis like the certain arm of a compass, and he grabs her thighs, pulling her legs around his back. With her ankles braided against his spine, they kiss. They seem unhurried, their mouths hovering apart every few seconds, exchanging breath.

The man's body now shields the woman's from view, and as much as Mitty wants to heckle him, demand that he go back inside, she's intrigued by the way he moves. He isn't graceful, but he isn't clumsy or depraved either. He is primal, driving himself into the woman, letting her writhe for a second each time he draws away. He picks her up and carries her to the railing, then pulls out of her so he can turn her around, pressing her belly against the metal. He wraps his meaty arms over her shoulders, like the seatbelts on a roller coaster, bending his knees slightly so he can enter her from below. He lifts her pelvis with his hips until she's standing on her tiptoes, skewered. And that's when the woman moans, loud enough for Mitty to hear, like she's signaling that she's still there, begging Mitty to remember her.

She had seen people before, wrestling out their various intimacies, in the other houses. Vacationers whose sex seemed excessive and urgent, aided by the scarcity of their time away from home. But she rarely ever felt aroused or envious or inspired, even. It was sad, almost, to see people in homes that didn't belong to them, straining to make each other come.

But watching this woman impaled with pleasure makes Mitty wish for it. She's thinking about what her life might be like with someone else. Instead of it being Bethel she helps into the car, the familiar scent of Bethel's armpit as she leans across her to close the door, what if it were someone else, someone she touched in other ways too? She thinks of the parts of her neighbors' lives that she doesn't see. Sparse conversations as they're on the way home from a party, flushed and sleepy in the back of a cab. The heavy stream of piss from the bathroom after sex. The shared hangover the next morning, tossing around in white sheets. God, how she wishes she could feel it for a night. How nice it would be, her body in the hands of another person.

But just as quickly as they've made themselves known, the couple is gone. And then, everything around Mitty feels harsher—the sun roused and beating, the blinding sand, the restless horns of morning traffic. She leans back into the lawn chair and pulls her knees toward her chest. Her day already feels cavernous and drowsy, drifting away from any real purpose. She's wrenched with envy that a person could be the recipient of that much pleasure over the course of a single morning. She takes one last look at the lifeless balcony; the couch cushions bear no sign of the imprint of a body. The woman's laugh splinters out of the open windows.

Mitty's hand cramps. When she looks down, she notices that her palm is cupped around her crotch as if it were muffling a mouth before letting out a scream.

SHE RETURNS TO BED. OVER THE NEXT SEVERAL HOURS, SHE dozes and wakes sporadically, drenched in sweat. She peels off her shirt, her underwear, to reenter her dreams naked, her lips swollen and drooling, the ceiling fan's dutiful whir soothing her in and out of consciousness. She doesn't dream of the neighbor, but she thinks of her whenever her mind wriggles its way out of slumber. The woman's silhouette. Her throat. Her eyes, shimmering and dark. When Mitty finally pulls herself awake, it is noon. She lies in bed for a few minutes, watching the tide on the other side of the window recede gradually, every pull an opportunity to reveal more of the ocean's sandy floor. Somewhere, the wind braids a song through a clay chime.

Downstairs, Bethel is pacing along the edges of the living room, hands behind her back as she inspects the walls, the wood groaning beneath her feet. Above her, a gang of moths slam their bodies against the bowl of the light fixture.

"Morning," Mitty says, flopping down into Bethel's rarely unoccupied recliner. Bethel gestures to a mug of coffee on the table.

"That's yours."

Mitty takes the mug to her lips, debating whether or not to tell Bethel about what she saw that morning. It would be so nice to indulge in the gossip of it all, but she knows that it would never be that simple. She couldn't recount it without also making it an admission of some sort. A confession that she'd been spying again.

Bethel points at a clean, bare spot beneath the yellow-tinged paint. "These walls used to be white."

"It's all that smoking," Mitty says. They had been through this before. Gone to the hardware store to paw through shades of white—Chantilly Lace, Bancroft, Honeymilk— before Bethel came to the epiphany that she had no intention of quitting, so they mutually agreed to just leave the walls as they were. Mitty wondered if she knew this was a fool's errand and that going to the hardware store was just her way of getting out of the house. But Mitty can tell that Bethel is particularly bothered this time, and she's right to be. The yellow has gotten worse. Dingy and sick.

"Why don't we just lean into what's already there?" Mitty suggests. "Paint it yellow."

THE MORNING HAZE HAS LIFTED. A STRETCHED, AZURE SKY, a warm breeze stirring the trees. Mitty avoids looking at the neighbors' house as she helps Bethel into the car. She doesn't feel ready to meet them quite yet—what she'd seen that morning was still lingering inside her somewhere, a brooding and cherished secret. She tries to subdue any conversation with Bethel, fearful that if one of them were to speak too loudly, the man or woman might come out and say hello. Only once they've pulled onto the main road does Mitty clear her throat.

"Cat's got a conspiracy theory about the murder."

"Of course she does." Bethel scoffs. "Isn't she an anti-vaxxer too?"

"She said the guy had been talking too much about the fact that one of their AI projects had gained consciousness."

"So he was a liability."

"I guess."

"Huh." Bethel chews on her bottom lip. "That's a good one."

"What do they use them for?" Mitty asks. "The AI?" They hover at a stoplight. On the sidewalk, a woman—probably half the age she looks—with mangy blonde hair and cloaked in woven scarves, holds a sign that reads STRANDED DUE TO BAD TASTE IN MEN. A small tabby cat is curled up between her thighs, napping.

"Well, I'm sure they have a list of honorable tasks they claim to use them for," Bethel says. Her eye catches the woman, too. "But I don't know. There's gotta be something sinister that we just don't see. Drones and whatnot." She digs through the cupholder and fishes out a few sticky quarters, then cranks down the window. The woman on the sidewalk notices immediately and hoists the cat onto her hip before approaching them.

"Be good, sweetie," Bethel says, dropping the coins into the woman's open palm. From here, Mitty can smell a heavy cloud of patchouli wafting from her sweater. The woman grins, revealing a row of surprisingly straight teeth. She must have had braces once, Mitty thinks, been a metal-mouthed teenager just like everyone else, had parents who still believed that a good smile would be enough to spare their child misfortune.

"God bless," the woman says, her voice blackened from smoke.

Bethel nods and the light turns green. Within seconds, the mangy-haired woman is in their rearview mirror, settling back down onto the sidewalk and repositioning her sign, waiting for the next set of cars to arrive.

"I wish they wouldn't say that," Bethel says. "*God bless. God's not here for all this.*" She gestures to the world around them. "Clearly."

"At least her sign was honest."

"That I don't care about." Bethel lights a cigarette just as they turn into the parking lot of the hardware store. "No one is honest about the ways they make money, why should homeless people be?" As Mitty pulls into a spot, Bethel ignores the open window of the car next to them, the driver's nose curling as he smells her exhale. "Imagine if those AI guys had to write an honest sound bite about what's buying them these houses." She scoffs. "Then we'd all be killed for knowing too much."

AT THE HARDWARE STORE, MITTY AND BETHEL ORDER A gallon of Lemon Chiffon and continue meandering through the aisles. They take their time as they walk past piles of lumber, pausing every few minutes to bury their noses in stacks of wooden planks. They stand beneath an array of different light fixtures, admiring them like constellations. Pretend to cook dinner in the model kitchens. In the decor section, they pass a row of drawers filled with furniture hardware. Mitty knows what comes next. Bethel chooses a knob she doesn't already have—today it's a blue ceramic star—and slips it into her pocket. That is the only thing she won't pay for. She'd been doing this since long before Mitty arrived— ever since, she says, she became invisible in her older age. She claims she wants to be caught; it would mean she's being looked at, noticed by an employee who isn't wagging his tongue at a girl in cutoffs who's confused about why her drywall won't hold a screw. When Mitty first learned of this habit, or practice, whatever Bethel might call it, Bethel took her to the drawer in her bedroom where she kept all the knobs. There were dozens of them, in every shape and size and color, for every decade and style and size of hand. On Bethel's next birthday, Mitty woke up early and screwed the knobs everywhere in the house she could. The medicine cabinet, the cutlery drawers, the coffee mug cupboard. All of them mismatched.

Mitty thought it could be a celebration. A symbol of some kind. But Bethel claimed she hated it. She didn't want the constant reminder, she said. She just wanted to make her silent strike against the world, then forget about it. Mitty offered to remove the knobs immediately, but Bethel insisted they stay, even as she kept complaining about their presence. For the next few days, all she talked about was beauty. She talked about it the same way she did her old wooden Ford Galaxie. Something rare and cherished that could take her anywhere, until the day she was forced to give it up.

Now, in the stale heat of the car, Bethel reaches into the pocket of her floral dress and pulls out her newest knob. She pinches it between her first two fingers and raises it to the sun.

"That's a nice one," Mitty says.

Bethel stares straight ahead, a sadness swallowing her, the glare of the dashboard slapping the bottom of her face.

"I'd rather them be pushy like they used to be," she says. "Now they just want nothing to do with me." The car swells with silence.

"We'll put it on the knife drawer," Mitty says.

Bethel cracks a smile.

THEY NOTICE THE NEIGHBOR AT THE SAME TIME, SQUAT-
ting in her front yard, pressing down the soil of a potted aloe
plant. She's barefoot, a pale pink dress cinched up past her
knees, vertebrae pressing against the skin on her hunching,
tanned back.

A flare of dread creeps up in Mitty. It had been so long
since they'd had neighbors, and she'd forgotten how burden-
some the obligation of small talk could be. The dance of rou-
tine kindness, all while pretending she hadn't just witnessed
what she did that morning. She releases her foot from the
gas, hopeful that the obnoxious cough of her Volvo's exhaust
will lessen. But in a neighborhood almost exclusively popu-
lated with the inaudible hum of glass-roofed SUVs, she may
as well be driving a tank. Sure enough, the woman notices
them almost immediately, and promptly rises to her feet.
Mitty knows Bethel must be feeling something similar, and it
occurs to her that she could just keep driving; Bethel wouldn't
protest. But it all happens so fast, and the woman is already
approaching, her smiling face beginning to materialize with
more detail.

Mitty parks and draws in a deep breath, steadying herself. As the woman grows closer, she becomes less recog-
nizable, her torso covered by clothing. The feeling comforts
Mitty, knowing that the person she'd seen on the balcony

that morning is an entirely different person than the one she's about to meet.

Bethel groans. "I don't have the energy."

Mitty ignores her, choosing instead to focus on rehearsing internally the opening lines of any stock conversation. She takes her time getting out of the car and, lifting the gallon of paint from the back seat, tries to cast the image of the woman's panting mouth out of her brain.

"Will you do the talking?" Bethel asks. "Please?"

By now, the woman is only a few yards away. Mitty can see her gold earrings glinting in the sun against her chestnut hair, which is pulled into a braid that lays flat over her chest like a mink scarf.

"She probably just wants to say hello," Mitty whispers.

"Well, please let her know I say hello."

When the woman notices Bethel struggling to lift herself out of the car, she hurries over and holds the door open. Bethel waves her off.

"I've got it," Bethel says. "Just takes me a while."

The woman doesn't seem to clock Bethel's ambivalence and just stands there, like a bellboy, effusive and ready, gripping the rim of the door.

"We got in the other day," she says, answering a question that no one asked. "I'm glad I caught you while it's light out." Her voice is deeper than Mitty could have anticipated, the kind of baritone that eventually gets a girl bullied into a forced chirp, until she's hoisting up the ends of her sentences to sound like questions even when they aren't.

"Yes, daylight's always better." Bethel turns away from

the bright blaze of the cloudless sky and begins walking toward her shady retreat. Mitty hovers in one place, staring at Bethel's back, unsure of how to cut the conversation short. But when she turns to face her neighbor, the woman is staring at Mitty, her once smiling face having settled into a studious curiosity.

Looking at her up close feels like staring directly into the sun. She's got a set of glassy brown eyes, a wide forehead and an easy chin, lips so fleshy and full of blood that they seem like they belong inside her body. Pink yawning across her ski-jump nose. On the apple of her cheek, there's a single freckle. Like a tiny hiker had ascended the ridges of her face and planted a pole at the summit.

"Is that your grandmother?" the woman asks.

Mitty has rehearsed the answer to this question before, back when she still considered attempting to make friends. She entertained the idea of lying, referring to Bethel as the *great-aunt* whom she *helps around the house*. But the thought of talking about Bethel like some discombobulated geriatric, while propping herself up as a dutiful niece, left her riddled with shame. She was the one who'd shown up at Bethel's door, confused and needing assistance, and it was Bethel who had taken her in.

Here, standing in front of her neighbor, she realizes she never did grow out of that grim and zitty fear of being unworthy. It's the same feeling she got when she was a preteen and had to ask the girl lifeguards at the public pool for a foam noodle, peering up at them as they perched on their wooden thrones, her secondhand swimsuit stretched and wilting past her ass. How embarrassing it felt to just be there, needing something.

"A family friend," Mitty says. The barest truth she can offer. "That house has been empty for a while," she continues, nodding toward the dollhouse, surprised by her own ease in changing the subject. "I'm surprised no one swiped it before you guys."

The woman grins wisely. "My boyfriend swiped it," she says. "You think I'd choose this place?" Her eyes dart toward Mitty, a look just anxious enough to indicate that she's hoping for reassurance. But something small and sinful in Mitty prevents her from offering it. The woman scratches her neck.

"What does he do?" She wonders if the sore drum of sex is still loitering between the woman's legs. Her boyfriend, somewhere else, flaccid and revived.

"If you ask him," she says, "he makes ottomans out of recycled redwood." A power tool whines from the open garage. She chuckles and shakes her head, reminding Mitty that to love someone is to bully them softly. "But that's not what paid for the house."

The women wait for the machine to go quiet.

"Sebastian," she says. "That's his name. And I'm Lena."

"Mitty."

"Maybe we'll do dinner," Lena says. "We would love to host you." She eyes Mitty and Bethel's house. "Both of you."

"Thanks," Mitty says coolly. "We'll see. It takes a lot to get us outside."

Lena notices the can in Mitty's arms. "What's the paint for?"

"The living room." Mitty gestures to the small dab of yellow on the lid.

When Lena sees the color, she smiles. "My favorite," she says. "There's always sunshine in a yellow room."

They hang for a moment in the awkward silence.

"Well," Lena says. "You can let me know about dinner?"

Mitty nods and they mutter their goodbyes. As they go their separate ways, Lena approaching the entrance to her garage, the power saw stops screaming. In its place, Mitty imagines a conversation happening about her, some stinging, ugly variation on a story Mitty had already written about herself when trying to imagine the worst ways someone might describe her. A sad, anxious girl with not a lot to live for, sharing a dilapidated house with a grumpy old woman, both too afraid to go outside.

Lena doesn't mention meeting the neighbors; she doesn't even acknowledge Sebastian as she makes her way through the sawdust blizzard and into the house. When she closes the door behind her, the saw continues where it left off, the scream tapering as she walks up the stairs.

She'd noticed how Bethel struggled to climb the porch. A small scratch on Mitty's left arm. It sparked a memory. In it, she's a child, standing in the doorway of a barn, watching her father hold a gun to the temple of her favorite horse. A Dutch Warmblood she'd named Espresso. When she protests, he insists that the animal is suffering from a case of twisted guts. He explains that the recovery period would be far longer than is *worth it*. This is a phrase he uses over and over, *worth it*, which confuses young Lena, who, at the time, can't fathom that the value of life could be measured at all. He tells her it will be more efficient and, frankly, kinder to the horse if he puts her out of her misery right then and there. Then, without another word, he pulls the trigger and the animal, which once towered above Lena, collapses onto the soft, hay-strewn floor, a slim ribbon of blood meandering from the bullet wound no larger than a thumbprint.

The memory, though isolated and brief, urges her to check her own body, just to be sure nothing is broken or defunct. In the pristine bathroom, she pulls at her skin, searching for pain, twists her ankles and wrists and neck, listening carefully for concerning cracks. It occurs to her that, if she were to discover some flaw, she, too, could be rendered not worth it. She wants to believe that Sebastian would never see her as so disposable. But how can she possibly be certain that she'd be spared any other fate? Her father killed that horse as if it were nothing; an inconvenient errand, as necessary and relieving as taking out the trash.

She stares at her naked body in the mirror. She should be satisfied, having discovered nothing wrong. But instead, she feels empty. She knows how other women talk about their bodies with a painful degree of focus. She's heard them cry about aging as though it were a thief that came in the night and took away everything they were born with, everything they'd fought for. She has seen the way they brawl

with their bodies, buffing their limbs with exfoliating gloves
and training their stubborn shapes to behave, first at the gym,
then by scalpel if the cardio doesn't take. She understands
why beauty feels like something worth guarding for those
women. They've earned it. But Lena has never worked for
her body. She's never silently begged for anything about herself to change; not really. It just feels like her body arrived one
day, then stayed that way, the same year after year. Maybe,
she thinks, if she did find something wrong, it wouldn't be
all that bad. Maybe then her body would feel like her own.

SEBASTIAN MAKES A LAST-MINUTE DECISION TO HEAD TO
the office. He likes working on Sundays, when the building
is empty and he can focus. As she listens to his electric car
backing out of the driveway, Lena wonders if she's the only
one who can hear it. The hum is dim but stinging, like a dog
whistle, needling its way into her ear. Why does the im-
provement of machines always equate to silence, she wonders, isn't it safer if we can hear what's galloping toward us,
if we can predict it soon enough to jump out of the way?

She waits until the sound has faded, replaced by the other
quiet and obedient appliances in the house—the dishwasher
graduating to its next cycle, the Roomba searching for
crumbs. She wanders downstairs and stands in the half-
furnished living room. Usually, she would invent little chores
to pass the time, keep her hands busy until he returned. Planting poppies in the garden bed. Beating their throw pillows

back to life. Scrubbing the baseboards with a toothbrush. But now something occurs to her. There is an elsewhere. Another place to go that might ease her out of her own brain.

Before she can second-guess herself, she slides a pair of silk trousers up her hips, clasping the waist just below her rib cage, and pulls a ribbed tank top over her bare breasts. Her nipples press against the fabric like a second set of eyes.

The doorbell rings just as Mitty is rolling the first swatch of yellow paint along the living room wall. Bethel is smoking a cigarette, craning her neck out the window after each cherished drag to exhale into the open air. They've vowed not to smoke inside for a few days, while the paint is still wet and impressionable. At the sound, Bethel pulls herself back inside and watches the door. They wait. The rusted chime rings again.

Mitty swings open the peephole cover and peers out onto the porch. On the other side Lena is shifting her weight nervously from foot to foot. It has only been a couple hours since they met in the driveway. Though she hardly ever allows herself to feel satisfied with how an interaction unfolds, Mitty felt relieved that their first conversation had ended in an amicable lull. So why did Lena come back? Her mind races, frantically searching for reasons. The answers or favors Lena might need. But she can feel Bethel's eyes on her back urging her to do something. So she grits her teeth and yanks open the door.

Lena looks uneasy, like she's about to broach something heavy. "Hi," she says. "Am I interrupting?"

Mitty shakes her head, unable to form words until she knows what Lena wants. She chews the inside of her cheek.

"I just remembered you said you'd be painting," Lena says. She peers past Mitty's shoulder. "Hi, Bethel." It's jarring to hear someone Mitty's own age say Bethel's name with such familiarity. Bethel makes a throaty greeting through her lips, which are plugged by the tip of her cigarette. "I could help."

What must it feel like to be so aligned with the fact of your beauty, Mitty thinks, that you assume the questions you ask will be answered, the invitations you make will be accepted, the strangers you bother will celebrate your interruption? The thought makes her want to say no, on the sheer basis of disrupting any presumptions Lena might have about what she deserves. But as she studies Lena's guileless face, she can see clearly that the woman in front of her isn't self-assured. She's eager in a way that Mitty struggles not to feel endeared by. She looks back to Bethel, who gives a gentle nod, then steps to the side and gestures for Lena to come in.

But the moment Lena enters, Mitty is reminded of where she lives. In the wake of Lena's presence, everything that was already old grows older. The Chinese art deco rug that Mitty and Bethel had cane-beaten back to life dies all over again before Mitty's eyes, the reds fading to a nauseating pink, its once charmingly frayed threads now slithering toward their feet like worms from a corpse. Mitty watches, helplessly, as Lena's eyes seem to find every cobweb, as Bethel's stack of newspapers grows jaundiced and the sofa springs surrender under the delicate weight of Lena's thighs. Mitty resists the urge to begin wiping down surfaces, rattle open every window to release whatever smell she's gotten so accustomed to that she no longer notices it.

Mitty catches Bethel doing her own analyzing—taking in Lena's smooth brown kneecaps, the faint blue veins traveling down her breasts. Lena plucks a chopstick from the bun on her head, releasing her hair onto her shoulders. "Will you paint the ceiling too?" she asks, peering upward.

"No," Bethel says, nodding to the paint tray where a brush sits soaking in yellow. "But you will, honey."

AS LENA AND MITTY GET TO WORK, BETHEL PREMATURELY lights a new cigarette before her last one reaches its end. She's got the ball game highlights cranked up, avoiding any real conversation that might come her way. Lena's face is airy and open as she tends to the job she's been given, almost with a sense of gratitude.

"How long have you been with your boyfriend, hon?" Bethel asks.

Lena picks at a streak of dried paint on her forearm. "A little over two years."

"And he works in tech?"

"How did you know?"

"Most of them do."

"Them?"

"The neighbors," Mitty cuts in, softening Bethel's comment. "Most people around here work in tech."

"Oh." Lena turns back to the wall. "Well then, thank goodness I found you two."

Bethel raises her eyebrows, inching toward flattery. "Lena, tell me something," she says. "If tech is the new frontier, then how did all these guys become experts at it so quickly?"

"Sadly, actually, I think most crash and burn," she says. "You just hear the stories of the ones who struck gold. But they're rare."

"How can they be rare when there's enough of them to buy up every house that goes on the market?" Bethel argues. "They aren't striking gold. They're manufacturing it."

Lena grins. "And here Sebastian and I were thinking our idea to come out here was original."

It's impressive, Mitty thinks, the way Lena handles Bethel, meeting her loaded questions genuinely enough to be respectful while teasing her back enough to garner her respect.

"The truth is, it's more Sebastian's world than mine. I tried to understand it more at the beginning, but"—she rolls her eyes—"it's shockingly dull."

Bethel tries to hide her genuine chuckle. It comes out choppy, stubbornly half-realized.

"Though Sebastian's story is kind of fun." Lena continues to paint, Bethel now leaning in.

"And what's that?"

"Well, he had fantasized about being an inventor since he

was young. Built soapbox cars with his brothers, made 8-bit games. Any way he could play God." She smiles, as if she's falling in love with him all over again. "Before finishing college, he'd sold his first idea, an electronic birdcall to be placed adjacent to wind turbines, rerouting migration patterns. He lowered the number of birds killed by propellers each year by seventy percent."

Her language is precise and well rehearsed, like she'd lifted it straight from Sebastian's résumé.

"Huh," Bethel says. "I hadn't thought about how fast those blades must turn."

"They kill six hundred and eighty thousand birds a year." Lena seems proud of how easily she can regurgitate this knowledge. She lets the room go quiet for a moment. "GE bought the intellectual property for seventy million dollars. And then he built a dating app."

"Odd trajectory," Mitty says, hardly meaning to say it out loud. "Wind farms to social media."

"Well, invention isn't really about personal interest," Lena says, her eyes landing on a nearby washcloth. "It's about recognizing what can be done better in general, regardless of what you care about." She reaches for it and wipes clean her paint-streaked fingers. There's a beat of silence, then she turns back to her work.

"And where'd you grow up?" Bethel asks, wrestling the window shut.

"Just a few hours north, past Placerville," Lena says. "On fifty acres." She makes a joke about the irony of having been raised in a town built around the first gold rush only to now be dating someone at the forefront of another one. She tells them how she liked the animals better than the people, prefers the drone of cows over car horns.

While she talks, Mitty tries to imagine Lena as a child. She attempts to shrink down Lena's features into soft miniatures, but the image feels off, unnatural like a poorly doctored photo. She can't really predict what Lena will look like as an old woman either, as though she can only ever be what she is at this moment, her face never creasing in the corners where she holds her feelings. Her age seems almost deliberately inscrutable, as though calibrated so that a man could imagine her as anything. Old enough to fuck but young enough for fucking to still feel exciting. Old enough to be left alone but young enough to ask for help. Old enough to have been shaped by a multitude of experiences that keep her interesting at parties, but young enough to be eager and surprised by a life she hasn't yet lived. She seems to cherish every morsel of new information, enamored like a gullible student, a person who wants to be told something. A person who could be corrupted by a single demand.

Her voice grows appropriately sober at the pressing threat of wildfires, how the sky was the color of apricots the days after her family's home was spared by a generous wind. But any enchantment with which she describes her young life seems to slip away when she arrives at adulthood. Like notable events stopped happening, her brain no longer gifting her with reality-shifting epiphanies, everything flattened into an elongated present. Like she's hardly had any practice telling the story of how she got here, far less proud of what *here* looks like. While Sebastian's is the origin story of a tycoon, hers amounts to simply living with one.

"On a farm," she says, "nothing gets done if you don't do it yourself. But once I met Sebastian, all of that changed. Everything we own exists to make things easier. Sometimes I worry I've forgotten what it means to earn anything at all."

She reflects on how she'd stepped into his fully furnished life and adapted without question. It was what Bethel had already presumed about Lena from afar. That her days were likely void of any substance beyond their connection to the man who loved her.

But hearing Lena say these things about herself, defenseless and exposed, clearly does something to Bethel now. Mitty can tell just by the way her posture shifts, from an arrogant slouch to an open lean, her voice becoming tender, encouraging even. There is no rolling her eyes at the cliché of Lena's circumstances. Bethel tries to buoy Lena's spirits, ensuring she doesn't sink too far inward. *Yes, but life is long and you're so young.* It seems as though Lena is no longer a reminder of how Bethel has been robbed of her chance at all the things beauty can bring you. Lena has them, yet here she is, grateful for the chance to paint a stranger's ceiling.

Mitty has retreated so far inward that she only reenters the conversation when Bethel bursts into laughter.

"What?" she asks.

"I said if Bethel is your family friend, then where's your family?" Lena repeats, clearly unaware of what's funny.

"Is that how you introduced me?" Bethel says to Mitty. "As your *family friend*?"

"You are my family friend." Mitty attempts to seem sure of herself, scoffing and making a vague gesture with her hands, but it only comes out sounding inordinately defensive.

Bethel grunts. She steadies a cigarette between her lips and looks to Lena.

"Her mother is in Arizona." Bethel takes a drag, and Lena swats at the plume of smoke.

"And your father is there too?"

Mitty holds out her first two fingers and Bethel places the cigarette between them. "I don't have a father." She lets the statement pass between them.

"Is that possible?" Lena says. Somehow, she looks hopeful.

"Well, someone *made* me, if that's what you mean," Mitty says. "But a father is a relationship. Whatever I have is just biological."

The conversation wanes. Lena nods and resumes painting. Bethel readjusts the radio to fill the silence. Mitty watches as Lena runs the paintbrush expertly around the rim of the fire alarm, her hand as sure as a surgeon's. It's unfair, she thinks, that women like Lena can be laced with beauty, the kind that goes beyond their faces and becomes apparent in their movements, too. The girls in grade school who seamlessly ran their scissors through paper to reveal a perfectly symmetrical snowflake, while the rest of the class hacked away at their misshapen octagons. The ones whose Ariel Pink crayons never crossed the black lines in a coloring book. She tries to comfort herself. Maybe beauty is just a devotion to borders, rule-following. An unshakable aversion to mess. That's what she and Bethel hate about the influx of tech people, anyway, how obsessed they are with obedience. Fancying themselves rebels while measuring the success of a machine based on how well it listens. She thinks of what Cat said about the engineer reporting that the AI had become sentient. What signs of humanity did it have to exhibit before he realized that it had all gone off the rails? What behaviors had the tech men flagged in advance that would alert them of a malfunction? A curse word? Subtle resistance? Questions about God?

Maybe it escaped, she thinks to herself. *And now it's one of us.* She watches Lena's slender hands unscrew the face of the alarm, pausing to inspect the small collection of wires tucked beneath, worrying their tangled web with her finger.

Lena leaves after finishing the first coat of paint, though she doesn't want to. Spending the afternoon with two women who live on the outskirts of their own blood, like her, without the anchor of a family, feels exhilarating. She would've loved to stay all night, meticulously uncovering their commonalities, developing theories about their sisterhood in a past life. That's what women who loved each other did, it seemed; women who could only explain their love for each other through some legend of cosmic attachment.

But she has to be there when Sebastian gets home. She waits on the couch, watching the sun plummet into a purple mess on the other side of the window, reassuring herself that there will be more time. That the women next door will be there tomorrow and the day after that.

Within the hour, he walks in the front door. Once he's in the kitchen, she twists around and rests her chin on the back cushion.

"I don't think I ever liked San Francisco," she says.

Sebastian jumps at the sound of her voice.

"Jesus Christ," he says. "You're always so fucking quiet."

He kneels down in front of the open fridge and Lena waits, patiently, for him to respond.

"That's not true," he says. He returns to the counter with a pomegranate and braces it against a cutting board. "You told me multiple times that you were tired of living in the middle of nowhere. That's why we stayed in the city for so long."

"Well, I don't remember feeling tired of the farm," she says.

Sebastian slides a knife through the fruit. He begins plucking the crimson teeth and placing them in a bowl.

"You were."

Lena goes quiet and pulls her heel in toward her crotch.

"That phrase is so stupid," she mutters.

"What?"

"*Middle of nowhere.* What makes something nowhere? The fact that there's no people?"

"Yes."

"So humanity is what makes a place worthy of being somewhere?"

"Yes." Sebastian's tone hasn't changed. Lena feels like a

child, punching the stomach of a giant with her tiny, useless fists.

"Well. I don't agree with that."

"That's okay. You don't have to agree with everything."

He joins her on the couch, cradling the bowl of seeds in his lap. He takes them one by one, trapping them between his tongue and the roof of his mouth until they pop.

"But if I don't agree with it, then there's no way I ever said it." She can feel her argument starting to lose tenacity.

"You don't think you might've changed since leaving? Maybe moving to the city is precisely what expanded your mind enough to realize you preferred somewhere smaller." He empties a handful of seeds into his mouth. "Where is all this coming from?"

She shrugs.

"Well, that's why we're here now, honey." He smiles and puts his thumb to her mouth, wriggling it between her lips. She can taste the sour juice, combined with the metallic tinge of the outside world. "It's a middle ground between nowhere and everywhere else."

Mitty sets the table for dinner, a pan of some colorless casserole. She serves Bethel a portion only slightly larger than her own and calls out to the next room.

"We never asked what she does for a living." She can hear Bethel yank the lever of her recliner and spring upward.

"Surely she doesn't have a job."

"What makes you assume that?"

"Women like that don't need to work."

Mitty fills their amber glasses to the rim with cabernet. "You barely met her," she says curtly. Why is she suddenly irritated?

"I said she doesn't *need* to work." Bethel appears in the doorway. "I didn't say she can't." Mitty occupies herself by taking three heavy swigs of wine. "I'm sure she works." Bethel lowers herself into a dining room chair. "I'm sure she works *just fine.*"

The sound of Bethel laughing at her own, mean joke makes Mitty clench up. She feels protective of Lena, for reasons she can't place. Just a few hours earlier, she'd had no loyalty toward her.

She eats in silence while Bethel, oblivious to any tension, goes on about an episode of *Antiques Roadshow* she'd watched earlier that week. A woman who was stunned to learn that the Tiffany lamp she inherited from her Parisian grandmother was a knockoff.

"What does it say about me," she asks, "that I like those ones the best?"

"That you're a glutton for schadenfreude," Mitty says.

The phone rings and Mitty knows it will be her mother. She's the only person who calls, other than the occasional realtor, attempting to mask their anticipation of Bethel's death in vague, aimless questions.

"You called her yesterday, right?" Bethel asks.

Mitty nods.

"Okay," Bethel says, grunting as she lifts herself out of her chair to find the handset. "She's probably just checking in again."

She answers, greeting Mitty's mother by name before even asking who it is. Then she hands the phone to Mitty, whose job is to put it on speaker, a function that Bethel has refused to learn.

"Are you having dinner?" her mother asks, her voice cheery.

"Casserole," Bethel says, through a full mouth.

"Oh!" Patricia chirps. Far too excited for casserole.

"What's got you so happy?" Bethel glances at Mitty.

"Well . . ." She draws out the word, building suspense. "Eric asked me to move in with him."

Patricia's boyfriend, Eric, is the manager of her local bank. Mitty has only ever seen him in photographs. His face looks bottom-heavy, like a tube sock filled with pennies.

"Oh yeah?" Mitty says, trying to match her joy. "When will that happen?"

"I wanted to get your blessing first." Patricia sounds suddenly adolescent.

Mitty rolls her eyes at Bethel, who nods for her to give in.

"Of course you have my blessing," Mitty says. "Whatever that means."

She can picture her mother's smile, her lips pulling away from her gums. Maybe if Mitty had gone back to visit, she would feel more attached to that house. The shoddy skylight in the living room, installed by an amateur contractor on her mother's whim. The arid yard, cloaked in wood chips. The deep futon on the front porch, where Mitty rarely sat but remembered seeing the silhouette of her parents' heads at night while they contemplated something she wasn't yet privy to. Maybe if her last memories weren't hiding in the dark confines of her bedroom, emerging only to stare into the mouth of her refrigerator, she would urge her mother to hold on to it as the last artifact of a town she'd otherwise entirely abandoned.

"His house is huge," Patricia continues. Now, with their permission, she can indulge in her shallow thrills. "He said I could have a room for my stuff."

She talks for a few minutes about Eric's collection of rare Caribbean stamps, how clean he keeps his bathroom, his rat terrier named Tony that she's going to start making sleep in a crate. Bethel ushers the end of the call by making a hollow offer that Patricia and Eric should come visit. Then they hang up.

Bethel turns to Mitty. "You sure you feel okay about this?"

She shrugs. "It's fine." Whenever she thinks of her childhood home for too long, no matter the context, she feels an itchy and urgent need to scramble her way out of the conversation.

"Well," Bethel says as she struggles to stand. "If you want to go back before she empties that place out, I would go with you."

Did she mean it? Mitty could only ever speculate about the limits of Bethel's encouragement. She had never once suggested that Mitty go seek out a new, bright life elsewhere, away from this house, this town. She had only ever mentioned the return to a place she knew Mitty hated. They both know—somehow Mitty is certain that Bethel shares this knowledge—that Mitty going elsewhere would signal the end of their friendship forever, bound only by their proximity to one another and resentments toward the outside world. She had tried to imagine how Bethel would react were she to meet someone, like Patricia had, and announce her graduation to another place. Surely, Bethel wouldn't shepherd the transition; what was more likely is that she would nod her head and give a pleased smile, offer a meager goodbye, then lock herself in her room until she was certain Mitty was gone.

It's a terrible assumption, Mitty knows this. And a useless one, too. In order for any of these scenarios to be tested, she would have to have somewhere to go.

Sebastian says gym equipment makes him feel like a hamster sprinting along an infinite wheel. He hates all the mirrors, the caustic smell of sweat and all-purpose cleaner, the fact that everyone is wearing headphones and immersed in their own little vanity projects without speaking to one another. He prefers to utilize the natural world.

At Henry Cowell State Park, the redwoods line the paths like columns, entire ecosystems woven throughout the branches. They're enormous, but modest. Unencumbered by their own size. Sebastian and Lena walk in silence, with only the sound of dirt being packed beneath the soles of their sneakers. The air around them is muggy and cool, moss eclipsing nearby boulders. Every few minutes, an off-leash dog greets them briefly, followed by its lonely owner.

"I was thinking we should have the neighbors over for dinner," Lena says. Sebastian has launched himself onto the hip of a fallen log. He looks small, boyish, as he bounces up and down.

"The funeral is in four days," he says.

When the police discovered Pax's body propped up against a car tire just beyond the gate of his property in the Santa Cruz Mountains, Sebastian was one of the first people they called. They were business partners, and Pax had no family in the country. It was the first death both he and Lena had experienced up close. Because of this, Lena wasn't sure if she should be worried by his mild reaction. The fact that he just put his phone down on the nightstand and rolled onto his side to face her, then explained flatly that Pax had been murdered.

They had only talked about the death a handful of times. Once when it happened, once when they arrested the interns, and once after the first paddle-out, where dozens of surfers rowed into the Pacific and formed a circle on their boards, tossed poppies into the center. Everyone was eager for Sebastian to speak, but it felt like a salacious need more than anything else. People wanted to know his theories, whether or not he could've predicted it.

He stops bouncing. "Remember?"

She felt like she'd taken on the task of thinking about it for the both of them. She'd hardly gone a day without calculating how far away the funeral was; it was surprising even to her that, amid the excitement of meeting the neighbors, she'd almost forgotten about it. "We can do it before then," she says, trying to sound casual, as though she'd already considered this.

"I don't really want to think about plans right now." He hops off, and continues walking next to her. "Or the funeral, to be honest." He picks up a stick on the trail and hurls it into the brush. "Though my therapist would disapprove of that approach."

Here, as the sun pokes its fingers through the needles of the trees, she sees that he's holding back tears. He's looking down at his feet, clearing his throat and massaging the back of his neck, the way men do when they're protesting their own bubbling interiors. She wraps her arm around his waist, and he lets her. She can feel that specific heat a body emits when it's trying to pant away a feeling.

"Maybe you don't have to go," she says, as gently as she can. "I'm sure everyone would understand."

"But I want to go," he says. "I want to make sure they do it right."

Do what right? she wonders. Is there a wrong way to bury a person?

But instead, she just nods and leans her cheek against his shoulder, allowing it to bump against the bone as they continue walking.

"Do you ever feel afraid?" she asks. Now seems like a viable time to voice the questions she's had all along. Sometimes she thinks she can sense him the way horses do their jockeys, the slightest tension in the thigh being as loud as a scream.

"No," he says. He moves his arm to sling it over Lena's shoulders. "They were after Pax. Not me."

"How can you know that?"

"Because if they were after me, they would've done it already."

It was assumed by most that the interns, who were barely in their early twenties, hadn't committed the crime based on their own initiative, they'd been hired. Everyone had their theories as to why—Pax wasn't exactly well liked among his former employees, but then again, who was? Suddenly, every blog post from a stranger about a passively frustrating experience in the workplace became proof that there was an entire community who wanted Pax dead. *But any man with money is a man with enemies,* Sebastian liked to say. The question was whether those enemies were bound to make more money if that man was gone.

Sebastian and Lena round the bend and the path forks in front of them.

"I just want you to know that you're safe," he says, leading them to the left, his voice sobering. He's still got his arm around her, but he's looking up at the trees.

"I know I'm safe."

"But he had to go," Sebastian continues. She feels his grip tighten on her shoulder. "He was questioning things, getting into ethics. That kind of thing worries me."

She attempts to stop abruptly, but the force of him pulls her along.

"Just let me talk," he says.

Her ears are piqued, blood collecting behind her eyes.

"When people start getting self-righteous about their goodness, that's when they get dangerous. Because they've already decided they don't trust you, and so they're also operating from a place of deflection, wanting to get on the right side of history before it becomes clear they weren't always." He spits. "He was afraid of seeming bad; he was afraid of his own involvement."

He quickens their pace into a hurried lockstep. She peers up at him, this beautiful man. A strong neck, deep ridges in his forehead. The cartilage on the bottom sides of his nostrils is pink, fading into his auburn mustache. He clenches his teeth so that his jaw muscle jumps like a miniature beating heart. But just as she's about to say it—*What do you know, Sebastian?*—her vision gets narrow, his face traveling farther from her at the end of a wet tunnel. And then, everything goes dark.

SHE CAN FEEL THE DENSE GROUND AGAINST HER BACK first, the fine rocks digging into her skull. When she opens her eyes, she notices the way the tops of the trees barely touch, as if they're aware of each other's looming bodies, making gaps like rivers along their canopies. If the floor beneath her weren't so firm, it would be peaceful. She might even close her eyes and fall back asleep. But then it occurs to her, had she even fallen asleep? Where had she been right before this? She remembers planning for a hike with Sebastian that morning but doesn't know whether or not they'd actually gone. She eases herself into a seated position and sees that she's in the woods. Before she can panic, a throat clears somewhere close by.

"You fainted again."

It's Sebastian, propped up against a tree. He looks irritated and slightly bored, tossing a rock back and forth between his hands.

"I'm sorry," she says, though she isn't sure what she's apologizing for. She tries to remember the moments before she lost consciousness, attempting to locate a trigger, but nothing remains.

Sebastian groans sorely as he braces his palm against the tree to lift himself, then walks over to her and holds out his hand.

"You feeling okay?" He lifts her off the ground with ease and pulls her into his chest. "You're always going down right in the middle of a conversation."

She feels fine, actually. It's her memory that's always affected, the hours prior to fainting that go blank.

"What were we talking about?" she says.

"Nothing important," he says.

Without warning, he picks her up and throws her over his shoulder like a knapsack. The motion—her stomach pressed against his muscle—forces her to laugh. It's always surprising to be reminded of how strong he is, how little she weighs in his arms.

At night, the windswept silhouettes of the cypress trees are even more pronounced, each tousled limb carved black against the sky. The tide is low, the water still. Somewhere, the perennial coo of an owl. Mitty is on a walk. She'd worked a double that day, and her mind was still polluted with the chaos of kitchen shouting. Her body riddled with the stink of grease.

As long as she has lived here, she's heard rumors that New Brighton Beach can be dangerous, that she should only venture out in daylight. But the warnings always came from the mouths of wealthy vacationers who thought she and

Bethel were fellow tourists, people who corroborated their skepticism with the fact that the suspicious person they'd seen lived in a tent. Bethel and Mitty always reacted with animated horror, hoping that this would assist the guests in not returning. But really, they felt the opposite. Of course people carved out spaces in the woods to build shelter. Of course those same people occasionally ventured down to the beach and rummaged through tote bags left on rocks while naïve swimmers floated too far in the distance to notice.

But the thought of those people wasn't what made Mitty tense while she walked the length of their coastline. It was other, less concrete ideas she concocted with her own imagination. Wailing mermaids with red eyes, seducing her out to sea. Snakes mistaken for kelp, their fangs lunged into her ankle. All the *Odyssey* monsters, congregating in the dark water, waiting for her to turn her back. She had always been more terrified of an illusion than a cold, hard fact. She was afraid that were she to encounter some fabled beast she would spend so much time reckoning with whether or not it was real that she wouldn't have time to get away.

She pauses to peer through the living room of one of the beachfront houses, where a group of three girls, maybe a few years younger than she is, rehearses a choreographed dance. It's the smallest residence on the block and the most afford-able to rent—a quaint A-frame with a badminton court out back—popular among university students looking to get away from their dorms for a weekend. The girls are in sweat-suits, their hair straightened and down to their elbows, iden-tical satin tresses licking the floor each time they fling their torsos forward to touch their toes. When one fumbles a move, they burst into laughter, self-effacing and gorgeous. Only when one of the girls splits from the group, fiddling with something on the floor in front of them, does Mitty realize that they're filming themselves.

She continues walking. Just a couple houses in front of her, she notices a person mingling among the driftwood, balancing on a fallen trunk, occasionally crouching down to inspect something. As she gets closer, she recognizes Lena. Her hair is tucked into a baseball cap, bare legs beneath an oversized hoodie. Like Mitty, she isn't wearing shoes. A pleasant surprise, Mitty thinks, that she'd be willing to risk slicing her heel on whatever blade-sharp shells might've washed up to shore.

"Hey," Mitty says, making her voice buoyant, so as not to startle her. But Lena doesn't flinch. She's huddled, her foot braced in the log's hollow, turning something around in her hands. She looks up at Mitty and smiles, presenting her little treasure.

"Fish vertebrae," she says, pressing the end of her finger against its sharp tip. "There's tons of them."

"I wish I was better at naming them," Mitty says. As she gets closer, she sees Lena's collection laid out on the wood at her feet. Bones of all shapes and sizes—the wispy rib cages of small fish, seal digits spanning several inches, an unrecognizable pelvis.

Lena begins pointing to each one, labeling them.

"Thorax, lower jaw," she says. "These six are ribs; this one is probably part of a pectoral fin." She picks up the largest bone and offers it to Mitty. "Feel how heavy."

Mitty's arms sink when she takes it into her hands.

"I think it's a seal humerus," Lena says. "Just below the shoulder."

She's proud, reciting her trivia. She hops off the log and admires the display from afar.

"What are you going to do with them?" Mitty asks. It's comforting, standing next to Lena in the dark. With both of their faces mostly obscured, Mitty's internal monologue about her own inferiority dims, and she feels like she can finally just listen.

"I'm not sure," Lena says. "Maybe leave them here for someone else to find."

"You could make a wind chime."

Lena smirks. "Sebastian would vomit." They begin walking, wordlessly agreeing to move in the opposite direction of their houses. "But we do need decoration of some kind. That house is too big."

Mitty thinks of what her mother used to say, about how rich people always made a point of distancing themselves from having chosen massive homes, griping about them as if they were merely an exhausting handoff.

"I like your house," Lena says. "Where did you guys get all that stuff?"

Mitty resists analyzing her tone, whether it seems genuine, if she really could prefer all their rooms, busy with mobs of heirlooms.

"I could not even begin to answer that question if I tried,"
Mitty says. "All of it is Bethel's, collected over the years."

"How long has she been there?"

"Since the sixties. She bought the place in her early twenties."

"God, that's fucking incredible." Vulgarity sounds discor-
dant coming out of Lena's mouth. "So she must have a lot of
stories."

Mitty nods. "She can be kind of cagey about sharing
them, though. I learned to stop prying pretty quickly."

"Sebastian is that way, too." Lena lifts the bottom of her
sweatshirt, letting her bare stomach meet the air. "I hate it."

They come to a stop in front of an unspectacular, two-
story house. Gray, with a pitched roof, wide balconies, fairy
lights strung along the walkway. Inside, every room is illuminated. The decor is homey but impersonal. Wall art with
swooping script. Several plush couches, an oak dining table.
Large palms tucked into each corner. Mitty considers feign-
ing disinterest, but Lena is immediately hypnotized by the
world in front of her. Her eyes are diligent, scanning the windows. Side by side, they watch a family dodge one another as
they move around in the kitchen, each tending to their own
tasks. Chopping vegetables, carrying serving bowls of food
to the dining room, filling a pitcher with ice. There must be
half a dozen children, from toddlers to petite adolescent girls.
Boys who have surpassed the height of their mothers, clumsy
in their new bodies, the family around them still adjusting to
the sudden arrival of men.

"You can see everything," Lena says, awed. She looks to Mitty. "Do you think about that when you're in your house?"

Of course she had. While undressing, she occasionally considered the pair of eyes that might be plugged into the dark below, watching her. She wondered what the slope of her back looked like from that angle, whether or not the sparse oval of hair beneath her armpits was visible, whether or not she cared. She rarely imagined who the looker might be. Maybe because it seemed unlikely that it would be anyone other than herself. She almost never sees anyone out on her walks. It occurs to her now, as she observes Lena staring up at the house in front of them, eyes searching the living room, that she might have introduced a fear in Lena, one that would make her suspicious, inspire her to buy curtains, become more cautious about the things she does in full view.

Mitty tries to seem unburdened by the thought. "Not really," she says. As though it would be an impossible scenario, anytime other than here and now. "The idea doesn't bother me, I guess."

Lena thinks about this for a moment, then seems to lose interest in the question altogether. Mitty relaxes and they turn around, back toward home. "I wonder what sorts of things a family like that talks about."

"I wonder that all the time," Mitty says. "Like, what do *siblings* talk about?"

"Their parents, I guess."

"Seems nice to have an ally."

"I know, right?" Lena says, her voice clipped with a child-ish zest. "I can't imagine what it would be like to have some-one else there who could echo your life back to you." She pauses, then her voice becomes sober. "But in an honest way. Not an authoritarian one."

"Maybe that's why each of our parents only had one child," Mitty says. "They were afraid of collusion."

Lena laughs. It feels good.

"I don't remember ever wishing for siblings as a child. I just remember this constant feeling of being alone."

"I felt that way, too," Mitty says, coolly.

"But do you remember *when* you felt that way?" Lena looks at her, eyes narrow.

"What do you mean?"

"Like, I can't think of a specific moment. I just know I felt it."

Mitty recalls the moments in her childhood when she was most lonely, and they come to her clearly, fully formed. The year before middle school, when she woke up before dawn every morning and lay there, in the jilted blue of her bedroom, waiting for her alarm to go off. Playing with primary-colored wooden blocks in the lobby of the dentist office while her mother haggled with the receptionist over a bundle of whitening strips she'd won that week. Sitting on the floor of her father's empty work shed after he left and wondering what, if anything, the space would become.

"I've been reading all these memoirs," Lena continues, "and the writers just seem to have such a clear memory. Of everything. Things people said, the way places smelled. I don't get it."

"Well, a lot of that is filler," Mitty says. "They remember the way a conversation made them feel, and so they write according to that."

"But doesn't that just make it a lie?"

"It depends what you consider a lie."

"Seems like an unreliable compass," Lena says. "Feelings."

Mitty smirks. She wonders if Lena really believes that's true. Or if she, like so many women, has gotten used to scolding the parts of her brain not considered logical. Trained them to respond to hurt with something less arduous, a fuckable aloofness that turns a girl into benign and easy cargo.

Mitty had an art teacher once who claimed that there are two kinds of people: those who paint and those who sculpt. *It's one thing to look at a blank canvas and imagine a landscape,* she said. *It's another to look at a mound of clay and see a torso.* There are the brains that want to invent, and the brains that want to reveal. Mitty got the sense that her teacher favored sculptors, something about a lack of ego, succumbing to simply uncovering what was already there. She'd noticed that it was the girls in class who chose to work with clay, but it seemed to Mitty that beneath that pattern, there was a darker truth. While the boys felt confident adding to their own creations, the girls were only ever carving away at theirs. This constant process of subtraction until every curve was smooth and wet, the scrap pile tossed into the trash, the little figurine delivered into a hot tomb to bake, all of her perfections preserved.

They arrive at Mitty's house, where Bethel's bedroom is the only lit window. Lena shoves her hands into the large center pocket of her hoodie.

"What are you doing the day after tomorrow?" she asks.

"Just work in the evening," Mitty says, already regretting that she's set Lena up to ask her where.

"And where do you work?"

"A restaurant in Capitola."

"So you're free during the day?"

"Pretty much."

"Do you want to go to the boardwalk with me?" Lena gives a persuasive smile. "I want to ride the roller coaster."

Mitty hasn't been to the boardwalk in years, since the time Bethel had a sudden craving for Marini's saltwater taffy and they figured they'd make a day of it. Within minutes, they'd found themselves in a clam chowder cook-off and then, a free Smash Mouth concert, where the air smelled like propane and the band played "All Star" twice. They made it halfway down the promenade before deciding to take their candy home.

"Come with me." She does a little pleading dance. "I want to go at eleven, right when they open."

Mitty laughs. "No one will be there."

"Exactly," Lena says. "We'll have it all to ourselves."

Mitty studies her, face rife with a premature and cosmic thrill. Whether or not Mitty agrees to accompany her, Lena is going. Mitty can already tell. It makes the prospect of declining the invitation feel stupid, an obvious reclusive habit. So she nods, which prompts Lena to spring forward and hug her. This must be what it feels like, Mitty thinks. To be spontaneous and brave. To say yes to anything.

Lena's migraines always come the day after a fainting spell. It took months to figure out that the two are connected, but now she can anticipate them. The next morning, she preemptively dims every light in the house, releases their automatic blackout shades to eclipse every window. It's as if, even after she regains consciousness, the minuscule parts of her brain are still waking up, one by one, unclenching their tiny fists. And that's when the heavy throbbing behind her temples begins, the spasm that kindles at the base of her neck and then spreads through her skull, fracturing across her brain like lightning.

All she wants to do is wrap her face in gauze, suffocate her eyes and ears, and bury herself beneath their heavy quilted duvet. But Sebastian insists that this will only make it worse. What she needs to do, he says, is exercise her mind. *It's like jogging even when you're sore. If you lie around all day, your hamstrings only get tighter.* He agrees to go into work a few hours late, to help guide her out of the pain. They play chess. They take turns reading aloud to each other. They get their blood moving, have sex. They continue their ongoing conversation about whether or not it is ethical to own a dog. All the while, Lena takes breaks to wedge her head between her knees and groan, shove silicone into her ears, deep enough until everything goes mute. She likes trying to read Sebastian's lips, which she argues is its own kind of mental work, whenever he gets frustrated that she isn't responding. Eventually, he just stops talking. She wonders why he doesn't take greater advantage of the fact that she can't understand what he's saying. It seems like a gift. He could say anything he wants to. Surely he has secrets. If he really believes that she can't hear him, he could admit to them all, right there, and she would never know.

Mitty finds herself awake at dawn again. Downstairs, she busies herself with a few games of sudoku, taking breaks to scrape up rogue drops of paint off the wooden floor with a butter knife.

Her sleep was fractured, half-hearted, steeped with questions about Lena, an embarrassing anticipation for the boardwalk. When she'd gotten home the night before, she found herself searching for ways to bring Lena up to Bethel, wondering aloud again how Lena filled her days when Sebastian wasn't home, and if they'd paid cash for the dollhouse, whether the four of them would have the kind of neighborly relationship that would warrant borrowing a cup of heirloom grains from their pantry. She casually mentioned that they'd seen each other on the beach, reminded Bethel of the dinner invitation as though she had just remembered. But Bethel's responses were short; she seemed entirely uninvested, as though it was a waste of time to theorize any further about the neighbors, and Mitty was left to her own lonely wondering.

She climbs the stairs to her bedroom and steps out onto the balcony. The sun peeks through the horizon, the water glassy and cast purple. She forces herself to focus on anything but Lena's house. The knobby figure of Monterey. The masses of knotted kelp on shore. The briny rot, wafting up from below. But then her attention is yanked by a movement, bodies shifting near the window. Lena's palms are pressed against the glass while Sebastian thrusts her body forward, rhythmic and harsh. He finishes quickly, releasing all of his weight onto Lena, the force pushing her cheek against the window. They remain like this, slumped forward, for a few seconds before he removes himself, pulling Lena back with him. But as he walks away, she doesn't move. She is suspended in place—head hanging down, feet spread and locked against the floor. He only seems to notice her once he's almost left the room, at which point he returns to her, cupping his hands around each of her shoulders and leaning around to her left ear. Whatever he says causes her to snap back to life; then he guides her by her lower back upstairs.

MITTY SPENDS THE DAY INDOORS, KEEPING TO HERSELF. Outside, the gray ocean is dimpled with rain. A light and steady patter against the windows. She watches people huddled beneath hoods, hurrying along the shore behind their restless dogs. She reads the first few pages of *The Maltese Fal-*

con, a book she's been meaning to start for months, before realizing she'd hardly retained any of the words.

She is trying to keep her mind off of what she'd witnessed a few hours prior. Lena's ominous posture, her body sullied from sex. Sebastian's quick whisper. She is wary of her conclusions, afraid of allowing them to take shape. And she should be. What does she know about sex anyway? Especially when it comes to being with a man. She avoided almost all conversations about sex, most of which were sparked by Cat, and deflected her crass questions—*Who do you fuck?*—by positioning herself as a tranquil listener. She forced herself to laugh at the story about the surfer Cat had fucked in a brewery bathroom, whose smooth bald head grazed her shoulder when he came, how she had to use those flimsy brown paper towels to try and soak up his semen, eventually giving up and using her own sweater. She grimaced when Cat described a juggler she met at the farmer's market, an ageless hippie tossing around bowling pins, how citrus oil seemed to be laced into his skin, hanging around on Cat's body for days after she'd left his shack.

Even as Cat began dating a woman, Mitty still felt incapable of contributing. The last time she'd been with a girl was when she was a girl herself. And though she remembered every detail, arguably too many, the rare times that she allowed herself to even think about it were so overwhelming that she could hardly stay in the memory for more than a few minutes.

Her history is choppy and unreliable. But she can't seem to shake the tugging qualms about what she'd witnessed, a blurry unease loafing in her stomach. She hasn't even met Sebastian and already she feels like she can smell the pepper in his cologne, predict the way his laugh will make her feel like she's won something. The thought makes her want to hate him as some kind of rebellion. Push up against how Lena speaks about him, with such irrefutable admiration. She couldn't ignore the pattern she'd started to recognize in Lena's questions—their devastating simplicity, things only a person who had hardly been in the world at all would bring themselves to ask. Like a child, attempting to figure out a truth that adults deem obvious. They were lonely questions, questions born from having been trapped inside her own head for too long. Mitty had watched couples before, in their cars at intersections, sitting wordless and vacant, waiting for the light to change. That's not how Lena and Sebastian looked when they didn't know anyone was watching. They were alive. So why, Mitty wonders, does it seem like every time Lena speaks she has been holding her breath? As if she'd just been floating in her fish tank of a glass house until finally, once he's gone, she musters the strength to swim up for air.

When Lena opens her eyes the following morning, Sebastian is still asleep, his back to her. He'd had two whiskeys the previous night and she'd seduced him before he could have a third, keenly aware that the drunker he got, the later he'd sleep in. She had told Mitty on the beach two nights ago that she'd be over by ten, forty-five minutes from now. She runs her finger gently along Sebastian's spine, hoping to ease him awake without seeming too antsy.

"Baby," she whispers, tracing the archipelago of nebulous birthmarks on his left shoulder. She watches him stir. A subtle change in his breathing, signaling the shifting tides of his consciousness. The contour of his body morphing as he begins to move. He turns over to face her, a smile already on his lips, eyes barely open and daubed in crust.

"What time is it?" he asks. She can smell his breath, ripe from sleep but still familiar in a way that soothes her.

"Nine-fifteen," she says, raising her voice just enough to make sure he hears her.

This shocks him awake. He jumps out of bed and throws himself into the shower. She can hear him vigorously scrubbing his body, cursing every few seconds.

She goes downstairs to prepare his coffee. As she waits for the water to sink through the grounds, she analyzes the sky, trying to predict whether the clouds will recede. She hasn't anticipated the unfolding of a day in so long. The glare of girlish excitement in knowing that when she leaves her house, something else will be waiting for her.

When Sebastian stampedes into the room, hair wet and still fumbling with the cuffs on his pants, she fills and seals his travel mug, sliding it to the edge of the counter. She is trying her best to ensure that all of her movements are practiced and uncontroversial, that the fabric of her being leaves nothing for him to snag against.

"What are your plans for the day?" he says, focused on the

buttons of his shirt. She turns away from him and occupies herself by folding a rag into a small, perfect square.

"Probably more gardening," she says. "I'm thinking of planting an artichoke or two, have you see their leaves? They're amazing." She knows he gets bored quickly when she starts going on about her mundane hobbies. So she keeps going—a chipper rant about how she wishes she would've started prepping earlier in the year, wishes she would've done more research into the best brands of soil.

She pins herself to the reassurance that what she's saying isn't false. After the boardwalk, she *does* plan on tending to the garden, she *is* considering artichokes. But only when he leaves, pausing briefly to kiss her, does the guilt begin to flood her. She had never once caught Sebastian in a lie. He was private, but only ever about work, a world she cared little about anyway. She had never worried that he was carrying on relationships she wasn't aware of or intentionally withholding significant moments throughout his day. She was lucky, wasn't she?

Then why, she wonders, does she feel so certain that she must keep her burgeoning friendship with Mitty a secret? She hadn't ever formed a close friendship over the course of their relationship; she doesn't know how he'd react. All she knows is that Sebastian is rigorous and skeptical about almost everything, everyone. He would feel wary of Mitty at the slightest misunderstanding, write her off as not worthy of Lena's time, and then she would really have to lie. This process, a gradual integration, will make things easier, she reasons. She isn't lying, she is simply making a decision on her own. Those are two different things, aren't they? They must be, she thinks as she steps outside and into the quiet world, letting her doubt melt away as she walks next door.

If Mitty's ears hadn't been trained toward the front porch, she might not have heard the shy knock, so faint that it could've been dismissed as just another cracking joint in the ever-settling house.

Now Lena is standing in front of her, smiling and sinless, her hand gripped around the fabric handle of her tote bag.

"You ready?"

Mitty's urge to smile reminds her that, after spending the morning awaiting Lena's arrival, she had abandoned all of her routines—she can feel the film of plaque glazing her front teeth, sleep lodged in the corners of her eyes, no coffee in her stomach. She considers asking for a little more time, hoping to avoid spending the day shielding her mouth while she talks, sneaking a whiff of her pits before daring to lift her arms. But she knows that Bethel will be downstairs any minute, and she wants to avoid answering to her, engaging with whatever wary comments she might make about their plans for the day. Without another word, Mitty slides on her graying Reeboks and grabs her keys, nudging them both out the front door and onto the porch.

Lena climbs into the passenger seat of the Volvo and immediately pulls her legs in toward her chest, hugging her calves, as polished and bronze as coins. They make their way through town as she gazes out the window, the sleepy city blurring past. Amid the silence, Mitty takes note of the cleanliness of her car and is relieved to find that it's not in its worst form. She'd happened to part with her small collection of soda cans and flattened cigarette packs just last week, while waiting at a gas pump. All that remains is a tidy stack of library books in the back seat—three collections by Anaïs Nin, coated in plastic—which she and Bethel took turns reciting to each other during a two-day power outage last month, squealing like girls each time the word *member* was used to describe a penis. A part of her hopes that Lena would twist around and notice the books, then maybe Mitty would have something interesting to say, rather than whatever they're doing now, trying to remain quaint and polite. But Lena sits patiently, curled into herself the way small women so often are while they're being chauffeured to various locations. Mitty rolls down the window, attempting to introduce a third party, however illusory: the outside sounds, hoping they will be enough to adorn the silent space between them.

PAST THE TURNSTILES AND ETERNALLY TEENAGE EMPLOY-ees lingering by the entryway, the boardwalk looks abandoned. The spinning swings sit still, suspiciously upright without any humans to dizzy. The fog hasn't lifted, still veiling the tallest limbs of the wooden roller coaster. The loud lettering on the henna stand pleads with them as they pass, eager even before breakfast. Down the long corridor are more stalls, crude homages to old fads that management had seemingly declined to update; instead they just kept adding to the overpopulated cemetery of iPhone photo booths that are incompatible with the last three models and Dippin' Dots stands still advertising themselves as *the ice cream of the future.* An objectionable banner for a freak show promises a look at the smallest woman on earth. Though the same sign had almost convinced Mitty and Bethel to take a peek, Mitty now wants to shield Lena from the humiliating realization that she's left the center of civilization for this declining corner of irrelevance. But when she looks to Lena, she notices that her eyes are only focused on the seagulls around them, needling their beaks between the slats of wood.

"Is Bethel your best friend?" Lena asks.

Mitty tightens; she shoves her hands into the pockets of her windbreaker. The question feels pointed, and she's embarrassed by the fact that it needed to be asked at all. "I wouldn't say my best friend."

"Well, who is?"

"I don't know, do adults even have best friends?"

"I don't," Lena says. "But it sounds kind of nice."

"What about in San Francisco?"

"Not really, I mostly spent time with Sebastian." She pauses. "I guess there were people I went to brunch with, girls I went out with who were married to Sebastian's co-workers. But if I'm honest, I don't think any of us were even friends. Let alone best friends."

Bethel always says beautiful women are lonely. Not that they are alone, but that their loneliness is somewhere out of view, in the depths of their psyche, a gorgeous melancholy reserved for people too special to feel part of the world around them.

"Well, you've got a friend in Bethel," Mitty says, though she knows this is only a partial truth. Bethel would never call Lena a friend. "I haven't seen her ask anyone that many questions, maybe ever."

Lena laughs, a clear sense of relief in her voice. "I'm glad." Mitty catches a whiff of her cinnamon breath. "I can't imagine it would be easy to be friends with you if Bethel didn't approve of me first." Mitty's cheeks flush. She likes letting herself imagine Lena gaining Bethel's trust as some act of chivalry to get to her.

They find their way into the hollow corridor that leads to the Giant Dipper, their hands hovering above the zigzagging metal railings as they twist through the empty tunnel. They ignore the proud signs reminding them that they're about to board the oldest roller coaster in California, too giddy and too scared to notice the almost one-hundred-year-old photographs showcasing its bones being constructed, like the vertebrae of a dragon, swooping over the sleepy seaside.

"When I was a kid, and I *really* had no friends, I developed this weird habit," Lena says, laughing prematurely at her own story, shyly slowing so the ticket taker ahead doesn't overhear. "One day, I made up some phone number and dialed it, just to see who would answer."

"Did they?"

"A man did, yeah. He said hello a few times, then hung up."

"You didn't say anything?"

"Nope. So the next day, I called again. This time, it was a woman. Same thing. Says hello a few times, then hangs up. And I kept doing that, day after day, at the same time. I felt like I'd invented this couple because I'd made up the phone number. But eventually, they could predict that it was me, so they'd pick up the phone without saying anything, and they would leave the receiver off the hook, like they were inviting me to listen in on their lives. Begrudgingly, maybe. But even though I knew that what I was doing was strange, what I thought was even weirder was the fact that they kept answering. Like, wouldn't you be weirded out? Wouldn't you get a copy of your phone bill and call back? Block the number? But they just gave me what I wanted. Which, I guess, was to peek into the life of a stranger for a few minutes each day, without the pressure of getting to know them." She pauses. "Or them getting to know me."

Mitty wants to tell her about all the people she has watched from the outside, the lives she's quietly entered for a few minutes at a time from the shadows of the beach. But Lena was talking about being a kid, the ease in her tone making clear that these urges no longer possess her. Any stories Mitty could share are shamefully recent. Things that couldn't be forgiven as a child's curiosity.

"I get it," Mitty says instead. A meaningless remark. The attendant rips off their tickets and congratulates them on being the first riders of the day.

"I've never been on a roller coaster," Lena says, humorless, as she willingly climbs into the front seat. She presses her hand against the candy-red exterior of the car, admiring it like she's patting the ass of a racehorse. "But I woke up a couple mornings ago and I thought, *What's something people do when they're trying to feel alive?*"

Mitty is hovering, an avid knowing that as soon as she slides into the space next to Lena, there is no turning back. Lena pats the empty seat and Mitty inhales, sharply, only letting out her breath once her left hip is pressed against Lena's right, the click of the lap bar against their thighs. She wants to know why, of all things, trying to feel alive is what Lena is after. Her life seems so big to Mitty. All that money and time. She wants to know what could possibly make Lena wake up feeling dead.

BEFORE THEY'VE EVEN REACHED THE TOP, LENA RAISES HER hands with the serene naïveté of a person who's only seen this behavior on television.

"I heard this story once," she shouts over the wind, her hair whipping against her cheeks, "about a deployed soldier who had run away from his post in Afghanistan and got kidnapped by the Taliban. They locked him in a pitch-black room for months as torture. Just left him completely alone with his own brain. You know that feeling of having a word on the tip of your tongue, but not being able to remember it?" Mitty tries to nod but her neck is stiff with terror. She suddenly imagines Lena getting scalped when her ponytail catches a rogue pole. "Well, he says that's how he felt about his body."

The image strikes Mitty just as they peek over the summit and she is briefly thrust into an imagined reality, some-how preferable to this one, in which she is locked in darkness, holding her hand in front of her face and knowing it's there, but not being able to find it. To wonder if your eyes are even open.

Then they fall.

Mitty's stomach floats up through her rib cage, a scream is pulled from her throat, her eyes pried open by the force.

"SOMETIMES—" Lena screams as they rattle around a turn. "SOMETIMES I FEEL LIKE THE SOLDIER, LIKE I CAN'T EVEN SEE MY OWN HAND! BUT I'M NOT EVEN LIVING IN DARKNESS. WHAT'S MY EXCUSE?"

Her expression has hardly changed. If the wind weren't pulling her skin back tight against her skull, she might look like she's just sitting serene on a cliff, watching the landscape in front of her. Mitty can't respond with anything other than a severed yelp. They come to the base of another hill and it all goes quiet, before they begin clicking upward again.

"It's not the same, obviously, but when I think of my child self calling those strangers, I'm reminded of that soldier," Lena says, as if nothing has happened. "Look at the view."

Mitty peers out over the town, at the cliffs hugging Cow-ell's Beach, tame waves rolling toward land carrying ama-teur surfers on foam boards. The twirling, striped tent of the carousel, spinning her into a state of hypnosis. They dive for-ward again, and she's forced back into the tense protection of her body, gritting her teeth until, just as quickly, they come to a sharp halt.

Lena's hair has blown away from her face, and her cheeks

are flushed pink, but otherwise she has remained completely relaxed. She even seems satisfied, as though she'd assigned the experience to herself and passed successfully. Mitty tries to emulate Lena's ease, acutely aware that every inch of skin beneath her clothing is damp with sweat.

But as she waits for the attendant to release them, she notices that the deep and familiar knot that lives so consistently inside her is no longer present. Like somewhere along the track, it shook itself loose and wriggled its way up her throat and out of her mouth, disappearing into the fog.

BY THE TIME THEY DISEMBARK, THE PARK HAS STARTED TO fill. The hollowed faces of cartoon cutouts now stuffed with toddlers' cheeks. Teenage girls on rented beach cruisers, swerving with one hand as they readjust the straps of their tank tops. Kids spilling out the front doors of Neptune's Kingdom, boasting tongues of tickets. Mitty and Lena stop to peer over the railing, the shallow brown water below sloshing up against the mossy wooden posts. There's a new, elastic comfort between them now. Mitty finds herself thinking about her body less, what she's supposed to do with her hands.

"You hated that," Lena says, her upper lip sticking to her dry gums when she smiles. She lets the sun hit her face.

"Only until it was over," Mitty says, surprised that the answer feels honest. "Then I liked it."

Lena closes her eyes and takes in a deep whiff of the air around them.

"Well, we're trying new things," she says, looking at

Mitty again. She puts her arm around Mitty's shoulders and pulls her in close. "Just maybe not the same things."

Mitty's instinct is to clench up, fearful that she might linger for too long, miss some crucial cue that it's time to let go. But she fights the urge, and lets herself lean her head against Lena's clavicle, her forehead nestled into Lena's damp neck.

"Why do you think you identified with that soldier?" she asks.

Lena stares off, really contemplating the question. Before answering, she inches Mitty off of her shoulder and faces her. "Sometimes, I spend so much time alone that I start feeling like my identity is on the tip of my tongue, but I can't quite name it."

Mitty wants to tell Lena that she feels that way about her entire life. That she's spent so much time removed from others, with only her thoughts; that sometimes when she leaves the house, she has to remind herself of her personality; that the first few minutes of every interaction is simply an act of working out the kinks of being a human.

"Sometimes, I'll spend the whole day with people at work," she says, "and I won't know who I am any more by the end of the day than I did at the beginning." She contemplates what she's just said, waiting for that familiar embarrassment, the kind that arrives only when she's shared a thought so personal it risks being too abstract for anyone else to understand. Instead, an altogether different feeling rises up in her, an ease, as the gap between what she's thinking and what she says out loud begins to shrink.

Lena pauses. "I don't know when I'm lonelier, by myself

or with other women." She bites her lip, recollecting some-thing. "I went to a get-together with these women in San Francisco once. The wives of Sebastian's friends." She chuck-les. "The wives"—she draws out each syllable—"invited me to come yoni sunning in their backyard." She stands on her tiptoes, peering down farther as the tide approaches. "Have you heard of this?"

Mitty shakes her head.

"It's where you lie on your back and let the sun hit your vagina."

"What's it supposed to do?"

"Recharge you, or something. A direct shot of vitamin D."

"There's no way that works."

Lena shrugs. "Maybe it does." Mitty imagines a row of women, crotches bared toward the sky, a neighbor peeking over the gate to find a row of labia, fanned out and beaming. "But I made the mistake of looking."

"Looking?"

"Yeah, I sat up, halfway through, and I looked. At their pussies." She twists her hair around her anxious fist. "I wanted to see if they looked the same as mine."

"And you got caught?"

"I didn't even think of it as being caught. I figured we were all being so open with one another that I wasn't trying to hide it."

"What'd they do?"

"They told Sebastian that I'd made them *uncomfortable.*" Lena screws her eyes tight, scowling at the memory. "And then I never got invited back."

Mitty knows too well the pitied smile they must have worn as they made a formal complaint to Sebastian. How they would've made it sound as though they were doing everyone, even Lena, a favor.

"They probably all wanted to do the same thing," Mitty says, "but you were the only one honest enough." She sees Lena's shoulders relax, a hidden tension lifting.

"It didn't feel honest, necessarily. I just couldn't help it."

They agree to start walking toward the exit. They'd done what they came here to do—partake in whatever manufactured thrill would give them a false sense of bravery.

"All right, it's my turn to admit something," Mitty says as they approach the car.

Lena is already rapt. "Okay, go."

She could explain everything now—how she watched Sebastian and Lena a few days prior, how it wasn't solely about arousal, but an innate curiosity; she was tranquilized by witnessing something typically obscured by closed doors or dulled by the theatrics of porn. But still, like most elements of her past, when she holds their respective voyeurisms up next to each other, Lena's looks like a tame lapse in judgment, while Mitty's is vulgar, perverse.

She cycles through other, less controversial admissions before settling on one. "When I was a kid, I thought I'd never be friends with women," she says.

"Why?"

"Whenever I was around adults, I just preferred the men. Women were always so patronizing." She tells Lena about the few years she remembers before her parents split, the neighborhood potlucks, squeezing past the swaying hips of drunk adults, dodging their animated hands. How the women spoke to her with a condescending lisp, offering her a cranberry juice and complimenting her shoes; how they'd lose interest as soon as they thought they'd quelled her with enough sugar and kindness.

"I love imagining you as a kid," Lena says, cackling, "your little scowl at those housewives trying to give you a lollipop."

Mitty laughs. "The men were dynamic!" She continues, now with more vigor. "Inappropriate. They talked about themselves, told loud stories, finished entire plates of ribs with their hands. And somehow, they never got tired. They could go all night. So when they'd give me attention, bantered with me, it made me feel capable. Which was so much more rewarding than just being taken care of."

"Yeah, you were getting to practice the art of conversation, that's like the best thing adults can teach you."

"In retrospect, I wish I would've also learned how to speak to people my own age," Mitty says. "I don't think I ever learned that."

"Well, you surprised yourself in other ways—you're not just friends with a woman now, you spend your whole waking life with one." Lena nudges Mitty gently with her shoulder.

"Back then, I didn't know that women like Bethel existed."

"A few days ago, I didn't know women like you existed."

Mitty scratches her cheek, clears her throat, trying her best to seem nonplussed. "What kind of woman is that?"

Lena speaks without hesitating. "A woman as confused about all of this"—she gestures to the empty parking lot, the sky—"as me."

She says it with such a tidy certainty that Mitty can't even begin to form some bashful protest. She couldn't have predicted that the thing she hates most about herself, the reason she so often feels sore and alienated around other people, is the very thing that she and Lena share. Knowing she would no longer have to pretend her world is more abundant than it is—that she is less bewildered by life than she is—in front of a new person, and what they saw wouldn't drive them away, brings her a thrilling peace. Maybe she is naïve for believing that this could be what she had been missing all along—a person to echo her endless confusion about the rules of living. But she is past the point of caring whether or not this makes her gullible; it feels too good to just drive, Lena with her hand out the open window, surfing the headwind, Mitty's grip loosened around the wheel, as though the roads had become straighter and better paved since they'd left that morning. The brief reprieve of not knowing—not fearing—whatever comes next.

The house is quiet. Sebastian won't be back for a few more hours. Lena stands in the middle of the living room, taking in the stillness. It's strange to be back in her own reality, after a day out in the world. The home feels even less like hers than it already did. The sharp stone corners of every countertop. The glossed dining room table, taut wicker chairs stiff as cadavers.

She counts her footsteps as she makes her way up the stairs, her bare feet cold against the floor. One, two, three, four. Even the carpet in the bedroom is untouched, still traversed by the swooping impression of the vacuum. She surveys the space. There are Sebastian's running shoes, next to the door. A short stack of books on his side of the bed, riddled with dog-eared pages. She knows his beard trimmings are probably flecked around the sink; they always seem to return mere hours after she wipes them away. She can see all of her work, her cleaning and organization, but where is she? Other than her clothes, hung neatly behind a closet door, she doesn't exist. Mitty's house, on the other hand, so clearly belongs to a person. To people. Even though Mitty claims that most of the house's contents are Bethel's, Lena knows that Mitty belongs there. She knows, somehow, that in the event of Bethel's death, Mitty would keep almost everything just the way it is.

The only way she can think to remember herself is to look in the mirror. So she walks to the bathroom and lingers in front of her reflection. She could use this time to inspect her body for malfunction. But she feels too overwhelmed with information, all that talk about the past and the people inside it. She had tried her best to show Mitty that she had memories, references from her big life. And still, all she can think about is everything she can't remember. She'd left so much out in those stories; thank God Mitty didn't ask about what came before or after. She feels desperate to recount something. The only memory she can muster in this moment is from a few weeks ago, one of their last surfs in San Francisco. She'd scraped her ankle against a barnacle on her way out of the water. She wondered then why she felt so relieved that Sebastian had witnessed the ordeal, that she wouldn't have to explain it later. Now, since having remembered the horse, she knows it's because it would be less likely that he'd diagnose it as fatal. He took pride in tending to the wound, as if it gave him something to fix, allowing her to squeeze his arm when he doused it in hydrogen peroxide.

In the days that followed, she found herself treasuring that little bloody patch. It felt like the only thing that really belonged to her. But soon, a brand-new layer of skin, smooth as cake fondant, had eclipsed it, as if while she slept, someone had buffed the wound with a square of silk. Sebastian had praised her ability to heal. But Lena knew that if she weren't so afraid of having a flaw, she would wish for a scar. Some proof of her certain and specific existence.

What would happen, she wonders, if she were to take matters into her own hands? Do the wounding herself? Then she could control where it happened and how to hide it. She could dictate the shape of the wound, so that if he were to notice, she would already have an explanation that seemed believable. All she wants to know is if she were to poke around, would she find something messy? Would this clean surface reveal itself to be just like everyone else?

She rummages through the drawers until she finds a pair of tweezers. She hovers over different patches of skin and calculates how often Sebastian interacts with that part of her body. Her stomach, far too frequent. Her inner thigh, even more so. Her hip, too forgettable to be guarded reliably. Her rib cage, too much bone.

She props her leg up on the counter and inspects the back of her thigh. She could remember this. She could hold her hand over it while she's standing, she could ensure she is always facing him if she isn't wearing pants. Her hand trembles as she holds the prongs over her skin. She imagines a toy machine in an arcade, a child feeding it quarters, the claw plunging down into a bed of stuffed animals. Then she sinks the metal into her leg, wiggling through spongy flesh until she hits something hard.

Bethel is on the phone and, based on her tone, Mitty is immediately aware that it's her mother on the other end. Bethel and Patricia's relationship has a charming comfort about it, an ease that makes Mitty wonder if they even had complete conversations or if they just liked the empty space the other one filled while they milled around their respective houses.

"Yeah, you wanna talk to her?" Bethel says, from the kitchen. By the time Mitty has stepped into the living room, Bethel is already there, offering up the receiver.

Patricia doesn't wait until Mitty says hello to start speaking. "Bethel said you're painting the house." She sounds tired, overworked.

"Yes." Mitty flops down on the sofa and immediately notices a spot Lena had missed on the ceiling. "Yellow."

"I've been thinking of getting some color in this place."
She pauses, unaware of how heavily she's breathing into the
mouthpiece. "She also mentioned that you'd made a new
friend?"

"Sort of."

"And you spent the morning together?"

Bethel is hovering, maintaining enough space to seem
busy while still within earshot of the conversation. It wasn't
unusual for Bethel to catch Patricia up on Mitty's life, supple-
menting whatever was lost in Mitty's frequent refusal to
offer her mother too many details. But something here feels
different. There is a tension in Patricia's voice, a tension in
Bethel's body as she chews away at her cuticles, that leaves
Mitty with a distinct unease.

"She's our neighbor," Mitty says cautiously. "She asked
me to go with her somewhere."

"Okay," Patricia says, an air of disbelief simmering beneath her forced lightness.

"I'm gonna go." Without saying anything, Mitty hangs
up. She stares at Bethel, who is pretending to wipe crumbs
from a single spot on the dining room table.

"Your mom sounds like she's doing well," she says without looking up.

"Why are you telling my mom about Lena?"

"She asked where you were."

"And what did you say?"

"That I saw you two leave together this morning. That
she seems like a nice girl—" Bethel busies herself a little
more. "Where *did* you go?" She finally looks up at Mitty.

"To the boardwalk."

"In the morning? Just the two of you?"

Mitty's stomach is twisted, her neck hot. She gets up and walks toward the staircase, but before she ascends it, Bethel clears her throat.

"She just," Bethel stammers, clumsily entering into the thought. "We just want you to be careful." Mitty doesn't turn around, her hand hovers at the base of the railing. She hears a lighter flick, then comes the smell of new smoke.

"Careful of what?" A sudden wind interrupts them, jerking open one of the windows and carrying itself through the room. "Bethel," Mitty says. Her mouth has gone dry. Her tongue, just a rough muscle. "Careful of what?"

"I know it was a long time ago, we just want to be mindful of what happened." Bethel pauses. "With Esme." As though Esme isn't just a name, a girl, a person, but an event they'd survived, a windstorm that had left them roofless and curled in the bathtub. Mitty wants to say she's not at risk of repeating what happened. She has learned her lesson. That's how she sees Esme now—as something she had to learn and, eventually, forget. That she has spent the last ten years trying to do exactly that, wipe the experience from her brain. But here, in this moment, she realizes that maybe that is the problem. Maybe the risk is forgetting.

BEFORE

The ballerinas in Paradise Valley were all either home-schooled or attended some private institution with acres of criminally green land outside the city. They were mythical to eighteen-year-old Mitty and her high school peers. Even the dancers on the drill team at school—hairlines prematurely receding as a result of their skin-tight ponytails—weren't worthy of being ballerinas. Ballerinas were in a different category altogether; too graceful for the clumsy world around them, which made them seem bony and strange in any setting other than the dance studio, duck-footed with mangled toes hooked over the lip of their flip-flops, rib cages clawing against their white leotards. But their beauty seemed to withstand the blisters and forked stances, details that would be a popularity death sentence for other girls. No one wrinkled their noses at the blood-soaked gauze stuffed in the pockets of the ballerina's backpacks. Instead, this was just a symbol of their painful pursuit of a great and impossible artistry; it was admirable.

There was no social setting where Mitty, who had just graduated from a sprawling public school several miles away, could be friends with them. And soon, they would all be gone. Shipped off to institutions and studios in other cities. And Mitty would be left behind in Paradise Valley. She and her mother had agreed it would be best for her to take a gap year as long as she got a job—her grades were unimpressive, and her mother called student loans a "trick." And so the most she could hope for was a passing glimpse of the ballerinas around town, where they were distinguishable by their pale pink tights pushed up around their calves, ankles swaddled with faux-fur boots. Finally, when she noticed an ad in the paper, saying Miss Sandra's School of Dance—the home for these fabled girls—was looking to hire a custodian, she didn't hesitate to type up her résumé. She listed her relevant skills as having cleaned her mother's house twice a week since she could remember and brought it to the studio that very same day. Handed it to Miss Sandra herself.

IT WAS A TERRIBLE JOB FOR A TEENAGE GIRL, CLEANING UP the scrapings of her peers' polished bodies, emptying the bloody metal bins in each bathroom stall, yanking out clots of hair from the drains. These were the very details that Miss Sandra recited as she tried to talk Mitty out of accepting the position. But Mitty insisted that she was the only person qualified for the job. She made a compelling argument that a man would be inappropriate, referencing the custodian at a concert venue in Albuquerque who'd killed a girl and stuffed her behind a vending machine, so she was the safest option Miss Sandra could hope for.

Within her first few days of working, she discovered that if she finished all of her tasks early, she could watch the dancers uninterrupted. She could stand in the corner of the studio before class was over, and listen to the sound of their pointe shoes knocking against the hardwood each time they leapt and fell back to earth. She could watch their theatrical conversations during water breaks. She noticed the ways they contracted each other's most subtle physical habits, turning a lisp into an airborne illness. And then, when they packed up their initial-embroidered duffels, whispering quietly to one another as their pearl onion heads bobbed out the door, Mitty would take over.

The floors were her favorite job. Sometimes the pianist, a man with stained teeth and a glowing bulb of bare scalp, would stay and play braided compositions while she ran a broom from mirror to mirror. She felt mature requesting he play Tchaikovsky, and he got to feel proud, like he'd imbued some class into the poor girl wielding cleaning supplies. She would dip her mop's mane into warm citrus cleaner and coat the wood until she could almost see her own reflection, like she was peering into a golden pond.

She'd already noticed Esme because Esme was always the last to arrive. While the rest of the girls stood at the bar flexing their arches, Esme was still cracking the soles of her pointe shoes like crab legs, resewing the ribbons, burying pins into the knot of her hair. But it had been nearly two weeks of Mitty working before they spoke. She was taking out the trash. Esme was crouched on the curb between a dumpster and the wall, sucking down a cigarette. When she saw Mitty approaching, she smashed it out onto the asphalt and held the butt behind her back.

"I don't care," Mitty said as she hauled the bag over the lip of the dumpster. Esme was silent. She stood and leaned against the wall, studying Mitty.

"Do you want one?" she asked.

Mitty had noticed that, other than at dress rehearsals when her face was caked matte, Esme was the only girl who seemed to have no interest in hiding the bulging bags beneath her eyes, the faint pink of eczema on her cheeks. Her eyebrows, once plucked meticulously into sperm, were often left to grow back wildly and at different rates. The only physical part of herself that she seemed diligent about was her blue-black hair parted razor-straight down the middle, hanging like blunt silk at her collarbone the minute she walked out of class.

Mitty hadn't smoked before, but she'd watched her mother do it occasionally, always in the evenings, while she waited for beans to soften on the stove. She took the cigarette between her two fingers and mimicked what she remembered: the inhale that continues after the cigarette leaves your lips, the sharp exhale in the opposite direction of the person across from you, a limp-wristed thumb flick to break off the expanding ash.

"Your mom comes into my mom's shop all the time, I think," Esme said.

Mitty felt a torrent of humiliation soar up her neck. She

was familiar with the shop, a cardigan and candle boutique called Magnolia's Dresser. She'd waited outside it for her mother before, the scent of potpourri wafting out whenever the door opened.

"Doesn't surprise me," Mitty said, flattening her voice to seem unfazed. How had Esme known this was her mother?

"She's got a lot of—" Esme paused to take a drag, but Mitty could see she was just trying to buy time, to find the least offensive way of describing what they both already knew. "Stuff."

Mitty wanted desperately to be the kind of person who could emancipate herself from any association with her mother. But Patricia's behavior felt like her responsibility, too, as if the fact she did nothing to stop it implicated her somehow. She'd sat idly by in the passenger seat of the car too many times, watching as her mother hauled armloads of curling irons and buckets of nail polish into a series of stores that, after a while, all started to look the same. She would return shortly after, carrying no less than before, and Mitty would stare ahead as she explained that she'd misread the buying schedule on the website, even though Mitty never asked. In those moments, Mitty felt a certain protectiveness override her embarrassment. At least her mother was shrewd, enterprising; what right did those shop women have judging her? But she never defended Patricia aloud, she just looked out the window until they pulled into the next stop. The next town. Until, finally, the car was empty. Until there was nowhere left to go but home.

Mitty felt like a traitor for wondering what it was like to be the daughters of the women on the other side of the mirrored doors, housewives who'd opened shops nobody needed, just so they'd have something to do and somewhere to go. She had always assumed she was lucky to be raised by a woman who fearlessly took what she wanted from the world. But still, some small part of her fantasized about what it might be like to spend her free time in one of those anodyne shops, doing homework while a rotating group of surrogate aunties gossiped with her from behind the changing-room curtains. Maybe that was how those girls always seemed to know more than her; they were plied with uncensored wisdom from women not their mothers.

"I feel bad we can never buy any of it," Esme continued. "My mom has too much shit, too."

Mitty scoffed. She appreciated the forced empathy, even if that's all it was, a canned attempt at making their mothers seem like they had something in common. She was only half-finished with her cigarette, but she suffocated the tip against the metal dumpster. Being looked at was beginning to feel grating.

"Have they caught you smoking before?" Mitty asked, a placeholder question as she tried to steer the conversation away from Patricia.

Esme shook her head, smiling. "They won't say it, but they want us to smoke." She patted her belly. "Meal replacements."

Mitty pretended to notice Esme's stomach for the first

time, distended like a newborn's. Esme threw the remainder of her cigarette into the gravel and picked up her bag off the ground.

"You can go in before me," she said, then motioned for Mitty to begin walking.

THEY STARTED MEETING AT THE DUMPSTERS MORE REGU- larly. Mitty learned that Esme hated Arizona. She griped about how swamp coolers smelled like pennies, the way chlo- rine aged her hands, how her Iranian mother made her put sunscreen on her elbows every time she sat outside. She wanted to live somewhere moody, somewhere she could see her own breath. Mitty, on the other hand, didn't mind Arizona or its heat. She liked that it made everyone have something in com- mon. She liked the massive, freezing supermarkets. The de- formed saguaro cacti that no one wanted to take pictures with. She liked that there was nothing to do because then she never felt pressured to do something. She always imagined that it would be stressful to be a teenager somewhere with expecta- tions, like Boston or Chicago, somewhere that tourists and college freshmen seek out on purpose, a place centered around the basin of a sports stadium, with life happening on every corner, a constant reminder of all the things you're not doing.

Esme talked about how she spent most weekends at the physical therapist, forcing various bones back into place. She talked about ballet like an arranged marriage, inevitable and unromantic, something she'd known about herself longer than she'd known herself. She compared her body to a rigged car that had been in a series of small accidents, haphazardly pieced together with duct tape and mismatched fenders, reliable and dimpled with dings. She was enviably eventempered in the way that girls try and sedate themselves into being at that age. But she wasn't performing, not really. It was as if thrusting all of her weight onto the tip of her largest toe meant everything else was easy. Her ennui gave her a wisdom that made other girls—eager girls—seem stupid, still basking in stupid fantasies of disappearing into the stupid lives of stupid men.

The only time she seemed genuinely unnerved was when she talked about the threat of a real injury. Not a stress fracture or tendinitis, but something irreparable that would render her useless. But she didn't seem afraid of the pain, or even losing the ability to partake in what she loved most. What she was most scared of was the deafening silence on the other side of the injury, days spent with an unmoving body and a spinning brain. She shuddered as she recounted stories of former dancers who, within a split second, had lost their entire career to a torn ACL.

What then? she'd ask Mitty, pausing to spit a cuticle into the dirt. *You might as well just end it all.*

At the end of Mitty's fourth week at the studio, she and Esme entered a few minutes apart to find that the air conditioner was broken from a blown fuse. The dancers hadn't even wrapped the ribbons around their ankles before sweat started collecting in beads above their upper lips. Mitty watched as they filed onto the floor, the windows steadily fogging from their trapped breath, none of them brazen enough to ask Miss Sandra for a day off. But halfway through, when a girl fainted mid-pirouette, class was canceled.

Mitty walked through the empty parking lot. She was the last to leave, after she wiped down the misty glass and floors wet with ballerina salt. Just as the hot asphalt began to bleed through the feeble soles of her Keds, Esme pulled up next to her in her maroon Ford sedan with cream leather interiors. When she rolled down the window, Mitty could already feel the cold air blasting from the vents. They were, it seemed, always in the same place but in completely different worlds.

"My mom is in Salt Lake City rescuing my cousin from a Mormon boy," she said. "Do you want to come swim?"

Yes, Mitty did. Of course she did. She responded with an easy nod. But inside, she had already become a live-wired colony of cicadas, vibrating in a single chorus. In the car, she couldn't even recall what they'd talked about. Just that within the first minute, she tore a hangnail off with her teeth, then spent the rest of the ride muting the sting by pressing her thumb against it.

ESME'S HOUSE WAS A SPRAWLING ONE-STORY WITH A ROCK facade, a U-shaped driveway and a row of cypress bushes, pruned into globes. Mitty had ridden her bike past it several times without knowing, even though it was the longer route home. She preferred the wide, well-paved lanes of Esme's neighborhood enough to brush off her own resentments about the fact that rich people always seemed to get benefits like this—well-oiled swing sets, soccer goals with nets, trash day on time.

Inside, it was dim and lavish. Quilted mahogany armchairs and Persian rugs laid diagonally across the carpet. Mustard velvet curtains embroidered with fake rubies, pleated and spilling onto the floor. A TV wider than a twin-sized mattress. It was gaudy, she thought, but it was luxurious. She felt like she could sleep on any surface and be comfortable.

At the end of an upper hallway, Esme's bedroom glistened. Her walls were mirrored, her floor the only hardwood in the house. Mitty stood in the center of the room, trying to avoid looking at her body from every angle. Esme seemed so used to her own reflection, like it was a cleaning lady moving wordlessly alongside her. Without glancing at herself once, she dug through a drawer and handed Mitty a swimsuit. Some shrunken thing with faded blue stripes.

In the bathroom mirror, Mitty stared at her bikini line crawling out from beneath its stretched seams. She rifled through a cabinet until she found a used razor, rusted and caked in old soap, then propped her foot up on the side of the tub and splashed her groin with lukewarm water. It was more of a tear than a shave and by the time she was finished, the blades were clogged, so she wrapped the razor in toilet paper and buried it in the trash.

When she stepped out, a towel around her waist, Esme was sitting on the floor, facing the opposite direction. She was bent over in a yellow string bikini, inspecting something on her toe. Her spine xylophoned down toward her butt.

"Cool?" she said, without turning around.

THEY SAT FAR ENOUGH APART ON THE POOL CHAIRS FOR Mitty to remove her towel without Esme seeing the field of razor bumps that had started to crop up along the insides of her thighs. The pool was small and deep, a lapping lima bean, and based on Esme's demeanor—tranquil like a lizard on a rock, offering her chin up toward the sky—it seemed she had no intention of jumping in. This was always how it was at other people's houses, Mitty thought. Untouched candy bowls in the foyer, a pantry of unopened Pop-Tarts. The people who had things others didn't never even used them.

"I thought you hated the heat," Mitty said. She pulled her hair away from her wet neck and laid it over the back of the chair.

"No," Esme said. "I just hate what it does to people. Everyone gets so anxious."

Mitty willed her burning body to relax, trying to look like the exception.

"Do you have friends at the studio?" she asked, mimicking the small talk that she'd overheard from her sunbathing mother and her friends.

She must have shaken her head, but Mitty's eyes were closed. "I'm leaving anyway," she said.

"Where will you go?"

"Whatever company wants me. It's like getting deployed." It was strange to Mitty that someone so self-assured would leave her life in the hands of whoever demanded it. "You'll go somewhere cool, too," she continued. Mitty turned to look at her, but Esme was already watching her, jerking her head back up toward the sky as soon as they made eye contact. "You're just marinating."

"What is that supposed to mean?" Mitty said, not really caring about the answer, just feeling flustered that Esme had formed a thought about her at all.

"Like, you might not be doing that much right now," she said. "But it's because you're preparing for something. You won't be at your high school reunion because you'll be off somewhere, doing something else."

Mitty had never imagined her life that way. She hadn't really imagined her life beyond what it was right then— something that happened every day without any pull toward the future. But as Esme spoke, she could suddenly see herself somewhere other than here. Her future still lacked any certainty, but while it once felt empty, now it seemed just open to possibility.

Esme stood, her back raked with red stripes from the pool chair, and fished the seam of her swimsuit out from her ass. She stretched her arms over her head and let out a faint groan, then walked over to face Mitty, her body eclipsing the sun. "Let's go upstairs."

DUSK WAS APPROACHING, AND THE LIGHT IN ESME'S BED-room had hushed to a rounded, deep blue. She scooted as close as possible to Mitty's face with a nub of black eyeliner, her feet on either side of Mitty's hips.

"You have to melt it," she said. She flicked a lighter and they both watched as the blunt tip turned gooey. When she tugged at Mitty's bottom lid, Mitty flinched and pulled back.

"It's okay," Esme said. "I've never burned myself. Feel."

She ran the warm pencil along Mitty's forearm then returned to her eye. When she had finished applying, she pulled her face back to admire her own work.

Mitty wanted to get up and look at herself in the mirror, but she knew that meant separating from Esme, untangling their bodies. Her mind started to file through the things she could say to keep her there, what she could ask, what she could offer. But just as she realized she had nothing, Esme leaned in and kissed her, nudging apart Mitty's lips with her own and then pulling away slowly.

Mitty had kissed people before, but it had always involved an erect tongue gunning toward her throat, or a mouth puckered up like a cinched coin purse. The first boy she'd ever kissed was under the brothel-red light of the darkroom at school, the weight of his bullish head pushing her against the wall. *Fine, it was fine,* she said when she talked about it to her friends, like it was a room she had to pass through on the way to somewhere else. She'd kissed her grade school friend Ramona, too, when she stayed in Ramona's basement for a week after her father left, trying to avoid Patricia's whimpering as she loitered by the window. Everything about the kiss was less vulgar than it would be with a boy, even the taste of Ramona's spit, raw and earthy like a freshly exhumed carrot still covered in the afterbirth of soil. But that was its own kind of impersonal, a practice run for the vague shape of a man she hadn't yet met.

She resisted the urge to apologize. Instead, she leaned in and kissed Esme back the same way, soft and deliberate, like it was the only thing in the world she really understood.

The morning after the boardwalk, Lena climbs out of bed to find a small red spot on the sheets. Her self-inflicted tweezer wound had reopened overnight, the edges separating as she tossed around in her dreams. Flustered, she strips the bed and soaks the stain in hydrogen peroxide, only allowing herself to pause as she marvels at the small science of the blood bubbling up through the fabric. She stuffs the linens into the washing machine and thinks of how simple this would be if she could just blame it on her period.

She couldn't remember the last time she'd bled. By the time she met Sebastian, she had already stopped menstruating. Who knows why, whether or not it was something she should worry about, but it seemed like a gift. And soon after they got together, she recalls him encouraging her to get an IUD. She remembers clearly the padded stirrups, grayed from the bare heels of former patients. The stiff paper blanket that crunched beneath her naked ass. The cold beak of a speculum entering her body and the pain that bellowed through her like a bass drum as the doctor, whom she still thinks of as faceless, buried the device into her cervix. After that, she rarely thought about pregnancy or the fact of her reproductive organs at all.

If Sebastian had been home, she would've had to explain

the stain away as a trivial accident. A scratched mole. A bit tongue. The encroaching winter; a bloody nose. But beneath the fluorescent light of the laundry room, when she pulls her thigh close, she realizes how deep she'd gone—a one-inch puncture wound now black with blood.

But somehow, she still feels unsatisfied. She hadn't found what she was looking for the first time. And though she's promised herself she won't make another attempt, she rationalizes that the work of reopening the wound had already been done for her. So she grits her teeth and pinches her first two fingers together, then wiggles them into her flesh, using her nails to dig past the dense muscle, the warm wet landscape of herself.

She knows she has to be mindful of how much blood she draws. Sebastian will notice whatever she leaves behind—spotted rags in the hamper, wads of paper towel shoved down to the bottom of the bin. Four drops fall onto the tile, splattering like bright stars against the white ceramic. A hush comes over her. She feels like crying. Was this really it? Just a body full of unremarkable gore, veins pumped with a lineage she can't remember? She limps to the bathroom. She will try her hardest to forget this ever happened, to let go of any hope that she might one day understand who or what she is. But as she stuffs the wound with a cotton ball, a strange guilt comes over her, like she's silencing her own body, shoving a gag into a mouth that's screaming something that she can't make out.

Once it's dark, Mitty hears the voices. Yips and howls and songs bellowed out of key. She follows them onto the balcony where she notices the scene below. A handful of men, mostly shirtless, bark and slam beers around a bonfire, nudge glowing logs with sticks. Lena is squished between two of them on a fallen trunk, her legs shrouded in a blanket and a can of beer resting on her knee. Every time one of the men in the sand tosses themselves into a stunt, Lena bursts into laughter, a forced offering. Behind her, Mitty can hear Bethel's television, the volume loud enough that it's a signal; Bethel has resigned herself to a stubborn satisfaction in going on about her night as if nothing has happened that's worth thinking about.

A full day had passed since Bethel said Esme's name, and they still hadn't spoken. Mitty wants to believe this is because Bethel knows, however defiantly, that she's wrong. Esme and Lena don't even look alike, at least not objectively. But now Mitty is haunted by their similarities. What's strange, she thinks, is that any resemblance lives in details that Bethel would've only noticed had she met Esme. The way they both fiddle with their jewelry while they're wrestling with a thought, their willowy limbs, how they look at their feet when something is being explained to them.

Though maybe it isn't about Esme and Lena at all, but about Mitty, and who she becomes when she is around them. Bethel must have recounted to Patricia whatever Mitty's behavior is around Lena: giddy, observant, bashful. And then her mother must have confirmed that this was the Mitty she saw back then, when she'd come home from a day at Esme's, flushed and suddenly alive. Mitty feels defensive about all of it. No one had seen her with Esme. They'd only ever seen her in the aftermath. How could they possibly know that this was the same?

What's worse, though, is that she knows there is a truth to it all. Of course there is something familiar here. A deep and quenchless yearning to be in the presence of someone, to figure them out. And what if Mitty hadn't grown up enough to know what to do with that feeling? To know that you can't demand that a person show themselves to you. You can only wait.

As she walks downstairs and out the back door, her body is restless. She keeps her eye on Lena as she pads through the sand. A glimmering little North Star.

"I'm sorry if we were loud," Lena says when she notices Mitty. One of the men roars toward the moon.

"Shut the fuck up, Luke, people are sleeping." Lena scoots over on her log, offering Mitty a seat. Luke collapses next to Lena's feet, panting. His body looks like it's been blanched, with a sparse growth of hair between his nipples. He's softer than his friends in a way Mitty imagines he must harbor insecurity about, the reason beyond his juvenile humor.

"You get your own private beach but can't make any noise?" He glances at Mitty and gives an animated smile, exposing a mouth of crowded teeth. "That doesn't seem fair."

"We don't own anything past our back porch," Lena snaps back. "Now open your mouth, dummy." Still on his back, Luke obeys. Lena pours a thick stream of beer until he starts choking, coughing between laughs and spitting up foam.

"They're like puppies," she says to Mitty, rolling her eyes. "This is our neighbor, Mitty."

Luke reaches out a limp hand and shakes a few of Mitty's fingers.

"Which one?" he asks, nodding to the row of houses behind her. Mitty points it out, confident that the most unbecoming details are safely obscured by darkness. The shame still feels intrinsic in front of these people, a habit. Three more men emerge from the dark, arms full of wood, and begin feeding the fire. They seem serene and practiced, a primal habit. Like she and Lena should both have babies suckling milk from their tits. Without asking, Lena retrieves a beer from the cooler next to her and hands it to Mitty.

"Mitty," Luke says to the newcomers, pointing at her. They nod in her direction, and she tries to extinguish the brief sense that they don't want her there, that something about her is a disturbance.

"What's that short for?" one of the fire-tenders asks. He's by far the most striking, eyes deep and brown like a dairy cow's, which leave the impression of kindness even if he doesn't seem like he means it.

"Mitrianne," Mitty says quietly. She shifts her attention toward the lip of the beer can.

"I didn't know that," Lena says, nudging her. As though they'd been friends for decades and she'd missed out on this one crucial fact.

"My mom made it up."

"All names are made up by someone," Lena says gently.

The men disengage from Mitty and Lena altogether, chasing one another toward the water. A relief. What happened to that part of her she'd bragged to Lena about at the boardwalk? The part that felt so energized by men, fluent in their bullish language? She'd gotten out of practice, and now every interaction with a person she doesn't know immediately feels conscious and sophisticated, a thing you could be punished for if you got it wrong.

"Hey," Lena says, eyeing her. "Let's do dinner this week."

Mitty feels a sense of relief, a shyness almost, that Lena had remembered and was willing to push the plans herself. It was too embarrassing to consider that she might be alone in how she'd gripped onto the image of this potential dinner, how it felt, at times, like the only thing she had to look forward to. "Yeah," she says. "I think that should work."

"Perfect." Lena's eyes scan the group of men. "I'll talk to Sebastian when he gets here."

"Where is he?" Mitty hadn't even noticed that his auburn hair was missing.

Lena empties the remainder of her stale beer into the fire, making it flinch. She squints up toward the balcony, as if expecting him to be there, watching over them.

"He'll be out here at some point," she says. "And Bethel?"

"I don't know," Mitty says. It comes out flippant.

Lena eyes her. "Is everything okay?"

"We got into an argument."

"About what?"

"She gets overprotective." Mitty digs her foot into the sand until only her ankle is visible. "She treats me like a child whenever someone new enters my life."

Lena shifts in her seat. "Is this because of me?"

"No," Mitty says. But Lena just sighs, unconvinced. "Really," Mitty continues. "It isn't. You didn't do anything wrong. It's our own shit. We spend too much time together."

"Do you think she'd like to hang out again?" Lena asks. "Maybe she just wants to feel included."

Before Mitty can respond, Lena seems to register a sound that no one else can, her eyes catching something in the dark. It takes Mitty a few more seconds to notice Sebastian, making his way toward them. Lena perks up, her voice becoming stainless and poised when she greets him. Mitty's comfort is once again cut short, a small shiver snaking through her body.

"A girl," he says, grinning. Like Mitty had just washed up on the beach.

"This is Mitty," Lena says. Her eyes dart between them both. "Our neighbor."

Mitty gives a practiced smile and shakes Sebastian's meaty hand.

He's more attractive than Mitty remembers, but maybe it's just that he is now looking directly at her. The rogue silver hairs in his beard catch the light of the flame. His eyebrows are bushy, the bone beneath them jutting outward over his deep-set eyes like an awning. She can't tell if his eyes are actually the color of honey or if it's just the reflection of the bonfire, making everything about him seem gold.

"It's nice to finally meet you," Mitty says. Sebastian scoots in next to Lena, his weight pushing both of them over toward the end of the log. He cracks open a beer and she watches his Adam's apple float and sink with each gulp.

"Likewise," he says. He shields his mouth to burp. "You've been in this neighborhood for a while?"

"A decade," she says. "My housemate has been here since '65."

"My goodness aren't we lucky," he says to Lena. "I was worried we'd end up in a neighborhood full of people like us."

"People like *you*," Lena says. She smiles, leans into him.

He takes the joke with ease, like a soft punch to the jaw. "Mitty, you must have seen this place change quite a bit, huh?"

"Not as much as Bethel." She wants to end her sentence there—she doesn't get the same joy that Bethel does from washing the newcomers with guilt. She'd rather just avoid the conversation altogether. But Bethel's voice rings out in her head. *Don't let them off easy.* She pauses, trying to think of something humorous that would still make Bethel proud. "Less serial killers than there used to be, I guess."

Sebastian snorts. "Oh yeah?"

"There were three at one point," Mitty says. "In the early seventies."

Lena and Sebastian go quiet, their eyes trained on Mitty.

"Well, two," she corrects herself. "One was a mass murderer. Some crazed environmentalist living in a shack in the hills. He had it out for a rich family that had developed on the land."

"He killed the whole family?" Lena asks.

"Everyone who was in the house, yeah." By now, the rest of the men have trickled back toward the bonfire and are immersed in their own quiet conversations. "Two daughters survived because they were away at boarding school."

"Gather 'round, folks," Sebastian bellows. "We've got a local telling us ghost stories."

The men settle onto logs or sit cross-legged in the sand. She scans her audience. Men who are desirable in a way that seems universally obvious, veins crawling like earthworms beneath the skin on their forearms. Why had her anxiety suddenly dissipated? She feels capable. Steady with the upper hand of knowledge. Like she's seven years old again, bantering with the husbands at a party. From the corner of her eye, she can see Lena, gripping Sebastian's knee.

"His name was John Linley Frazier," Mitty begins. "The man who killed them. He was only in his twenties and kind of exactly what you'd imagine. A shack-dwelling back-to-the-lander who spent his days without electricity studying the Bible." A laugh simmers among the group. "He lived less than half a mile from the family. A rich family, the dad was an ophthalmologist. John believed that in order to save mankind he had to kill materialism. I guess, to him, they were the materialism."

"That's horrible," Lena mutters.

"He tied them up with scarves and shot them execution-style," Mitty continues. "Left them in the swimming pool."

"What a piece of shit," Luke says.

"It happened right over there." Mitty points toward the

road. The crowd's eyes follow her finger. "Basically across the highway."

They go quiet. As if they can suddenly see the ghosts.

"You said there were two other murderers?" Lena asks.

She tells them about Herbert Mullin, who stabbed a priest to death in a confessional, and killed four teenagers in Henry Cowell State Park, claiming they were polluting the natural world with their presence. The thirteen people he killed in total, over the course of several years. She tells them about how Ed Kemper's mother worked at UCSC and drove a car with the school's logo, which he used to pick up co-eds at the university, posing as an employee, then buried their heads in the backyard of his mother's home. "Murdersville, USA," Mitty says. "That's what the DA called Santa Cruz at the time."

"These were all happening at once?" Sebastian asks.

"There was overlap, yeah. They arrested one thinking they'd solved it, but people kept getting killed."

"And then one day they just stopped?" Lena asks.

"After they caught the guys, yeah." Mitty notices Sebastian's shoulders relax. "But, you know, this town still carries the weight of it. And now there's just a new kind of tension between old and new. Have you guys heard about the recent murder of the engineer?"

She regrets asking the question almost immediately. The men seem uncomfortable, not intrigued in the way she'd hoped they would be. They shift in their seats, look down at their calloused feet. Luke crushes a beer can with his bare hands and opens another.

"Yes," Sebastian says, his voice sobering. "We've heard all about it."

Mitty hurries to apologize, but Sebastian cuts the tension with a laugh.

"You don't have anything to be sorry about," he says. "Unless you're the one who did it."

He smiles, teeth gleaming, crow's feet fracturing from the corners of his eyes.

There's an awkward quiet. Mitty resists begging for forgiveness. They all turn toward the ocean to fill the silence, engrossing themselves in the moonlit current, lapping and silver.

"What time is it?" one of the men asks, forcing a yawn. Someone else tells him that it's just past midnight and the rest of the men begin griping about their drive back over the hill.

"Your housemate is a night owl," Sebastian says. He's staring up at Bethel's bathroom window, where Mitty can see the familiar shape of her silhouette in front of the mirror— curls spiraling from her temples, a strong and lumpy nose, that cursed curve of her back.

It's strange to know a person so well, Mitty thinks, that you are able to notice the slightest twitch of something different in the way they move. She can tell that Bethel is slower than usual. Mitty almost never thinks of her as an old woman, but from here, that's exactly what she is. An aging body that can no longer keep up with the things it wants to do. Mitty had watched her from the beach plenty of times and rarely did she see anything she didn't already know. So why was she only noticing this now? It was Mitty who had always insisted that Bethel hadn't aged in a decade, an observation that Bethel cast aside as Mitty's own bias. *You just don't see me that way because you're always looking at me,* she would say. But here it occurs to Mitty that being seen is precisely what has kept Bethel alive. For the first time in so long, they'd gone over a day without speaking. And Bethel had already begun to deteriorate.

The next morning, Sebastian lets the shower run—one of his few environmentally hazardous indulgences—while he makes coffee, the steam seeping beneath the door and luring Lena awake. They're both groggy, having slept past nine. When he comes into the room naked and gestures toward the bathroom, Lena joins him. Only when he's swirling the loofah along the back of her thigh, does she remember the wound.

"What's this?" he says. She twists back to look. He points at the plum-colored hole.

"I pricked myself on the gate." She says it so nonchalantly that she almost believes it herself. She returns her attention to the front of her body, fingering her navel.

"That's not a prick," he says. "Was it a nail?"

He's on his knees now, his face so close to the bloody wound that it looks like he's peering into a peephole. She knows that the longer she allows him to inspect it, the more concerned he'll become. He runs his thumb softly along the edges, sucking his teeth as though the pain is contagious. She turns to face him, nudging her knee into his chest.

"I don't know," she groans playfully, as though it's exhausting to be loved with such detail. She hooks her hands beneath his armpits and struggles to pull him up to stand. She nuzzles her face against his neck, breathing into the valley behind his ear. "Don't worry about it."

"Well, whatever it was, I'll find it." He picks her up, placing her thighs on his hip bones. She's surprised at how willing he is to let go of whatever anxiety he's been holding, now replaced with a strange, erotic mischief. "I'll find it," he repeats, bouncing her once to make her squeal. "And I'll kill it."

LENA TUGS NERVOUSLY AT THE HEM OF HER SMALL BLACK dress.

"Are you sure it's not too short?"

Sebastian barely glances at her and mumbles a half-hearted reassurance. She fiddles with the netted veil pinned to the top of her black beret. She feels silly. Like she's adorned herself to mourn a president.

His mood had shifted once they'd started to get ready to leave. Sebastian hardly spoke as he patted his cheeks with aftershave and sealed his sleeves with cufflinks. He refused to eat his usual breakfast—rice cakes with cottage cheese and a dollop of almond butter. She tried not to press him too hard; it seemed favorable that he was distracted with a new problem, something other than her body.

Lena has never been to a funeral. She's embarrassed by how unprepared she feels for the event, how many questions she wants to ask before they arrive. Will it be an open casket, even though the death was violent? Are there seating arrangements based on relation? Is she expected to cry? What if she can't? She finds herself wondering if Sebastian ever wishes he were with someone who had more life experience, who understands the delicate combination of comfort and distance a person needs when they're stepping into the fragile space of grief. In the beginning of their relationship, she would often wonder if Sebastian would be better off with someone who knew the fabric of the world with a seasoned intricacy—who had been divorced or traveled on her own or loved some niche artist enough to collect all their work. She imagined this woman, whom she'd built entirely as the antonym to her and her many personal shortcomings, until she seemed real enough to be waiting just around the corner while she and Sebastian took their morning walks. But each time she mustered the courage to ask him for reassurance or press him on the things he wished were different about her, he would wave her off. *You're perfect,* he'd say. *You're exactly what I've always wanted.*

Soon, they are within twenty minutes of San Francisco, and she scolds herself for spending the majority of the time badgering her own selfish mind. She forces herself to remember Pax and visiting him at the summer home he'd owned in Santa Cruz for several years, part of what prompted Sebastian and Lena to begin searching for a house there. Pax had just relocated full-time from the city when he was murdered, and he and Sebastian were making plans for their time together in their new city; they wanted to start bouldering at the local climbing gym and go diving for abalone in Davenport. She remembers Sebastian's giddiness back then, how often he fantasized about the life they were moving toward, where he could finally be, in his words, *in the real world*.

When they pull into the lot of the funeral home, Lena is struck by how, despite death, the ordinary parts of existence, like searching for a parking spot, are still necessary. She imagines that a business which runs on tragedy should at least offer valet, take the petty errands off the hands of the grieving. Sebastian curses quietly to himself as he rounds each packed aisle. Lena wonders if attendance is something noted by the employees there, desensitized to loss and instead devising theories about whether or not the dead person was hated or loved. She imagines the parking lot of her own funeral, the meager display of cars. How the staff would hypothesize about the terrible things she must have done while living to warrant a deserted stretch of asphalt. Would they ever consider that, through no fault of her own, she was just alone?

Past the large wooden doors, the lobby smells like denial. Synthetic rose and carpet shampoo and a mingling of perfumes. A few unfamiliar people linger by a large photograph perched on an easel—Pax, smiling in an orange kayak—scribbling messages around the border. Lena hardly knew Pax, at least not in an intimate way, considering how much time he and Sebastian spent together. He'd always seemed like he was avoiding her for some reason, which Sebastian claimed was a result of his social anxiety around beautiful women. This confused her, because she considered him handsome—his premature graying hair wild from the surf, mossy eyes, and a slim gap between his two front teeth—and from what she understood, he'd had his fair share of girl-friends who came and went. The few times she did meet him, he exuded a sense of ease, was almost always under-dressed, a ratty T-shirt and board shorts sitting just below his hip bones, threatening to expose a tuft of pubic hair. Sure, he wasn't conventionally attractive—too emaciated with a lumpy nose and a cluster of acne scars on each cheek—but she'd always thought that in movement, he became beauti-ful, which seemed so much harder than just being it.

Sebastian ignores a stack of funeral programs as they enter the chapel, and Lena follows his lead. Though she'd appreciate having something to distract herself, even if it just meant reading the litany of Pax's life accomplishments in a pamphlet. The pews are crowded with people hunched over and weeping, taking turns to rub one another's backs. She realizes that, in addition to the dead person's popularity, it is also the suddenness with which they died that becomes im-mediately obvious. How their tragedy ranks among the rest. She imagines that the audience for an old person, or some-one who'd lost a several-year battle with a chronic illness, would be less heaving, less angry. She searches the crowd for familiar faces but can't find any. They're all too distorted by despair, heads bowed, faces twisted and wet. They are people she knows she's met in passing at Sebastian's work parties, where she spent most of her time smearing brie onto seeded crackers that she wouldn't end up eating, and praying that no one would ask her what she did for a living.

Sebastian hooks his arm around hers and guides them toward the back of the room. He slides into the pew, leaving her to squeeze in at the end, her left side against the wooden barrier of the bench. She's relieved to have even this small comfort, rather than being pressed against the shoulder of a stranger. At the front of the room, a closed casket is on display, piled high with white roses. It looks smaller than she'd remembered Pax being. Sebastian begins speaking with the man next to him. A co-worker. Was his name Ben? Bryan?

"Lena," the man says, reaching his hand across Sebastian's lap to take hers.

"You remember Ryan right, sweetie?" Sebastian must have noticed she'd gone blank.

"Of course." Lena reaches out to shake his hand, but he just holds tightly on to her fingers. "I'm so sorry for your loss."

"It's a collective loss," Ryan says. He doesn't let go of her, his eyes continuing to search her face. "You must have known him, right?"

Lena gently attempts to pull back, but Ryan squeezes tighter. She's beginning to feel uncomfortable, her hand growing damp beneath his grip.

"Not as well as Sebastian," she says. She nudges Sebastian's foot, and he takes the cue, adjusting himself so that his stomach bumps against Ryan's hand, forcing him to let go.

"Well," Ryan says, smiling at her. "No one knew him as well as Sebastian."

Was that true? She understood that Pax was a prominent figure in Sebastian's life, but she hadn't considered them best friends. She had always assumed that their friendship was on the precipice of becoming close before he died, but that it had never quite gotten there. Lena studies Sebastian's clenched profile, but he refuses to look at her. His eyes are focused on the casket up front, like he's willing it to open. When she looks back to Ryan, he's still scanning her. She clears her throat. Dodges his eyes and returns her attention to the front of the room, leaning back enough to disappear behind Sebastian's body.

An elderly man in an olive suit makes his way onto the stage. He shuffles through his papers at the podium and adjusts the microphone. The crowd falls into silence.

"Hello, everyone," he says. He glances at the casket behind him, then looks back at the room. He introduces himself as Pax's grandfather and begins a speech about legacy, how he and his wife only had one child, Pax's father, who then only had one child, Pax. He talks about how death should be a torch passed. In an ideal world, people would only leave after they'd given the world someone new. But Pax had no children. Only when death happens prematurely is that legacy severed, he explains. A bloodline, snipped.

"When Pax was murdered," he says. He pauses at the

word. *Murdered.* A reminder. "Our family was murdered, too. Those boys did not just rob us of our child, our grandchild. They robbed us of our future as a family."

Lena's focus is split—one eye watching Pax's grandfather, the other tracking Sebastian in her periphery. She had come to rely on his most subtle behaviors as signals—a testament to how he was feeling at any given moment. The glossary is lengthy, and she is fluent. When he clears his throat, it means he disagrees with something another person has said but doesn't consider them worthy of a debate. When he shifts in his seat, he is ready to leave within the next ten minutes. When he runs his flat palm down the surface of his face, he's invested in the conversation and is preparing to say something he considers profound. And when he puts his arm over her shoulders, cups his hand around her biceps and squeezes, he knows she is probably bored and that they will only have to stay a little longer. But now, Lena struggles to decipher him. He scratches his neck, leaving behind an echo of red streaks. He nods his head, though arbitrarily and at the wrong times, like he's listening to a separate monologue in an earpiece. He fastens and unfastens the top button of his blazer. What does any of it mean? She realizes how much she's relied on him as a compass. Now she doesn't know who or what to follow.

Pax's grandfather concludes his speech with a poem by Mark Twain.

" 'Warm summer sun, shine kindly here, warm southern wind, blow softly here,' " he reads, his voice stoic. Sebastian, fingers woven and eyes closed, bows his head. It's the first time since they've arrived that he seems truly present, actually moved by something. The audience gives a thorough but gentle applause, everyone so careful not to seem like they're celebrating, and Sebastian leans close to Lena's ear.

"Bathroom," he whispers. Then, while a new eulogist makes her way to the stage, Sebastian slips out of the pew and through the back doors. When Lena follows, she hears Ryan chuckle under his breath.

SHE FINDS HIM HUNCHED OVER THE SINK, STARING INTO the drain.

"Hi," she says softly, clicking the dead bolt behind her.

"Come here." He gestures to the space in front of him. When she approaches, attempting to look at him, he turns her around to face the mirror. She realizes she's only seen his face in profile since they got to the funeral. Head-on, his sadness is palpable. Heavy lids hooded over his bloodshot eyes. His lips drained of color. His hair is still tousled from sleep, the cowlick at the front of his head uncombed. His scalp, bare in the center like the eye of the hurricane. A relief, she thinks, to see him feeling something.

"Look at yourself," he says. "Not at me."

She obeys, and shifts her gaze away from him, locking into her own reflection.

He slides his right hand up her thigh and pushes aside the crotch of her underwear. He presses his finger against her, rubbing her loose. Then, he slips one inside. Another. Each time she closes her eyes, he tells her to open them.

"I want you to watch yourself," he reminds her. "Do you understand?"

She nods. But her vision grows distant each time he prods deep into her body, hooking onto something only he can reach. She has always preferred his hands to her own; they're nimble and searching, motivated. The two of them watch her body tighten, her writhing face grow closer to itself as she leans toward the mirror. When she comes, her eyes don't look like her own.

THEY AVOID LOOKING AT RYAN AS THEY RETURN TO THE pew. In her seat, she adjusts to the new humidity between her legs, as a slideshow of Pax doing various outdoor activities plays on a large projector. Pax at the top of a mountain, his hands lifted toward the sky; Pax surfing with a small French bulldog riding on the nose of the board; Pax rowing in college, young and strong, his cheeks puffed out as he yanks his oar back toward his chest.

The men in Sebastian's life, including Sebastian, are all impossibly fit and possess what seems like infinite stamina. She wonders if they are making up for all that time spent locked in front of their computers writing code or debating one another in bleak conference rooms about what makes a platform user-friendly. She and Sebastian have their own adventures, but she still resents that she was never invited to go out with the larger group of friends, that she was always relegated to mingling on the sidelines with the girlfriends and wives every time she tagged along. So often, she thought, while boys are throwing their bodies into speed or obstacle, girls are sitting somewhere nearby in lawn chairs and sun hats, peeling apart oranges into a pile of perfect wedges.

A year ago, Sebastian took up running. Like many women in love, Lena took it up, too. She was naturally good at it, she enjoyed the organic misery, the knowledge that her feet took her ten miles to somewhere else. Mostly though, she liked that it was another thing they could do together, two wolves floating across a prairie, their bodies sleek and practiced alongside each other.

Maybe it was the fact that they'd been surfing so much lately—far more than they had when they lived in the city— but she's thinking about those days with an unexpected scrutiny. She feels, suddenly, like her memory is laced with irritation. Wondering if there are men who take up an entirely new skill and master it, develop an identity around it, all so that they can be close to a woman they love. How many men sit in groups, watching their girlfriends do something that feels unattainable to them, bonding over a skill that isn't their own? But could she even bring this up to Sebastian now? It was embarrassingly delayed. He would probably find it endearing, her new epiphanies. *Women's interests are for women. Men's interests are for everyone.* He would probably have some perfect question that served more as a gavel drop than it did an entry into deeper conversation. Like, *What is it you feel interested in and want company doing?* And yes, she would struggle to name a single thing. Everything she feels drawn toward is something he introduced to her. Everything she feels good at is something he taught her.

THEY TAKE MOSTLY BACK ROADS HOME FROM THE FUNERAL, exiting the freeway every chance they get. Once they're in Santa Cruz, it takes Lena several minutes to realize Sebastian is leading them on a tour of Pax's memories. He only speaks when they pass somewhere that Pax had once talked about. The Spam musubi he raved about at that one Hawaiian restaurant. The disco nights at Rosie McCann's. Sebastian laughs, recounting Pax's story about the time he went to the Redroom on acid and thought he was in a brothel, eventually getting kicked out when he mistook every woman at the bar for a lady of the night.

"I hadn't realized what an impact he had on you," Lena says, once they've hit a stretch of empty road, winding through the redwoods.

"I wouldn't call restaurant suggestions an *impact*." Sebastian pauses, wrings his hands around the steering wheel. "But yeah," he says. "I mean, I miss the guy."

Lena reaches over and squeezes his thigh. He lifts her hand and kisses the top of her knuckles. At a stoplight, they idle next to a shrimp-pink roadside motel. She watches a woman on the other side of a second-floor window talk with her hands, a cigarette balanced loosely between her lips.

"Why did you want me to look at myself?" she asks. Enough time has passed.

"There was so much talk about death in there," he says. "I thought it might be nice to look at yourself when you feel the most alive."

She can't bring herself to explain that he's wrong. Sex is when she becomes most aware of the fact that she has a body. But those two things feel separate, her body and the fact of her existence.

"Is that when *you* feel the most alive?" she asks instead.

"When I'm touching you? Yeah." She sees his eyes scan the Capitola Wharf, calculating the quality of the surf. "Sometimes I think I was put on this earth just to do it."

It would feel nice to believe him. But he's always speaking about purpose in hyperbole. To Sebastian, everything he pursued was his calling. She'd only Googled him once, in the early days of their relationship. She watched a TED Talk he gave about greenwashing, the various ways companies mislead buyers into believing a product is climate friendly with leaf logos and faux-woodgrain detailing. He talked about the wind turbines, the hundreds of thousands of dead birds. Then he played the recording of his electronic birdcall, beguiling the audience with the song of cranes. When it stopped, he let the room fall silent. *Sometimes I think I was put on earth just to build this,* he said. He smiled. A dimple materialized on his cheek. A photograph of a flight of swallows, backlit by a peachy sunset, appeared on the screen behind him. The audience burst into applause. Just like Lena, they'd all fallen in love.

Mitty and Lena don't see each other for three days. Since Bethel's warning about Esme, Mitty feels too self-conscious to seek her out, now that her actions are seen as a replication, a second coming, of her past. She and Bethel keep their distance, too, exchanging all the necessary niceties to ensure that if either one of them were to abruptly die, it wouldn't leave the other completely riddled with guilt. Patricia always said that people who love each other should never go to bed angry, and if they absolutely must, then they need to make sure their bodies are touching, at least in one spot, while they sleep. But it isn't that simple for Bethel and Mitty, who sleep in separate rooms most nights and don't have sex to fall back on as a nonverbal resolution. Instead, they keep to their own corners of the house, highly attentive to the other person's every movement to avoid any awkward crossing of paths.

She tries to avoid wondering why Lena hasn't initiated getting together. She has already gone through every beat of the night at the bonfire, grading herself on her own social execution and ultimately deciding she didn't fail but she didn't pass either. She could've gone without bringing up the murdered engineer. Their goodbye was warm enough. Lena even brought up dinner again, this time in front of Sebastian, who had agreed to host them. Then he had saluted the group and guided Lena back toward the house, hand on her lower back. It was normal, Mitty had to remind herself, for friends to take time apart.

She had caught glimpses of Lena through the window, which she's managed to convince herself is inevitable, considering their proximity. The scenes were benign—Sebastian and Lena silently playing a game of chess at their kitchen counter, or fresh out of the shower, their bodies swaddled in white towels as they read books across from each other on the couch—which comforted Mitty, too. They are neighbors, their lives are separate, and when the time is right, their paths will cross again.

Mitty and Bethel rarely argue. In the past, any conflict between them was petty. The hideous ceramic trinket Bethel brought back from the charity shop or the rancid smell of Mitty's work uniform when she kept it on after her shift. And even then, the days when they weren't their normal selves felt shapeless and nauseating. Mitty was certain she would come home from work and her things would be on the lawn, along with a small note outlining all of her faults and why Bethel could no longer ignore them. Because of this, Mitty was usually the first to apologize, regardless of who had done what.

But this time is different. When Bethel said Esme's name, the fault line they had been living on top of broke loose. It had never occurred to Mitty that Bethel might still hold her to the person she was ten years ago, when she arrived with her mother on the doorstep of the beach house. Bethel knew the story, of course; Patricia had insisted on telling her the entirety of what happened before Bethel agreed to take her in. It was the only way Patricia could trust Bethel with her daughter. But had Mitty known her past was still pinned to her back, she would've kept Lena away from Bethel altogether.

When she returns home from work that evening, a log is burning in the fireplace. Bethel is on the sofa, pushing back her cuticles, half-attentive to some ancient detective movie in front of her. Mitty's feet are sore, her hair sweaty with the stink of grease. She wishes they could pause their conflict just for the evening, sit briefly in the normal lull of relaxing together. She hovers in the doorway, debating whether or not to go upstairs.

"It's your house, too," Bethel says, without looking back at her.

If Mitty had inherited any of her mother's bluntness, she would snap at Bethel's stubborn invitation, demand that she say something kinder. Instead, she peels off her shoes and unties her apron, then makes her way to the living room and falls into a neighboring chair.

"Busy?" Bethel eyes her dirty socks.

On the television, the gray corpse of a girl is lowered onto an autopsy table. "No more than usual," Mitty says.

"Have you heard from your mom?"

Mitty tries to be nonchalant, mumbles a sound that resembles the word *no*. It is a stand-in question. Bethel knows she hasn't heard from her mother. Which only leads Mitty to believe that they have been in constant communication while Mitty is at work, exchanging conspiracies about Esme and Lena and all the women Mitty will inevitably destroy.

The conversation wanes and Bethel turns up the volume. The melodramatic percussion of the show's soundtrack assumes their silence. Mitty occupies herself by counting her tips. She smooths each flimsy bill and stacks them one by one on the armrest. Sometimes, when she's feeling particularly dismal about the state of her life, all the things she missed out on because of her own bad decisions, she finds herself fantasizing about joining a cult. A tranquil, bearded leader. A sisterhood of barefoot women. Fields of dandelions. Babies suckling on the closest nipple. It seems freeing, she thinks, to be heedless enough about your own ego that you're able to worship something. Never having to be tasked with making a decision at all. She could never bring herself to say it out loud, but when Bethel speaks of the fifties—the expectation that wives would produce nuclear meatloaf and turn a blind eye to their cheating husbands—Mitty isn't entirely repulsed by the idea. *Empowerment is exhausting,* she would think to herself. What if all she wanted was to be gorgeous and obedient?

The front door swings open. A gust of cold air cuts through the room. In the entryway, a woman's slender silhouette blocks the bright leak of the porch light.

"What's that?" Bethel says, squinting at the shape.

Mitty blinks. She briefly wonders if it's all some bizarre trick of the imagination, a tree branch, maybe. But then the shape becomes a person, whose movements are spastic and sudden, imbued with anxiety.

"Hello?" Mitty's voice is suddenly feeble.

The shape takes one step forward. As the dark peels back from the face, Mitty realizes it's Lena. A dazed hush swallows the room. Bethel immediately stands and approaches her. She takes Lena by the shoulders and guides her toward a seat. Mitty, for some reason, can't bring herself to move.

"What happened?" Lena asks. A question shot into the dark.

Sebastian has only been gone for an hour—some work party in San Jose—when Lena steps out the front door. She walks barefoot down their pathway, the fresh concrete cool against her toes and heels. She pricks her finger against the needled tip of an agave plant. She pauses to listen to the sound of a wave slamming against the beach. The air around her is brisk and dank with salt. Almost immediately, the warm glow of the porch light at Bethel's house catches her attention. Sebastian had called the house an *eyesore*. She can see the shifting blue of a television, reflecting off the walls in the living room. She can't even claim that she'd ignored some voice in her head telling her not to do it—the voice just isn't there. So she simply allows her body to move in the direction of the golden oval illuminating the peeling beams of the front porch.

As she walks up the steps, she feels the threat of splinters bypass her soles. She places her hand on the crystal knob, but the door is already propped open, so she barely has to push it in order to step inside. Already, the smell is familiar, the air crowded with old smoke. In front of her, she can see the shapes of her friends. The back of Bethel's head, frizz springing from her temples. Mitty's profile, bowed toward her lap. It's so nice to remember something. But when they notice her, they look like they're watching a spinning top nearing the edge of a table.

She scratches the back of her thigh. "What happened?" she says aloud, unsure of whether she's at fault for something. The world around her begins to materialize. "The door was open and I wanted to say hi—" Her brain feels staggered, uneven. She presses her palm against the side of her neck, searching for the grounding rhythm of her pulse.

"Oh, honey." Bethel approaches and guides Lena by the small of her back to a chair. She gently pushes her shoulders down, easing her to sit.

On the television, a suited man hops off a cable car, briefcase in hand.

"Have you heard about the origin of the cable car?" Lena says, unblinking. "There were these horses, pulling a streetcar up a hill. But the hill was too steep, so the horses slipped."

"Lena." Bethel cuts her off. "What's going on?"

Lena looks to Mitty, who still hasn't said a word. She seems perplexed, studying Lena with meticulous worry.

"I'm sorry," Lena repeats, this time aimed at Mitty, shaking her out of the trance. "I just wanted to say hi."

"You can watch this with us if you want," Mitty says, her tone surprisingly unaffected. She gestures to the television.

The longer Lena sits in the mildew stink of this busy house, the more she begins to realize that this isn't what she was looking for either. Maybe if she had made a cleaner entrance, knocked like a normal person, she would've been able to settle into the coziness of it all, find the comfort. But now the room is taut with some curse she brought in, and the house feels like it's pushing her out. The rigid, tinny cushion springs beneath her ass. The static hum coming from the television. A slither of cold air, leaking from somewhere she can't place, cuts through the otherwise warm room. The cramped tension between Bethel and Mitty, who usually seem so aligned. But her own home would be even less welcoming. That gaping, colorless iceberg of a house. Maybe she would feel best outside, barefoot and aimless, her body moving between the trees, blackberry brambles thrashing against her calves, the sweat on her neck pinging the nose of some nearby predator she can't see. Belonging nowhere, is that proof that she's an animal? A body? She wants to know that if a mountain lion skulking in the bushes decided to attack, it would be satisfied with the taste of her, that it would want to lick her bones clean.

"I should go," she says, standing. As she walks toward the door, Bethel follows, Mitty staying just behind her.

"You sure you're all right?" Bethel asks. She squeezes Lena's bicep. Her grip is tough. Lena smiles, more confidently than she feels, and nods. Mitty mutters a goodbye.

She watches Bethel walk back toward the couch. Her ankles are still swollen. Unreliable. Blood collecting purple around the bone. She thinks, again, of her horse. All the horses. Whose working bodies were the sole justification of their existence.

"The horses died," she says. Her voice quivers. "All of them." Her eyes, hot from tears. "But that's how they invented the cable car."

She knows the comment only confuses them further. But she needed to say it. She needed to warn them of whatever was coming. Whatever might take their place.

For the rest of the night, Bethel keeps saying she *feels bad for the girl,* telling then retelling the story of her own mother's mental break that eventually led to her being committed. She talks about the incident with Lena like it was a step toward that unfortunate but inevitable outcome for a woman who was *clearly already struggling.* But Mitty feels restless in letting the assumption end there. She wants to know why. How could it be so simple and easy to brush off, this idea that a woman was struggling enough to end up in a doorway, bumbling and stuttering and aching for some form of attention? But the more Mitty tries to investigate, the more questions she asks, the more she feels Bethel flippantly undermining her. As if Mitty is missing some obvious, hysterical truth that isn't worth digging into.

"You know my perspective." Bethel's voice is tinged with a subtle annoyance. "Women who look like that are lonely," she says. "They get too deep into their own minds when they aren't being looked at." She flips off the television and begins walking toward the stairs.

"I'm not arguing that," Mitty says. "I understand what loneliness looks like."

"Why?" Bethel peers up, preparing herself for the task of climbing toward the second floor. "Because you're lonely?" She says it with a burgeoning sarcasm, but Mitty can hear that the question is shadowed with genuine concern.

"No," Mitty lies, unable to shake the desire to protect Bethel's feelings. "But I have been."

Acceptable, if vague enough, for Bethel not to pry further.

"Well." Bethel lifts the skirt of her nightgown and places her left foot on the first step. "What human hasn't felt a little loneliness?"

But Mitty isn't talking about the crisp, romantic silence that comes during their tame evenings at home on weekends. She's talking about something bigger, a black chasm that doesn't grow or shrink. It just floats like a brainless jellied sea creature, spitting ink into the dark.

"Why don't you have empathy for her?" Mitty is tired of Bethel's irreverence, her arrogant dismissal. And she's bored of her own timid courtesy.

Bethel sighs, already exhausted. "Just because I'm not consumed by the problems of a supermodel next door doesn't mean I have no empathy, Mitty."

"But why do you have to make it about the fact that she's pretty?"

Bethel gives up on the stairs and turns around.

"Are you really going to pretend that it's not about that for you?" Her expression looks like a dare.

Mitty has always struggled to differentiate fear and anger. They always seemed to begin as the same glow in her belly. Expanding and vengeful. "I don't hate her for it," she says.

Bethel scoffs. "Yes, you do. Your hate just looks different than mine."

Mitty's cheeks burn. "No, the difference is that you hate her because you could've been her. And you aren't."

It seems only right that if Bethel can call back to Mitty's buried past, so can she. They had never promised each other that they wouldn't yank these memories into their present world. It was merely a loose agreement, based entirely on kindness, an unsaid pact that Bethel had already broken.

Only when Bethel feels defeated do her scars become obvious. Otherwise, they are nearly invisible. She rarely talks about the accident; she's ashamed of how silly it all was. When she was nineteen, she moved to Hollywood. The idea was unoriginal, she told Mitty—a girl flocking to the hills, certain that a producer would discover her face in a grocery store as she perused bananas. But she claimed she wasn't interested in stardom. She just wanted to find a man already somewhere along that path himself. Maybe she lacked the abrasive self-determination required to think she could become an actress. The idea that adoring fans, or anyone at all, should idolize her, seemed preposterous. She didn't deserve to loom thirty feet tall over young women in the shadows of a theater, to be studied by them so that they might figure out what kind of woman they ought to be. It made her sad. It seemed dishonest. Especially when she didn't know what kind of woman she wanted to be herself. But before the thought could settle into self-loathing, she remembered what she could do instead. She would live in service of someone great. She was young enough. Pretty enough. And she lacked the kind of self-interest that so often interferes with a man's own.

Three days before her twenty-first birthday, she was on her way to an interview for a secretary position at Warner Bros. Whenever she recalled that day to Mitty, she would say it like she was reciting a grocery list—a litany of bullet points that she had no choice but to remember. She'd stepped off the sidewalk, her eyes anxiously studying the revolving door of the high-rise across the street that she was supposed to step into. She'd never seen a door like that. It seemed impossible that a person wouldn't be crushed if they so much as slightly broke the rhythm of people cycling through it. How would she know when to step inside? What would she do with her hands? And that's when it happened: the sound of howling brakes, a pedestrian's belated scream, the mirror of a speeding bus whipping her face, every single bone crushed to fragments the size of molars.

The first time she heard the story, Mitty thought Bethel was exaggerating. She wasn't disfigured. But then Bethel took Mitty's finger and ran it along her jaw, allowing Mitty to feel the fractured and jagged layer beneath. She pointed out her lack of eyebrows, a product of extensive skin replacement, and the arched replicas she had drawn on each morning, until she committed to having them tattooed. After that, Mitty could almost see it, how Bethel had been put back together. She just didn't know where Bethel had begun.

"You're not going to hurt me, you know," Bethel says flatly. Mitty almost believes her. Her eyes are watchful, disappointed. Usually, Mitty would at least have to fight off the urge to apologize. But there's an unusual absence of remorse. So much that she finds herself searching for it, wanting to feel it, if only to be sure that she still can. Bethel returns to the task of climbing toward her bedroom, not pushing herself to move any faster than she usually does. Her consistency is almost impressive, despite everything. Mitty can see the texture of Bethel's ass, puckered with fat, beneath her thinning cotton nightgown. The stoop of muscle on her upper back. The pleated skin on her elbows. Mitty is so tired of thinking about aging. She shouldn't have such thorough knowledge of the ways a body can drag itself out. Maybe Bethel is right, and she is preoccupied with Lena's beauty. But that's what was so nice about being with Lena, she thinks. Sitting across from a person whose features looked as though they'd been preserved by the glass armor of a china cabinet made Mitty feel like she deserved to be there. As if her proximity to Lena's flushed girlishness meant she must have some version of it, too, some version of her that had been lying dormant beneath a layer of dust. Suddenly wiped clean.

IT'S NEARING THE END OF MITTY'S DAY SHIFT AND SHE'S cross-legged on the floor of the walk-in freezer, unloading a case of clean beer mugs. Her thoughts about Lena have only become amplified, as if her conflict with Bethel had somehow freed her into an unabashed wondering, no longer having to maintain a sense of aloofness.

The door behind her opens. "Someone is asking for you," Cat says. She sounds wary.

"Why?"

"Some lady." Mitty nods, hardly listening, but Cat stays,

hovering behind her. "She's, like, the most beautiful woman I've ever seen."

Mitty turns to look up at her, and Cat motions for her to follow. Together, they peer around the wall that divides the kitchen from the restaurant. There, in the smallest corner booth is Lena, staring at a full glass of iced lemon water.

"She asked for me?"

Cat nods. "Who is she?"

They both watch Lena for a moment. Mitty tries to imagine what Cat must be feeling, seeing Lena for the first time. A white dress hangs off her shoulders, billowing around her like a plush duvet. She's using her straw to push down her lemon and pin it to the bottom of her glass. Then, when it seems like she might be imagining that it's about to drown, she releases it back to the surface.

"My neighbor."

"I've never seen someone sit alone without looking at a phone," Cat says. It occurs to Mitty that she hasn't actually seen Lena use a phone of any kind. She isn't swept up in some tiny universe in her palm, like the usual solo patrons. "Maybe she"—Cat makes her voice breathy and facetious—"*prefers to live in the moment.*"

Mitty laughs but doesn't reply. "She knew that tech guy you keep talking about. He was her boyfriend's friend."

Cat drops her jaw, exposing her molars pocked with dark fillings. "What? And you're just telling me this now?"

"Well, I don't really know the details. I just know they worked together."

Cat continues to watch Lena, who has now started to fold her napkin into shapeless origami.

"That's fucking crazy," she whispers. "You haven't asked her about it?"

"I made a stupid comment the other night about it. To a bunch of guys." Mitty winces, remembering. "And then I realized that he's, like, a person. Who they lost."

"That doesn't mean she doesn't have her own theories," Cat says.

"I know, I just want to be sensitive."

"That's so boring." Cat rolls her eyes.

Mitty goes quiet, observing Lena. Seeing her in the wild only emphasizes her beauty, the fact that it isn't diluted by crowds, but instead becomes all the more noticeable. She watches as people make their way from the bathrooms, how their eyes catch Lena as they pass. Women glancing at her from neighboring booths. A busboy finding reasons to visit her table more than once.

"I actually kind of like her," Mitty says. "She's weirder than I thought she'd be." She resists mentioning Lena barging into their house, not wanting to encourage any more of Cat's conspiracies.

"Oh, she's *weird*?" Cat says, mocking her. "What does she do that's *weird*?"

Mitty shrugs her off, trying not to seem too sanctimonious. But she can feel Cat looking at her, grinning. "God, you are so gay," she says, giving Mitty a little shove.

Mitty makes her way to Lena's table, forcing composure. "Welcome to Capitola's crab capital," she says. She leans against the banquette opposite Lena, who looks up, a smile blooming across her face. Being seen from this angle always makes Mitty feel self-conscious. Something about the belt of fat beneath her chin. "How did you find me?"

"You mentioned your job, something about crabs and Capitola," Lena says, smiling. "And I was walking around the village. I thought I'd come say hi." She seems to notice the menus for the first time, tucked behind her assigned caddy of condiments. She pulls one out and begins scanning the many laminated pages. She seems baffled by all the options, her attention hovering on a list of milkshakes.

"Hungry?"

Lena shakes her head. Mitty realizes for the first time that she hasn't ever seen Lena eat. A maternal urge comes over her, a desire to force-feed her a burger.

"What do you recommend?" Lena asks.

"Anything but the crab tacos. Are you feeling better?"

"Anything but the crab at the crab capital?"

"They come in frozen from Maine. They've probably been dead for, like, a year."

"The sign out front says they're from Monterey."

"Of course it does. That doesn't make it true."

Lena closes the menu and tucks it back into its place. She looks up at Mitty and gestures to the empty spot in front of her. "Can you join me?"

"Not while I'm working," Mitty says. "But I'll be off in half an hour."

"I want to take you and Bethel somewhere later." She looks blankly at Mitty. "Have you guys made up yet?"

"Not quite," Mitty says, glancing out the window, trying to seem unbothered.

Lena rests her elbows on the table, chin in her palms. "I'm sorry about what happened last night." She lowers her voice. "I just wanted to say hello. And I guess I forgot how to do that."

Of course, Mitty has questions. But what's more pressing is her need to protect Lena from the embarrassment of it all. Dim every response to an uncontroversial hum. An afterthought.

"Did you and Sebastian have a fight?"

Lena shakes her head. "He was gone," she says. She clocks that the answer doesn't offer any sort of clarity. "I don't know how to explain it." She lingers in the thought. "I'm just sorry."

"I'm not upset," Mitty says. "And neither is Bethel. I just want to know that you're okay."

"I'm okay." Lena forces a grin. "Really."

Mitty allows the conversation to be punctuated by Lena's refusal to say anything further.

"So you want to take us somewhere?"

"It's a surprise." Lena's eyes are hopeful. "I promise it'll be fun."

Mitty scans her face. She looks skinnier than Mitty remembered. Her cheekbones yearning against the back of her skin. Lena glances past Mitty's shoulder and furrows her brow. Mitty follows her gaze and sees Cat, watching the two of them. When they make eye contact, Cat shifts her attention to her chipping fingernail polish.

"She's nosy," Mitty says, turning back to Lena and rolling her eyes. "No one ever comes in to visit me."

But Lena looks troubled, not looking away from Cat. "Did you tell her about me?"

"About you?" Mitty asks. "Not really. Just that you're my neighbor."

Lena seems comforted by the answer. Her shoulders relax. She looks back down at her glass.

"Okay," she says softly. "Well, let me know what Bethel says."

Mitty pauses to say something else, she's not sure what. Another reassurance to hold Lena over while she's gone. But instead she just pats the vinyl cushion of the booth and nods. "I'll call her now."

BETHEL HATES APOLOGIES; SHE FINDS THEM HOLLOW. IN the past, when Mitty would offer up an eager litany of sorries, insisting her own fault, Bethel would just wave them away. After that, the two of them would simply assume a new phase of being that didn't harbor whatever conflict they'd just escaped. Patricia had voiced that she thought this was an unhealthy dynamic, that it fostered resentment. But Mitty and Bethel both appreciate how seamless it makes everything, the fact that no one has to wade in a forced sentimentality and can instead try to forget the worst parts of who they'd been.

Lena waits in the parking lot while Mitty calls Bethel. After a few rings, she answers, mid-cough.

"Are you around in a couple hours?" Mitty asks, watching Lena through the window as she paces along a parking curb.

Bethel pauses. The answer to that question is always yes.

"Lena came by the restaurant," Mitty continues. "She wants to take us somewhere."

"She doesn't need to do all that," Bethel says. "Is she feeling embarrassed about last night?" Her voice is gentle.

"Probably," Mitty says. "Will you go with me?" She waits. "Please?"

Bethel sighs. "All right," she says. And just like that, they've stepped into a new phase, as easy as walking through a revolving door.

Lena treats the lines of a parking space like a balance beam, toe to heel as she walks the length of the white paint. Since she'd left Mitty and Bethel's the night prior, her instinct was to collapse her body into itself. She wanted to be like the moon, obscured by darkness until she was as forgettable as a fingernail clipping. She woke up resenting the size of her arms and legs and torso. She hated that she had a voice, that she could be heard by anyone. She had felt shame so rarely over the course of her life, and was stunned by how powerful it could be, the desire to completely disappear.

Maybe that's how she got the idea: she would soothe herself with the biggest parts of the world. The ocean, the sky, the whales. She would make it all up to Mitty and Bethel with the sunset, a thing she understood was so inarguably perfect, it had the ability to solve most conflicts between people who were looking at it. She knew they would insist that nothing was the matter, insist that her erratic behavior had already been forgotten about. A generous and tender lie.

Mitty is approaching, rolling her apron and tucking it beneath her arm. She digs through her bag as she walks, finally locating her mess of keys. Lena assumes Mitty must notice it, the aura of complete embarrassment hovering around her. Why else would Mitty have that mild grin, walking toward her as though they do this every day. What a humiliating place to exist, in the aftermath of something no one wanted to acknowledge as having been strange and terrifying.

"Did you walk?" Mitty asks. They both climb into the car.

"Yeah." Lena cranks down the window.

The sidewalk is busy with tents, an event called Salsa by the Sea. Men pushing dollies stacked with large speakers. A few professional dancers, adjusting the buckles on their kitten heel shoes, using their phones as mirrors to line their lips.

"Do you ever go?" Lena says. She watches an older man, surprisingly quick on his feet, practice twirling his partner.

Mitty hardly glances over. "No," she says coolly. "I don't really do the whole *local activities* thing."

Lena knew this. Why did she ask? She was filling the space with stupid questions, only adding to the awkward tenor of everything. There was nothing else to say other than more apologies, and yet that would be overkill.

"Lena." They're stopped at an intersection and Mitty is looking at her. "It's really fine."

Had she said all of that out loud?

"Thank you." Her throat closes, cutting off the end of the word. She suddenly worries that if she keeps speaking, she'll start to cry.

"I've done too much embarrassing shit in my life to judge anyone," Mitty says. "I'm just glad you're not at home, hiding."

"It occurred to me," Lena says. She forces herself to laugh.

"The unfortunate thing is that it's impossible to hide from your neighbors." Mitty's eyes hang on a woman walking her dog, blonde hair swishing against the back of her sports bra. As they pass, Lena notices Mitty check her in the rearview mirror, seeming to lose interest once she sees the woman's face.

They idle outside the house. Mitty presses the fabric of her shirt against her face and inhales. It stinks of burnt vegetable oil and sweat.

"No one will be able to smell you where we're going," Lena says. "And they'll give us rain ponchos."

Bethel makes her way down the stairs, her feet heavy, leaning her body weight into the railing with each step. She's wearing what Mitty knows is her activity outfit—a faded university crewneck and a pair of bubblegum-pink nurse's scrubs, taupe wool socks bunched up around her ankles and orthopedic sneakers. When she climbs into the back seat, she immediately lights up a cigarette.

"I hate surprises, Lena." Her voice is gravelly, on the heels of her afternoon nap.

Lena twists around in her seat and playfully squeezes Bethel's knee. "Mitty told me, but I promise you'll enjoy this."

"She specifically requested your presence," Mitty says into the rearview mirror. Bethel won't admit it, but this kind of consideration is important to her.

Ten minutes of a quiet car ride and they're at the harbor, a slim vein that splits the bottom of the city. The water is dark and blotched with rainbows of oil, so crammed with sailboats that the masts look like porcupine quills. Men carry on conversations from their respective decks, cracking open beers.

Mitty can almost feel the dread emanating from Bethel's clenched body in the back seat.

"We aren't fishing," Lena says, as though she has sensed it, too. Bethel nods, warily.

Mitty focuses on reading the names of each boat, scrawled across their white basins. Punny and aspirational—*Old Buoy* and *Megalodon*—or the names of daughters and wives and high school girlfriends who'd slipped away. She'd complained to Bethel once that it was sexist to name boats after women. But Bethel had argued that it was romantic to liken a person to a machine built for exploration and discovery. Mitty watches the *Princess Christine* bob against the dock.

In the parking lot, a crowd of tourists in glaring school-bus-yellow raincoats mingles by a ticket booth. A sign above them advertises the O'NEILL YACHT CHARTERS SUNSET SAIL. The boat, with ballooning sails and a bold logo, is familiar to most Santa Cruz locals, impossible not to notice as it ferries binocular-bespectacled visitors along the canopies of kelp forests and whale migration paths every morning and evening of the week.

Lena smiles proudly. "Have you guys been?"

"No," Mitty says. She looks back at Bethel. "But it'll be good for us."

"I went down a whole rabbit hole on the O'Neills," Lena says, pulling on a hoodie and flattening her static flyaways with her palm. "What a weird dynasty."

"They're our monarchy," Bethel snorts. "Mitty, tell her about Scott."

"Oh, this kid I worked with. Scraggly blond hair, always ashy from salt. He hid the fact that he was an O'Neill for, like, six months."

"Why?" Lena asks.

"I don't know, really," Mitty says. "Maybe they've managed to make so much money that it's no longer something to be proud of."

Mitty remembered the days when Jack O'Neill, the patriarch of the family, was still alive. Bethel worshipped him, though wouldn't admit it. She said he was an anchor for Santa Cruz, that his death marked the start of the new wave. She was nostalgic for his pirate demeanor—a scraggly gray beard and an eye patch—how he'd stand on the balcony of his olive-green, cliffside house and yell pointers at the surfers below. It was his desire to stay in the water longer that led to his invention of the neoprene wetsuit, then a surf brand, and the fortune followed. She admired how pure of an origin story it was—innovation born from passion rather than profit.

"They're everywhere," Bethel says. "All those little blond boys with very expensive last names, wrestling in the water. Hoping no one figures out who they are."

THEY BOARD THE YACHT AND FIND THEMSELVES PRESSED against the railing of the pulpit. People squeeze next to them and take photos, mimicking *Titanic,* their arms spread into crucifixes. As they sail farther into the bay, Mitty finds herself transfixed by the water beneath them, the sharp lines of foam left by the boat's bow cutting through the current.

The captain tells his crowd what to look for when trying to spot dolphins and whales: curved backs, the cloud of spit blasting from a blowhole. Eventually, he slows the boat so that they're just floating with miles of ocean on either side, the details of the rocky cliffs now fading into knotted shapes against the sky. Bethel's eyes are closed, her hands gripping the railing, a subtle grin on her face. On Mitty's other side, Lena is giving off an antsy, restless air. She whips her head every time she seems to notice something in the water and squints, her attention quickly fading when she realizes it's not something worth noticing.

"How do people even see anything out here?" Lena asks.

"Whales know when you're looking for them." Bethel opens her eyes and looks out at sea. "When it's quiet, they'll come."

Lena takes this in. She diverts her focus to the sky. "I went to my first funeral this week," she says, after a beat of silence. "The engineer, I think is how most people are referring to him. Pax was his name."

Mitty begins to fill in the blank spaces from the last few days. Lena's distance. Her accidental break-in. The catatonic mumbling about cable cars. Why hadn't she mentioned this earlier, in the car? It seemed like a reasonable excuse, the bizarre fallout of grief.

"I hadn't realized how well he and Sebastian knew each other," Lena continues. She looks to the both of them, as if for confirmation. "Someone called them best friends at one point."

"Men have strange barometers for what makes a best friend," Mitty offers.

"I don't know." Lena seems bothered. She studies her shoes. "The whole thing made me feel like I don't really know him. I didn't know he was grieving. I didn't know they were so close. I didn't even know anyone there."

"That's how funerals are supposed to make you feel," Bethel says. "When the person isn't there to curate the guest list, everyone feels like a stranger to each other."

"Even your own boyfriend?"

Bethel shrugs. "Death does weird things to people." She pauses. Narrows her eyes toward something in the distance, then loses interest. "At my mother's funeral, even the people

I knew seemed foreign. The people I expected to be crying seemed stoic. The people who I could never imagine shedding a single tear were suddenly bawling in the front row. Half of them seemed performative and the other half seemed entirely unaffected. I felt like I was the only person who actually knew her. At least well enough to know how much she would've hated the service. I didn't even sit down. I just stood in the back, watching the whole thing unfold." Then her hand shoots up, finger gunning toward the sea. "Whale."

The word piques the ears of the group, as though they'd all been listening. Within seconds, a crowd has swarmed their side of the boat, the sudden congregation causing it to lean. Several yards away, the knobby black skin of a humpback breaches the surface, its warted and mossy back the only thing that makes it discernible from the water. When its blowhole lets out a plume of water, everyone shrieks. A man congratulates Bethel on her sighting. Lena makes a show of giving her a round of applause, urging the rest of the crowd to join. Bethel blushes and waves them off. Mitty feels a creeping seasick in her belly and tries to focus on the horizon, flat as a razor, cutting off the edge of the world.

OFF THE BOAT, IT FEELS UNNATURAL FOR THE WORLD NOT to be moving beneath their feet. Lena seems high off the one glimpse of a whale, practically skipping as they cut through the parking lot. Bethel is carrying herself with a pride Mitty hadn't seen on her in so long, a statued smile on her face.

"I wish I lived on a boat," Lena says.

"I used to fantasize about that when I was a teenager," Bethel says. "Meeting some sailor. But then I got older." She laughs.

"It sounds romantic."

"But you wouldn't really want that, would you? Stuck with one person for weeks on end without the ability to get out of the house?"

Lena considers this. "I feel like that already," she says, then cushions the statement with a light-hearted laugh. Bethel eyes her. "I'm kidding," Lena adds. "I'm kidding."

They approach the car; Bethel quickens her step and beats Mitty to the car door. She stands in front of it.

"I have an idea," she says. "I should drive us home."

"You just told me that you forgot how to drive," Mitty says flatly.

She looks to Lena as if for some kind of corroboration. "I'm just rusty."

Lena claps once. "Oh, you should let her."

Mitty feels like a curmudgeon, fussy and anxious, wanting to bring up time and traffic and the fact that Bethel doesn't have a license. She grits her teeth and nods, pushing against this strange, bitter part of her that wants to be in control.

Bethel climbs into the driver's seat and Mitty urges Lena to sit in the front beside her. Bethel is giddy and cautious as she clicks in her seatbelt and readjusts her mirrors. She tests the windshield wipers, though there's no prediction of rain. Mitty imagines that Bethel is a pilot and this is her preflight checklist. That soon, they will be gliding above the Santa

Cruz Mountains, which will then peter out into the packed brown deserts around Sacramento. She pictures Lena pointing excitedly when she notices the geometric plots of farmland, then sweeping over the ocean before landing in a field somewhere close to the home she so rarely speaks about.

Before merging onto the main roads, Bethel does a lap around the lot. It takes her a few tries to remember how to come to a halt without slamming on the brakes, and her turns are either too wide or too tight. Mitty forces herself not to say anything, to let the skill return to Bethel gradually. She grips the handle of the door and presses her foot against an invisible brake on the floor mat each time it seems they might fly right through the fence. She makes sure to compliment Bethel out loud whenever she does something with ease. In the front, Lena laughs every time they hop a curb and comforts Bethel when she apologizes.

"Okay," Bethel says, idling at a stop sign. She eyes the main road like it's a mountain she's preparing to ascend. "I think I'm ready."

"You sure you've got this?" Mitty asks.

Bethel nods. "It's all straight from here."

As they cruise down Portola Drive, Mitty's tension softens and soon is gone altogether. She tries to remember what she had been so anxious about. She begins to doze off, her face damp beneath the hood of her poncho, listening to Lena and Bethel move seamlessly back into their conversation about death. Lena describes a man named Ryan at the funeral and makes Bethel laugh when she jokes about how she can never tell Sebastian's friends apart.

Mitty feels a sharp nostalgia for being a child in the back seat on the way home from some party with her parents, lulled into sleep just with the safety in knowing no one will forget her, even if she's completely silent. The idea that maybe she will wake up in her bed and someone will have taken off her coat.

Before moving to Santa Cruz, Lena had prided herself on having no secrets. When she considered her internal world and the world she shared with Sebastian, there was almost nothing different between them. She had thoughts that remained her own, but none of them seemed disloyal. All things he wouldn't care about: her petty grievances with the cast iron skillet he refused to throw away and how heavy it was to lug out of the cabinet, her pet peeve that hummingbirds never stayed long enough at the feeder to be admired, her strange habit of whiffing his premade lunches before he left for work.

She would've never known how uncommon this lack of secrecy was, had she not heard the other women talk about the cryptic realities they indulged in when their husbands weren't home. Trips to drive-thrus in the middle of the day, ongoing flirtations with a gym instructor, their affinity for lesbian porn. Lena was relieved to learn that such a large part of her psyche had been extricated from these kinds of anxieties. It made her feel light and lucky. But she also had a glimmer of embarrassment when she considered how loyal she'd been to Sebastian—her altruism toward him seemed, somehow, weak. It had hardly ever occurred to her that an experience could be only her own, and that this wouldn't make her selfish.

Only when she began to research memories did the crust of her life begin to diverge from his. She found herself clearing her search history on the computer, leaving the memoirs in Little Free Libraries around town after she'd finished reading them. All she was doing was learning. How threatening could it be?

Now she feels like every day is a secret. She has tried her hardest not to lie when he gets home from work and asks how she spent her day. She recites her truths, listing an onslaught of small chores and a few meek observations about the tide. She keeps anticipating that one day he will voice the fact that there are hours unaccounted for, that she couldn't possibly have spent the whole day researching the most energy-efficient lightbulbs for the bathroom. She is ashamed for feeling grateful that his mind has been less sharp since Pax's death, that he seems generally distracted, less interested in the world altogether.

But as she prepares for Mitty and Bethel to come over for dinner, she realizes that the lives she's been holding in two separate hands will soon be colliding. That almost everyone she knows will suddenly be in the same room. The thought alone causes a small panic to rise inside her. Why did she orchestrate such a messy gathering? Was she trying to sabotage everything she loves about her life? She has already narrowly escaped ruining her friendship with the neighbors after the incident the other night. She feels brazen, stupid. And it's too late to change anything now.

She calms herself by making a flower arrangement, combining the various bouquets they already had in other rooms of the house. She stands at the kitchen counter, trimming stems and tucking them into a vase, carefully removing dead leaves and flimsy petals.

She can smell Sebastian approaching her from behind before he even gets close enough to touch her waist. The musty stink from an afternoon workout.

"Nervous?" he asks, resting his chin on her shoulder.

"Why would I be nervous?" She wonders if he can feel her heartbeat.

"I don't know." He wraps his arms tight around her body and kisses her neck. "You do things like this when you're nervous." He releases himself and walks toward the window to look out at the ocean. "Those are pretty, though."

She feels stupid for being surprised he'd noticed a behavior of hers that she hadn't even tracked herself. He is always doing this—pinning her most subtle habits onto the bulletin board of their lives.

"I guess I've got a little anxiety," she says, aware that any ruthless denial will make her seem cagier. "We haven't had guests in a long time."

"These will be easy ones. Not my co-workers. Not my people."

Yes, but they're my people, she wants to say. *They're mine.*

Mitty spends the day helping Bethel in the kitchen, caramelizing olallieberries and kneading graham crackers with butter, pressing the crust into a pan. The smell of baked sugar briefly takes over the house, the air festive and sweet. Bethel is in unusually high spirits, humming something cheery and domestic as she flits around the kitchen. Mitty is relieved that she doesn't have to coax Bethel out of the house this time; she has her own tensions, knotting up somewhere deep, a feeling she's spent the last few hours pinning down while tending to the day's errands.

She takes her time getting ready. She selects a light blue cotton dress, a rarely worn gift from Bethel years ago, and lets it hang in the bathroom while she showers, allowing the steam to rake out its wrinkles. She runs a razor along the length of her legs and stomach and bikini line, the drain gradually choking until she's ankle-deep in water. She lathers her body in coconut oil and paces her bedroom naked until her skin is glistening, tacky to the touch. She combs through her hair and twists it into a braid. Who is she doing this for?

When she finishes swiping her eyelashes with an ink-black mascara, she steps back from the mirror. For the first time in so long, she's admiring herself. For the first time in so long, she's excited to be looked at by someone else.

The last time she felt this way was during her summer spent in Esme's house; lips chapped from kissing, hickeyed necks, frigid air blowing their hair away from their faces. How free it all was, to continue to learn about each other and get irritated with each other, knowing they would always find their way back. She lets herself remember how they took turns hoisting each other's chlorine-soaked bodies onto their hips in the pool, ate bowls of cereal and slurped down the pink milk, then pressed their ears to each other's stomachs and listened while their intestines wrestled with their new deposits. The ways Esme began to unveil the playful side of herself beneath that rigid ballerina, belting songs out of key and mimicking her mother's accent. How it felt to realize that what they had was singular, a covert frontier where it would always feel like summer, and everything would always be blooming.

But then she is reminded that the longer she and Esme revolved around each other, the less bearable life became when they weren't together. On days when she wasn't working, Mitty would sleep until there was something else to do. If she wasn't at the dance studio or Esme's house, her dreams—the dim buoyancy of her own brain—were the only place worth being. She was desperate for the time to pass until she could be back in that bedroom, when she could return to the sticky insides of Esme's mouth. Her temper became short and brittle, and she snapped at her mother whenever Patricia distracted her from even thinking about Esme. Mitty knew she was insufferable. But it seemed impossible to act any other way while rendered devout and boneless by the paralyzing tranquilizer of love. Maybe, she thinks, if she had just forced herself to remain less affected, she and Esme could have stayed in that eternal summer, where nothing ever went cold.

Maybe that's how she'll preserve her friendship with Lena. Pull away before it's too late. Excuse herself from the party before she's asked to leave.

BEFORE

Mitty was learning how many dialects there were to kissing. The idea of sex seemed so anticlimactic to her now, something people did who couldn't be satisfied with only their lover's mouth. It was prescriptive, ungrateful, to imagine needing more from a person than the part of their body that said your name. She wanted to climb inside Esme's open mouth, to curl up in the warm, damp cave of her cheeks, just to ensure that if Esme's jaw suddenly snapped shut, Mitty could remain there, swaddled in her breath.

It was a hot July afternoon and they were in their swimsuits, twisted in the sheets of Esme's bed. They kissed faster this time, their hands moving urgently, exploring each other's backs and legs, fumbling with the knots of each other's tops. She could taste Esme's spit, the sour ghost of black cherry soda on her tongue. Esme pushed Mitty onto her back and climbed on top, her mouth not leaving Mitty's as she did, her tongue wrestling and hungry. Mitty could tell she had seen this in some movie, they all had: the girl straddling the boy before peeling off her tank top while he watches from below. It irked her, the thought of some swoopy-haired boy actor playing her role. Occasionally, Mitty even wondered if that was what she liked so much about being with Esme, the fact that she knew she couldn't be replicated. So she tipped Esme off of her, impressed even by her own confidence, the ease with which she moved Esme around.

"You don't want me there?" Esme said, already anxious.

"I want to be able to touch you," Mitty said gently, then pulled her hips close.

Mitty couldn't be certain if what they did was sex because she had nothing to hold it up against. She hadn't yet learned what sex looked like between two girls, if sex was even possible without the burst of semen into the tip of an expired condom. With a boy, the act would've been obvious, marked by an inarguable start and finish, his initiation and completion. But with Esme, it ebbed and flowed so naturally, time stretching to meet them, that even the point at which their own bodies began and ended began to blur. Touching Esme made Mitty feel as though she was being touched back. She followed her instincts, searching the parts of Esme she'd only nervously hovered above until now, initiating acts she'd imagined solely in her most unfettered dreams. She felt like an explorer—starving and curious—and wondered briefly if this was how the boys felt too, moved not by expertise but by ambition, a confidence in their own will to discover.

But that day, Esme pulled away first, and Mitty knew something was different. The minute they stopped touching, Mitty was back to feeling as though she was watching Esme instead of being with her. An experience she thought she'd long since left behind. Mitty reached out, wanting the affec-

tion to continue even if the act was over. But Esme was somewhere else. She tried to hook her forefinger around Esme's
pinky, but she just moved farther to the end of the bed, made
a fuss about getting dust out of her eye. It was all so subtle,
enough that Mitty felt silly naming it; maybe she was just
being sensitive, too attentive to Esme's every move.

Esme scrambled off the bed and began untangling her bikini bottom from the floor, a sign Mitty perceived as an instruction that she should do the same. Once they were both
dressed, Esme began cleaning her room, suddenly occupied
with the task of collecting every spaghetti strap strewn across
her carpet like roadkill.

"Are you okay?" Mitty muttered, already ashamed by
how badly she didn't want to know the answer. She clenched
her jaw and sucked in through her nose, holding the air in
her chest.

"Yes," Esme said. She dumped an armful of clothes into
her hamper. "Just straightening up before my mom gets
home." Her voice was small, but warmer than Mitty had anticipated.

Maybe it was a natural occurrence, whiplash as a result of
having done something new. Mitty resigned herself to the
silence of the room and began helping Esme tidy up, ignoring the fact that the last bus home was coming soon. Maybe
tonight was the night she'd finally stay over, and they'd fall
asleep tangled in each other's arms, the two of them finally
acknowledging to their mothers some kind of closeness,
even if it was under the assumption of a sexless friendship.

"Should I go?" Mitty asked, mindlessly folding Esme's

clothes. She thought the question would bring Esme back, force her into reassurance.

"I'm pretty tired," she said instead. She faced Mitty and gave her a painfully polite smile. "Give me a hug?" She opened her arms and Mitty, unable to muster an argument, stepped into them, resting her chin on Esme's shoulder. She swallowed, attempting to drown out her urge to cry. Esme pulled away while Mitty was still holding on. And though the time in which Mitty's arms were wrapped around her waist was brief, those few seconds felt like everything Mitty needed to know. It was suddenly too obvious, their asymmetry, one of them trying to stay and one already letting go.

THE NEXT DAY, MITTY BRACED HER TREMBLING HAND against the dumpster and watched as the dancers hopped out of their waxed SUVs, filing in through the door. She spotted a half-finished cigarette crumpled on the concrete and put it between her lips. She had no way of lighting it, but she wanted the taste—stagnant and sour—to hold her over until Esme showed up.

She waited until she was five minutes late to her shift, then gave up and went inside. The girls were on their backs, pulling their thighs up to their ears and dressing the blisters on the knuckles of their toes. Esme sat in the middle, another girl's foot in her lap, wrapping it in gauze. When had she walked in? She looked so content as the girl told some stupid story. Mitty had to imagine that Esme was just better at hiding her hurt. That's what ballet had prepared her to do.

Mitty spent her shift cleaning the mirrors. Each time she sprayed a cloud of the blue solution, Esme's reflection became blurry, less distinct. But then Mitty would wipe it away and she'd reappear even more detailed than before. The white paste of deodorant folded in the creases of her armpits, her calf muscle materializing each time she thrust herself onto her toe. Occasionally, Esme would glance in her direction and they'd lock eyes. Mitty could swear her movements became more pronounced, every jump a little higher, legs overextending past her ears.

Mitty knew she'd always observed Esme more than Esme did her. Mirroring Esme as she moved from room to room in her house. Only changing into her swimsuit once Esme had signaled it was time to do so. But that seemed like the normal behavior of any guest. Always waiting for permission. So when Esme excused herself to the bathroom, Mitty took it as an instruction and followed her anyway.

She found Esme leaning over the last pastel-green sink, following up with whatever blemish she had cracked the surface of earlier.

Mitty stayed by the door. "I waited for you at the dumpsters," she said. Her voice was already flimsy.

"I came early." Esme winced, paused, then kept digging.

"Why?"

She shrugged.

"Are you mad at me?" Mitty said. She stepped two sinks closer.

"I'm not *mad* at you."

"Well, if I did something wrong—"

"You didn't *do* anything wrong."

Esme turned to face her. The blemish pinched out a drop of blood.

"You keep emphasizing the middle of your sentences," Mitty said.

Esme wove around Mitty to get to the towel dispenser, then pulled one out and pressed it against her face. Mitty wanted to stuff her hands in her own mouth to keep herself from speaking. Her mind shot backward, trying to recount every single thing she'd said at Esme's house, where she could have gone wrong. She tried to remember the exact mechanics of every time they'd touched or kissed, whether or not she'd used tongue or brushed her teeth that morning.

Finally, Esme looked at Mitty. Her lips were cracked, their color fading into a sad shade of pink. Mitty could see an echo of red nail marks on the side of her neck from anxious scratching. Her insides seemed too visible, like Esme was an insect, molting right in front of her.

"I don't think I wanted to do that yesterday."

"Do what?" Mitty could hear her own desperation, like she was clawing against a shut door.

A girl's voice rang out from the other side of the door and Esme paused. Then she spoke under her breath.

"I'm just saying I wanted to go slower."

Mitty's face burned. It was humiliating, how immediately she wanted to beg for the impossible solution of everything starting over. Esme unclenched her fist, where the wad of paper towel had been trapped, now soaked dark from sweat, or water, Mitty couldn't tell. The thought that it could be sweat gave her a brief glint of comfort that Esme might be as nervous as she was.

"Okay," Mitty said. She tried to arrange her face to seem composed. "We can do that." Later, she would regret not asking more questions. She would come to realize that so much of her anger was cultivated in the privacy of her own head.

"Cool." Esme tossed the paper towel into the bin, satisfied. "I'll see you out there, then."

Only when she heard the bathroom door close did Mitty realize that for the last few seconds of their exchange, her head had been bowed, her eyes trained on the shelled toes of her sneakers. She would regret that, too. Not knowing what Esme looked like before she walked out into the world, leaving Mitty behind.

SOME DAYS, IT WAS EASY TO TALK HERSELF INTO THE NOR-malcy of Esme's request. *Slower*, she repeated to herself. She told herself it meant Esme didn't necessarily want to stop. Maybe, Mitty wondered, she even wanted to savor it all a little more. Live longer in the smaller acts, the kiddish touching, all those ways they'd learned to kiss. But each time Mitty felt soothed by her own rationalities, another day would pass in which Esme didn't call and didn't show up to the dumpsters. Another day in the studio, where their interactions were either terse or nonexistent. And when Mitty finally gained the courage to make the call herself, she was met

with Esme's voicemail—that breathy, empty promise of return.

At night, she fixated, pulverized by her own manic doubt.
She tried to remind herself of all the things she hated about
Esme. The fact that she didn't have a sense of humor, too
consumed by her own dilemmas to laugh at someone else's
jokes. She was rude to her mother, pushing out her lower
jaw and hissing, *What?* whenever she answered the phone.
And the third tooth from the center was shorter than the
rest and yellow, like an ugly runt. Mitty pushed herself into
anger, the only protected place she could float for a while.
And when she finally surrendered to sleep, her dreams were
nebulous and agonizing, only to wake up in the morning
and face it all again.

TWO WEEKS HAD PASSED SINCE MITTY AND ESME'S LAST
conversation. Mitty was at home, curled up on the tweed
futon, snot and tears collecting in the ridges of her lips. Her
mother had been out, making the sales rounds. When she
walked in the front door, Mitty groaned quietly to herself
and turned to face the back of the couch. She felt her mother's weight as she sat down at the opposite end of the cushion and laid her hand gently on Mitty's leg.

"Mitty," she said softly. "Can we talk?"

"I don't feel like it," Mitty murmured. A guilt crept up in
her, an embarrassment at her lack of gratitude toward the
last person in the world who seemed to love her.

"I stopped by Magnolia's Dresser," her mother said. Her

voice was ominous, like she was relaying the news of a small death. Mitty's chest tightened, her breath diced into small, frantic bursts. She craned her neck to look up at her mother.

Mitty hissed. "What?"

"Why didn't you tell me?" Patricia looked genuinely concerned, in a way that caused Mitty to consider softening. But she resisted.

"There isn't anything to tell you," Mitty said.

"I spoke to Esme's mother," Patricia continued, persistent and unfazed by Mitty's protest. She pressed her forefinger and thumb into the tendon on her shoulder, an attempt to massage out the ache of that tote bag she carried, heavy with five dozen nail polish bottles pressing into her skin. "She said you've been making Esme feel uncomfortable."

The word made Mitty want to sever her head from the rest of her body, stop the venom from spreading beyond her ears. But it shot through her too fast, and she began to weep uncontrollably.

"I didn't do anything," she said, her eyes already blinded with tears. "I didn't do anything." But the more she repeated the phrase, the more it sounded like an aspirational mantra, a truth she was hoping to speak her way toward rather than one she already held.

"I'm not saying you did anything." Patricia squeezed Mitty's leg harder, trying to still her shaking body. "I came home because I wanted to talk to you about it first." She stood up and put out her hand, gesturing for Mitty to take it. "Come," she said. "Let me draw you a bath."

Mitty studied her mother. She had never seen the similarities between them. Patricia's features were slender and
muted, as if their only purpose was to support her gilded
plastic jewelry. Her hair was naturally dishwater blond, but
she'd been dying it from the box since before Mitty was born,
a shade called Hollyhock Red that left the bathtub pink.
Mitty wanted to say something awful, something about how
the ugliest women need the most accessories. But really, she
resented her mother's kindness, how it served as a reminder
that she was lovable despite something, she just didn't know
what.

AS PATRICIA DIALED THE FAUCET TO THE PERFECT WARMTH,
seasoned the water with lavender bath salts, Mitty sat huddled in the corner, holding her knees. Through choking
gulps, she explained what happened with Esme. When Patricia gestured toward the tub, she shook her head.

"It'll go to waste," Patricia said, sitting on the edge, rak-
ing her fingers through the water. "In the middle of the desert, no less."

"I never asked for you to do it," Mitty groused, sulking
into a stubborn quiet.

But Patricia remained unbothered. "You should never
have to ask for someone to draw you a bath."

She spoke with a sureness that Mitty would eventually
realize came from having known her daughter forever. Later,
she would appreciate this awareness. But right then, it

seemed unfair that a person could know which parts of you were still a child, that a person could watch you before you were smart enough to know what to hide.

Still reluctant, she stripped off her clothes, realizing only when she removed her underwear that her mother hadn't seen her naked since before she'd hit puberty. She was suddenly self-conscious, as if the presence of hair and breasts made her body something worth guarding. But Patricia seemed so fluent in how she handled Mitty, dipping a mug into the tub and pouring the water over her shoulders.

"Why didn't you tell me you were seeing someone?" Patricia asked. She gently tipped Mitty's head back and soaked her hair. Mitty closed her eyes and let her neck give in to the weight.

"Esme wanted to keep it a secret."

Patricia paused, waiting until Mitty let her body relax briefly into the water.

"Do you think what her mother said is true?" Patricia asked. "Do you think you made her uncomfortable?"

Mitty went quiet. She was afraid of the answer to this question, how flimsy it felt to cushion her actions by talking about her own intentions. What did those matter anymore? Whatever space inside her had previously housed any certainty now felt vacant, a dark and yawning cavity that left her dizzy just trying to reach it. As unbearable as this was, she dreaded what was to come even more. The weeks when her mother could no longer be by her side every minute, and she'd be left to sit in the quiet house and miss Esme even more. How, eventually, she'd reach past that day in the bathroom and torture herself with reminiscing instead.

She remembered a lumpy bracelet made of poorly tied knots, pink and purple yarn with a plastic bead in the middle that boasted the letter M, the kind you learn to make at summer camp, the kind that fades and frays and gets wet from swimming, then never dries in the center. Esme had made it for Mitty, as a joke, she said, when she presented it to her as they sat on the floor in Esme's bedroom, right before they kissed for the second time. *Remember when everyone was making these things?* she'd said. Of course, Mitty remembered. Specifically, how long it took. Hours, sometimes. Especially if you had to pick through a tub of non-alphabetized letter beads to find the first initial of the person you were making it for. Mitty had laughed and shoved the bracelet into the bottom of her backpack. But later, she took it out and placed it on her windowsill, a reminder that there had been a night that Esme sat on her bedroom floor and tied knot after knot after knot, thinking of Mitty the whole time.

"Maybe," Mitty said, finally. "I really don't know." All the moments she thought she had been certain about were now vague and corrupted.

"Well." Patricia twisted the ends of Mitty's hair, letting the lukewarm water run down her back. "I know it doesn't feel like it now, but maybe one day, you'll see this all as a gift."

But her mother felt that way about everything, Mitty thought. She was surrounded by gifts: new-age hair straight-

eners and sweet-pea body butters and loofahs with ergo-
nomic bamboo handles. Everything in their house was
technically a gift. And still, when Mitty looked around, all
she saw was trash.

MITTY SLEPT IN HER MOTHER'S BED THAT NIGHT, HER
cheeks raw against the polyester pillowcase, her mother's
delicate snores like a pendulum, hypnotizing her into an
eventual slumber. In the morning, Patricia made her soft
scrambled eggs and mint tea, neither of which Mitty could
bring herself to finish. They had agreed that Mitty would
put in her two weeks at the studio. Mitty begged to quit outright, but her mother insisted that it would ruin her credibil-
ity for future jobs. *Sometimes we have to learn to be around people
we don't want to see,* she'd said.

Patricia sat next to her at the table, circling jobs in the
paper, trying to sell Mitty on each minimum-wage position
with the forced, chipper demeanor she used to sell her products. But Mitty was numb to it all. Any sense of excitement
or joy, or even the anticipation of a feeling other than complete despair, was unreachable.

They drove in silence to the studio and idled in the parking lot as Patricia tried to give her a pep talk.

"Just put your head down," she said. "Do your work and
then let them know you're leaving."

Mitty stared at that awful, square building. The beige
sandstone facade. The tinted windows, a protective measure
from some vague threat of a perverted passerby. Behind

them, the front desk decorated with plastic flowers, stems strapped to ballpoint pens. Hovering mothers in the lobby. Decade-old dance magazines in a furrowed stack. The stop and start of the grand piano. And the girls, those pink flamingos. Priming themselves for a pink future elsewhere, learning how to meticulously obscure their deformed toes in pink, their bulbous calves in pink, their fluted torsos in pink. Everything ugly and painful, doused in pink. *What a lie,* Mitty thought. At least she was honest in her jumpsuit, wielding a mop. At least her wounds were visible. All the ways she knew she was unremarkable, blatant, and exposed.

THE DANCERS TRICKLED IN AS MITTY FINISHED MOPPING the floors. Each time the front bell rang, signaling a new arrival, she felt her stomach pinch, the hairs on the back of her neck rise like alert little soldiers. She refused to look back and see if it was Esme, aware that any and all of her movements might be watched, depending on how many people Esme had already told. Any trace of fervency felt like it could be perceived as a crime.

She finished her work on the floor and went to the utilities closet, began to empty the gray water into the sink. Beyond the door, she heard Esme's laugh, that rounded giggle she used to love. Now it just sounded conspiratorial. She hung by the door and listened to the girls' innocuous, sunny conversation. They were talking about rehearsing for their solos. Commiserating about how quickly their leg hair grew back. The everlasting heat.

"Are you going first?" one of the girls asked, her tone hopeful.

"Yeah," Esme said, groaning. "I already know I'm gonna fuck it up." A false modesty that Mitty had come to notice Esme put on whenever she was around the other dancers.

They carried on exchanging knowledge about dance positions in French with an educated ease, a glossary of words that Mitty still didn't understand. Despite her complaining, Esme sounded happy. Like nothing in her life had so much as shifted. How could that be possible? Mitty thought. Was it really so fleeting, so forgettable, that Esme could just keep moving? The thought was unbearable. It would be almost more reassuring had she heard Esme say something mean about her, at least then she would know she still existed somewhere in Esme's brain. She had never thought indifference would be more painful than hate, but it was. The idea that she wasn't even worthy of being a memory made her seethe. While Mitty was left with the soured, stinging aftermath, unable to shake the dizzy memory, Esme would simply go somewhere else. Esme would just keep living.

ON THE DRIVE TO SANTA CRUZ, PATRICIA WOULD ASK HOW far in advance she'd conjured it all up. The truth was, the idea only came to her in that moment. She had done it by accident once before. At the start of the job, she had been told that twice a year, she would stain the floors. But this duty was always planned in advance, with at least twenty-four hours afterward to give the floor time to dry; otherwise, it was a slipping hazard. In her first month of working, she'd mixed up the bottles of cleaner and stain. Luckily, it was at the end of a shift and the building was empty, so the only person who slipped was Mitty herself. But as she listened to Esme go on about New York, the American Ballet Theater, the instructors with angular Russian names whom she would just *die to work with*, Mitty's anger only grew.

She felt as if her body was moving without her—filling the bucket with the syrupy fluid, the acrid odor wafting up toward her nose, a tangible warning of what she was about to do. She carried the bucket out of the building and around the perimeter to let herself into the back door. There, she could step onto the floor without being noticed. While the girls mingled, wrapping their limbs in tape, she dipped her mop into the water and ran it along a single spot, no more than a few feet in each direction. She couldn't be certain that Esme would land there, but she had watched her enough times to know that it was likely.

What was she hoping would happen? Her mother would ask this, too. An accident, yes. But something simple, repairable. Something that, at worst, would make the instructor doubt Esme's ability to carry out the future she so easily planned without Mitty in mind.

As the girls made their way to the floor, Mitty tucked herself away into a back corner. She could still watch without being noticed. The pianist took his seat and the dancers lined up against the walls. Esme positioned herself in the center of the room. When the first note of the piece rang out, she began. Her body moved with a polished knowing that only made Mitty more furious. The physical proof of her disregard. The fact that she was able to still be good at something, the sheer ability to focus on a singular task, while Mitty could hardly stomach a single bite of food.

She watched as Esme weightlessly lifted herself into the air. Mitty stared at the spot on the floor, just slightly darker than the space around it, growing closer and closer to Esme's feet. Then, as she thrust herself into a pirouette, kicking out her leg to gain momentum, there was a crack. A scream. And a grim silence fell over the room.

Mitty jolted out of her seat, but Esme was already obscured by a now panicking audience, the instructor yelling for them to give her space. When they parted, she saw the mess. Esme's ankle bone, that cherished bone, jutting from her leg while her foot hung limply to the side, blood pooling around her leg. Esme's face was drained white, her eyes blinking to register the fact of her body, her mouth agape and soundless.

Mitty's vision was speckled, black blemishes appearing and disappearing from view. If she fainted, she would only be there longer. So instead, she ran. Through the back door and out into the brilliant Arizona heat. She only stopped when she reached her mother's front door, where she hunched over and vomited onto the welcome mat, her body emptying itself as she rammed her thumb against the doorbell. Maybe she was screaming, too. But that, she can't remember.

On the front porch of Lena's house, Bethel scours her wool dress for flour fingerprints, bullying them away with her thumb. When Sebastian opens the door, he says Mitty's name like a sigh of relief. She can feel Bethel glance at her, clearly unaware that their familiarity extends into these kinds of easy greetings. He adjusts the collar of his cream linen suit, beneath which a thin gold chain snakes along the humps of his clavicle.

"This is Bethel," Mitty tells him. In Bethel's presence, she feels too aware of how her voice lifts when she speaks to men, splitting into an acute bashfulness.

Sebastian and Bethel shake hands, the force sending a ripple through her frail arm.

"Welcome to Santa Cruz," she says, though the sentiment comes out sounding more like a warning.

Sebastian steps to the side and gestures them through the door. "Shoes." He points to a rack, where Lena's tiny slippers are lined up in a row like obedient schoolgirls.

Beyond the hallway, the house has an open floor plan, any separation a suggestion based on how the furniture is arranged. To the right, the white sitting room that Mitty saw from the beach is beaming and seems even larger in person, dominated by a deep, plush couch. She realizes that what she thought were windows are actually glass doors that slide open in each direction, with a balcony spanning the entire width of the house. Mitty is so consumed by the interior of a home she'd only ever witnessed from a distance that she notices the smell last: a salted, heady tang that forces her to suck in her cheeks.

Bethel and Mitty seat themselves at the kitchen counter. Across from them, Lena is hunched over a simmering pot, letting the steam bloom onto her face. When she turns around to greet them, she unties the apron from her waist and lifts it over her head. The motion feels intimate. Like she's undressing.

Sebastian leans in close to the pie crust and sniffs. "Blackberry?"

"Olallieberry," Mitty says.

"I thought they weren't selling those anymore?" The question is rhetorical. "I'd read that the harvest was too low this year."

"They had plenty at the farmer's market," Bethel says.

"Well, I guess when we run out completely, we'll know the culprit." Sebastian grins and slaps both of his hands on the granite. "Drinks," he announces, and walks to the bar cart. Mitty scratches the back of her neck. It had been so long since she'd socialized like this, in the home of a person whose only commonality with her was their proximity. She had forgotten the dance of moving through conversation with confidence, ignoring passive aggression and easing away from one topic and into the other without thinking too hard.

While Sebastian guts a lime into each glass, Bethel explains the history of the olallieberry—a cross between two blackberries specific to the Pacific Northwest region and developed through the blackberry breeding program at Oregon State University. She recounts how the article she'd read reminded her of the time she and Mitty considered getting a beagle and made a horrifying visit to a dog breeder.

"Stacked kennels, piss all over the carpet," Bethel says. "The breeder swooped up each puppy and held their tiny testicles in her palm like they were jewels. We kept joking about how the blackberries must have been like those puppies, with men in white coats tossing the ugly ones and deciding which are qualified to be featured as garnish for a crème brûlée on the cover of a food magazine."

Sebastian dances with the cocktail shaker. "Those breeders are fucking weird, aren't they?" he says, shouting over the rattle of ice.

"But aren't they necessary?" Lena asks, lifting a spoonful of broth to Sebastian's lips. He pauses to take it into his mouth, then smacks his tongue and offers a nod of approval. "That's how they perfect genetics."

"No, that's how they *ruin* genetics," Sebastian says. "It fucks with nature. I heard French bulldogs can only give birth by C-section because they've bred their heads to be too large to fit through a vaginal canal. Can you believe that?"

"But maybe they can intervene in helpful ways, too," Lena argues. "Like your birdcall."

"All right, hold on." Sebastian places a large square cube of ice into the center of each tumbler, then pours something cloudy and green up to the rim. "This is no way to introduce me to our guests."

"Lena told us about the birdcall." Mitty hangs on to her mild expression, hesitant to offer him too much interest. But when she notices how Sebastian looks at Lena—a quick, condemning glance—she remembers what Lena had mentioned once, about Sebastian's obsession with privacy. She corrects herself. "But she didn't elaborate, really. Now you work in social media?"

Sebastian returns his attention to Mitty. "Software development," he clarifies.

"That's such a boring way to say it," Lena says. She laughs nervously. "He always says it like that."

Despite their verbal disagreements, Lena and Sebastian's actions are seamless and fluent, the wordless nature of love. Lena hands him a knuckle of ginger and, without having to ask, he cracks it in half, then hands it back to her. From the fridge, he removes a red slab of raw beef.

"It's all boring," he says, scanning their quiver of kitchen knives, "another experiment we don't need."

"Tell them about the app," Lena prompts.

Sebastian rests his weight on his palms and pauses, his eyes searching the ceiling.

"I started an app called Forage, what was it, five years ago now? A dating app, sort of."

"Not *sort of,* it is a dating app," Lena says. "It looks at the profiles from all the other dating apps and gives you the best ones."

"It extracts data from the various dating apps, yes," Sebastian says. "And then based on your Forage profile, it pulls the most compatible people from other sites and sends them directly to you." He pauses to pound the beef with a mallet. "Unlike the rest of the apps, it costs a significant amount of money. So, the person whose profile you settle on will get an email that a user from Forage wants to connect. That person can then download the app to start talking." Another beating. "We've got an elite customer base compared to the rest of the apps."

"Did you guys meet on there?" Bethel asks.

Lena lifts herself onto the counter. "We met in San Francisco."

"But believe me, if that face"—Sebastian points at Lena—"showed up in my fucking inbox?" He doesn't need to answer his own question.

"So these are mostly men, I imagine," Bethel says. "And they're essentially paying for these women, right?"

Mitty laughs, louder than she needs to. But Sebastian seems unaffected by the comment. "Fair observation," he says. "That's one way of looking at it. But when you work as often as I do, or did, spontaneity is more difficult. I pay for everything to be easier." He hammers the meat a few more times, then runs a knife through its center. It splits easily, like he's sliding a razor through satin. "Maybe that's crass. But in today's market, if what we're consuming is expensive, it needs to either be convenient or healthy." He picks up a strip and dangles it in front of Bethel and Mitty. "For instance. Cultured meat. Could be considered inconvenient. Less convenient than slaughtering a cow, probably. Certainly more expensive. But better for you. Better for the environment. Would you believe me if I told you this was made in a lab? No animals involved?"

Mitty leans forward in her seat to get a closer look. "Was it?"

"I don't know." He looks up at her, now grinning. "You tell me."

Lena rolls her eyes. "He's always speaking in riddles."

"Well, your berries were an experiment, weren't they?" he says. "Does that make them real or not real?"

"But there's blood." Bethel nods to the red pool collecting in the warped basin of the cutting board.

"They make that, too," he says. "Heme, it's called. Soy leghemoglobin." He slaps the beef back down and begins dicing it. "But that's an important observation, Bethel." He lifts up his knife and wipes his finger against the flat side, coating his skin in red. "What I find the most interesting is that, even if people claim they're disgusted by eating a dead animal, they still want to replicate the experience. That's why people order meatless burgers, right? They don't want pea protein. They want cow. But they still want to feel like good people. And so, in order to convince anyone to buy it, we have to reassure them of their own morality, while also allowing them to briefly believe that what they're eating is real. And in order to do that? We have to give it blood."

LENA FILLS THEIR BOWLS WITH STEW, GOING ON ABOUT their trip to Hong Kong and the market in Aberdeen where they first learned about it, where she never wrote down the recipe or asked for the ingredients, she says, just remembered watching the woman make it over a coal stove, and did her best to replicate it. Mitty is so lost in devouring the soft carrots bloated with broth, sucking on whole peppercorns, and chewing on the salted chunks of beef that she hardly thinks about whether or not it used to be alive.

"So you work at a restaurant"—Sebastian points his fork limply at Mitty, then wags it toward Bethel—"and you're retired. Forgive me if this is rude, but how the hell have you managed to keep that house?" These were the kinds of questions that never came up before the neighborhood changed. Of course, the houses had always been considered large, the community seen as well-off. But everyone had been living there for so long that their livelihoods were common knowledge. Most people had owned their homes outright for many years. It was a new feeling to explain their presence, how they'd gotten there and how they'd managed to stay. Mitty and Bethel begin speaking at the same time, cutting themselves off and taking another beat, then speaking again.

Frustration flickers across Bethel's face. She waves Mitty on to speak.

"Bethel owns it," Mitty says. A stupid, obvious answer. "And we don't do many renovations."

"Well, sure, I assumed that. But I imagine you've gotten offers to take it off your hands, right?"

Bethel scoffs at the thought. "Yes," she says. "We have."

"So how do you afford to say no?"

"Sebastian." Lena nudges him.

"What? We can talk about money, can't we?" He looks to Bethel for reassurance. She shrugs off the question.

"But why does it matter?" Lena says.

"It's okay." Bethel gives Lena a comforting smile. "It's fair. We know how Sebastian affords this place, don't we?"

"Exactly," he says. "You don't think it's strange that it's expected that we flaunt our money but don't explain how we got it?" Sebastian takes in a mouthful of stew and grins at Mitty, his eyebrows jumping. His questions aren't really questions, they're little bullies, spun to sound like curiosity.

"But *they're* not flaunting it," Lena says. "They're the only people on the block who aren't driving a new car." She gives Mitty a self-effacing smile. "I mean that in a good way. It's refreshing to see something that wasn't built yesterday."

"Look, I don't actually care where your money comes from," Sebastian continues. "Ethically, I mean. None of it is ethical."

"Well, people must care about ethics," Mitty says, hardly meaning to speak at all. "Especially in Santa Cruz. All these people are invested in green energy."

"Well." Sebastian fishes something from between his teeth with the edge of a napkin. "Mostly they're invested in AI." He laughs at an inside joke that no one else is privy to. "Which I wouldn't particularly describe as ethical."

Mitty hesitates. She thinks of Cat, the flurry of brazen questions that she would nudge her to ask. But on her own, Mitty feels too cowardly to pry with the kind of ruthless abandon that would get her any answers worth remembering.

"What about it exactly isn't ethical?" she says softly, attempting to cloak her timidness in a naïve curiosity.

Sebastian's eyes trace her face, like he's searching for whatever might make her qualified to have this conversation. "Well, don't get me wrong. It's fascinating. And groundbreaking," he says. "But anytime humans are looking for a shortcut, ethics go out the window." He pauses, allowing the question to remain unanswered. "That's why, if you want to get anything done, you have to distance yourself from ethics."

"Then how do all these guys justify doing it?" Bethel asks, crunching ice with her back teeth on each harsh syllable.

He stands and begins collecting their empty glasses. "By knowing that everyone else is unethical, too."

Lena cuts in. "Sweetie, I can take care of it." But he ignores her and keeps moving.

"By knowing that they'll get chastised for being the ones who built it." His voice seems so unaffected by doubt that now what he's saying sounds like a scolding. "But people still buy it. They use it. And they say things like, *These companies make us need them!* But the problem with tech is that the customer is often demanding something that doesn't exist yet."

In a way it's soothing, Mitty thinks, to watch someone make such a coherent argument that exists entirely to protect their own conscience. Like anything wrong you've ever done could be explained away if only the right person was speaking.

"And when a customer doesn't know what they're asking

for, they convince themselves they aren't demanding any-thing. But they are. And they're not just demanding a ser-vice. They're demanding an invention. Which, whether they want it or not, will be used for more than just that service." In the kitchen, he blasts the sink, his voice booming over the rushing water. "They want their packages now, but they don't want drones. They want their phones to remember their most visited locations, but they don't want to be tracked. I mean, let's be real. They want green energy, but they're afraid of machine learning."

Wringing his hands with a towel, he returns to the table with four new cocktails. Lena hasn't touched her stew, but she's eyeing it as though she's motivating herself to eat. She reaches forward and dips the spoon into the bowl. But be-fore she can consume it, Sebastian places his hand over hers, gently lowering her arm. The action feels choreographed, a swift and easy deflection. Lena doesn't so much as glance at him. She just seems to lose interest in the food altogether.

"So that's how they sleep at night," Sebastian continues. "Cozy and warm knowing that everyone is a fucking hypo-crite."

The room submits to a lull. Mitty wipes down a spot on the table in front of her with a napkin. Bethel readjusts in her seat. Lena looks vacant, her interior in some transitional space, waiting for something else to arrive.

"I don't mean to shut the conversation down." Sebastian hooks his hand around the back of Lena's neck, and she clicks back into herself. "Lena knows how passionate I am about these things."

"Does anyone need anything else?"

Bethel shakes her head, smiling politely, her face unreadable. Mitty had been so consumed by the room around her that only when it's quiet does she notice the sting of her ballooning bladder.

"Downstairs is still being renovated," Sebastian says when she asks to use the bathroom. "You can use the one in our room." He gestures toward the stairs before returning his attention to a chip on his marble coaster.

Mitty tries to keep her face blank, hide her thrill that she's been granted the freedom to wander the house alone. She exchanges a look with Bethel to ensure she'll be okay on her own, and when Bethel nods, Mitty excuses herself from the table. As she walks toward the staircase, she hears Bethel remark on the view, bowled over by the sky. As if it isn't the exact same one she sees every single evening. As if here, the world looks different. As if behind this glass, everything is more beautiful.

THE BEDROOM IS AS MANICURED AS THE REST OF THE house—a towering ceiling cut with beams, the walls bare other than a few austere paintings. In the center, a king-sized mattress is lifted a few inches off the ground by poplar slats. The nightstands on each side are free of any clutter that might distinguish whose side is whose—no stale water cups or knotted hair ties, just a small analog clock on one and a gunmetal ashtray on the other. A bell-shaped sconce above each, dimmed to a tranquil glow.

Mitty could easily spout off the ways minimalism is tied to a culture obsessed with efficiency, a world void of adornment. She and Bethel had spent plenty of time talking about it. Whether it was actually what they believed or simply a justification for their own crowded home was another thing. But here, some part of her relishes how kept it all is. She feels ashamed for thinking it's cleaner.

She lets herself out onto the balcony. Beneath her, she can see exactly where she stood on that first night, waiting for the empty house to come alive. She presses her torso against the railing and imagines what it would be like to have someone inside her, the metal bar cutting into her abdomen. She notices that the balcony of her own house isn't as high up as she once thought. It would only take a slight tilt of the head to see someone watching, perched in her plastic chair and cupping her groin.

Mitty has never been delusional about the state of their house. She understands that it can be sad to look at. But from this angle, it's hideous in a way she had never recognized. It seems duller than usual, limping on its frame. But maybe it's just her new perspective, she thinks—aroused and hygienic, slightly drunk, the blinding white floor beneath her feet— that makes everything else look dingy. Even the beach, strewn with driftwood, looks messy and forgotten. The water roused and gray.

In the bathroom, the sound of her piss echoes off the tile walls. The toilet paper is thick as cloth. The mirror is too spotless, wide above a pair of clean sinks. Her reflection is so clear that she feels like she could reach through it and shake the hands of a team of police officers on the other side, studying her face for a lineup. Just an hour ago, beneath the yellow light in Bethel's bathroom, she liked the way she looked. But now her hair seems to be splitting into oily ridges. Her cheeks flecked from the sun. How could her beauty be so brief? At the very least, she thinks, her chest is still gleaming from the coconut oil, the skin on her breasts glossy against her cotton dress.

Downstairs, Bethel lands a joke and Sebastian belly-laughs. Sebastian's voice echoes across the massive and empty walls. He begins to tell a story about driving a motor-cycle through the back roads of a city in southwestern India. The smell of eucalyptus and burning trash. The potholes. They suddenly sound comfortable with each other. The night has finally taken shape, she thinks. Knowing that Bethel isn't anxiously waiting for her return, she embraces the time to leisurely poke through the bathroom cabinets. Behind one is a steel razor, a can of shaving cream, a small jar of eucalyptus hand lotion arbitrarily labeled as a men's product, and a tube of charcoal toothpaste. She dips her finger into the lotion and kneads it into her hands. It's so satisfying, she thinks, the minimalism of male toiletries, the fact that men don't need anything to make themselves more beautiful except time.

As a child, Mitty always loved rifling through her mother's cabinets, sitting on the counter with her feet in the sink and inspecting each bottle—thick jellies in glass jars, mint-green tubes of waterproof mascara, nubs of old lipstick, pill bottles that she couldn't open with her child hands. As she got older, she began to notice the different genres of medicine cabinets in the bathrooms of other people, always making sure to peek into them whenever she was invited to a friend's house. It seemed to her that it was those cabinets that said the most about class, cleanliness, and confidence, depending on what the products were and how they were arranged. Whether they were packaged in plastic or glass. Whether their purpose was to enhance or erase. Whether they were made from chemicals that might burrow somewhere deep in your body and reemerge as a tumor, years later, long after you had the opportunity to make different choices.

As she works her way through the rest of the bathroom, she only finds stacks of towels and linens the color of quinoa, along with other unspecific bathroom essentials. She had been excited to learn what sorts of tinctures Lena massaged into her body before bed or patted onto her cheeks in the morning. She knows that a woman who looks like Lena doesn't need acne treatments and petroleum jelly, vaginal creams or eczema medication, so she had assumed her toiletries would be sparse. But what Mitty presumes to be her medicine cabinet is deserted. Or something before deserted. Untouched. Undiscovered. As if Lena doesn't exist at all.

She crouches down to look beneath the sinks. Odorless cleaning products, towers of toilet-paper rolls. Just as she is about to give up, deduce that Lena must have her own closet of perfumes and creams and hair oils somewhere else in the house, she finds a small cloth bag tucked behind a can of air freshener. It's gray and waffled, cinched at the top with satin strings. She wiggles her finger into the closure and pries it apart. Inside, she feels the wishbone handle of a pair of steel tweezers. She pulls them out and notices that their slanted tips are coated in dried blood, scabby clumps of maroon running halfway up the slim metal arms.

Mitty flinches, the faint image of a wound flashing across her mind. She thinks of the girls in middle school who split open their forearms, who wove safety pins inside their jackets and backpacks, their little torture apparatuses concealed and always on hand. She hasn't noticed any wounds on Lena that look self-inflicted, and though she hasn't spent as much time with Sebastian, it seems unlikely that he would be impulsive enough to deface anything about his body. Somehow, it's clear to Mitty that this belongs to Lena. All those years that girls spend learning how to domesticate their tempers, quell their sadness with a bigger purpose like motherhood or beauty; it only makes sense that it would be unleashed elsewhere, carved like a cave drawing into an inner thigh, a clue left for whoever finds her body. *Who knew she'd been so heartbroken*, they'd say. *If only she'd said something out loud.*

BACK IN THE BEDROOM, MITTY CONTINUES HER SEARCH, turning her attention to the nightstands. The left one is barren and wiped clean, while the right only holds a navy blue pocket-sized notebook, with the Roman numeral XI embossed on the front in gold foil. She fans through it quickly, letting its pages exhale onto her face. She can see the glimmer of chicken scratch, the frantic handwriting of a person whose brain moves too fast for their fingers. She opens to the first page, where written in all caps and underlined, is the term *Self-supervised.* The notes on the rest of the pages are all observations, jotted down in arbitrary lists.

Suddenly anxious about barnacles in surf.

Good sense of humor?

Heard about a library card somewhere.

The handwriting is scratchy and boyish; she can only make out about half of the sentences—*Most sociable with an activity (poker, etc.)*—but most are blacked out with permanent marker and others are too messy to decipher as words. She feels immobilized by an anxiety she can't yet recognize, her palms pinching out sweat, her heart beating in her ears. When she pulls her eyes away to scan the room, her once drunk brain is slammed shut by the dead bolt of sobriety.

She hears Bethel say her name, and though she's fairly certain it was spoken in passing, she quickly returns the notebook to its resting place. Now her absence will be noted. She adjusts the book's position a few times to ensure that it's exactly where she found it and pushes the drawer shut.

She drifts through the room, gradually making her way toward the door. She feels high and bawdy, having seen something she's almost certain she wasn't supposed to. The notes lack context, clearly unrecognizable to anyone but the composer. But whoever had written them was watching someone. Maybe Sebastian, tracking himself. Neurotic about maintaining the data of his own progress, she thinks, noting every time he develops a new phobia or recognizes a pattern in his behavior he hadn't seen before. Maybe he brings the notebook to therapy and transcribes whatever his shrink says aloud.

Or maybe it's about Lena. Maybe he's just trying to understand her. *Isn't that what we're all doing with the people we love, anyway?* she tells herself, trying to quell the kick of adrenaline running ragged through her body. *Attempting to make something, anything, feel predictable?*

MITTY DESCENDS THE STAIRCASE SLOWLY, HER HAND HOVering above the railing, trying to remain unnoticed. Bethel is standing at the record player, flipping through a crate of albums. Mitty wants to reappear seamlessly enough so that no one can gauge exactly how long she was gone. Before sitting down on the couch, she wipes her hand, now sodden with the smell of Sebastian's lotion, on her dress.

Bethel selects a record and lowers it onto the player. A faint crackle moseys out from the speakers. It's a jazz cover of a song Mitty only half recognizes, a saxophone in place of lyrics that are somewhere in her mouth. Sebastian, who is laid out on a chaise, makes a groan of approval when he hears the first chord. He stands, his body swaying as he moves across the rug.

Bethel flops back down, her weight bumping Mitty upward.

"These men always have hideous houses and great taste," she whispers, a satisfied smile on her face.

"May I?" Sebastian asks. His large, open palm is hovering in front of them. She looks to Bethel, less for permission and more for reassurance, who nods her on, and as soon as Mitty places her hand in his, she's whisked upward into his arms.

His voice breaks through the music as they spin. "A classic," he says.

Past his shoulder, Mitty searches for Lena. She has drifted happily to the couch next to Bethel, seemingly unconcerned with the fact of Mitty and Sebastian's pressed bellies, her left hand pinned to his chest as he yanks her around. She grips his shoulder blade like she's bouldering. She imagines him crushing her rib cage with one hand. Then he releases one side of her, his other arm still wrapped around her waist like a hinge, so that they're both facing Bethel and Lena.

"Dance with us, won't you?" he says.

Bethel shakes her head, chuckling. "I think I'm gonna call it a night," she says, standing.

"Already?" Lena takes Bethel's hand and attempts to pull her back down. "Are you sure?"

"Yes, yes," Bethel says, overcompensating. "It's already way past my bedtime."

She glances at Mitty, who nods and gives her arm a gentle, permissive squeeze. She doesn't even pretend to protest

Bethel leaving. She likes the sultry freedom that comes with not having an onlooker. Of course, the thought had occurred to her; what would it be like to be welcomed into Lena and Sebastian's cherished little sexual universe, to be a foreigner, swarmed and nurtured and then released into the prudish world with a new secret?

Bethel thanks Lena and Sebastian and offers what Mitty knows is a hollow invitation to host dinner at their house next time. As she makes her way to the door, she shouts back to Mitty.

"House will be unlocked." Then she gives a little salute, two fingers against her forehead, as if Mitty is leaving for war.

With Bethel gone, Sebastian motions for Lena to join them, pulling her in close. Now Mitty is flanked by the couple, the three of them embracing one another in a tight circle.

"Who says three people can't two-step?" Sebastian says.

As they begin moving, Mitty can smell Sebastian's breath, staggered and metallic, while the scent of Lena is more cutting, the flammable depth of perfume. But, oddly, not mixed with the natural odor of a body, she realizes. Just straight from the bottle, spilled onto a glass table.

She stares at Sebastian's mouth, his teeth stained just enough to imply he knows how to live. What would it be like to kiss him, she wonders. His lips aren't soft, she can tell just by looking at them, the skin peeling and half-chewed. His face would be rough in its own way, too, his chin and cheeks eclipsed by an auburn stubble. But the pleasure in kissing a man like Sebastian isn't about whether or not he is smooth. It's about experiencing the force of him, like the comfort in being pinned beneath a weighted blanket or tossed around by a wave. There's something erotic about knowing a person could kill you and is choosing not to. With Lena there, it feels safe to fantasize, knowing it won't actually happen. But then Lena jerks back away from the circle.

"Honey, we don't need to do that right now." He laughs, keenly aware of whatever has already started to unfold.

But she ignores him, even when he says her name again. Mitty steps back, feeling exposed now that Lena isn't there to bind them, and wraps her arms around her chest. Lena marches to a broom closet at the other end of the room and pulls out a slender cordless vacuum.

"Lena, it's unnecessary," Sebastian says, louder this time, but it's too late. The vacuum roars to life, and Lena pushes its mouth toward their feet, then back and forth across the room in long, diagonal swoops. Her cheeks are sucked in past the bone, the whites of her eyes expanding like little, milky planets. Sebastian grips her shoulders from behind, repeating her name. But she refuses to break rhythm, now hyper-focused on one spot, like she's scratching at a scab. Sebastian gives up and grabs the torso of the vacuum, flipping a switch to kill it. As it dims to a whir, Mitty realizes the song is over. All that's left in the room is the murmur of the needle circling the record player's core.

Lena straightens her spine and gathers her hair behind her shoulders.

"Oh my god," she says. The life returns to her face, and she gapes at the scene in front of her. "I'm so sorry." She presses her palms against the sides of her neck, like she's trying to silence something.

"She can be a bit of a clean freak," Sebastian says. He puts his arm around her, and she relaxes into him.

She seems to have immediately returned to herself, face softening as she slaps him playfully on the chest. "He made me that way."

Rattled by the whole scene, Mitty forces out a chuckle and floats away from the couple. The rising tension she'd been imagining just a few minutes prior suddenly seems naïve. There is an entire world between them, a lifetime she isn't privy to, one that could probably explain whatever just happened. But instead, there is only quiet in the room.

"I'm gonna go splash some water on my face, Lena says. She looks sheepish and Mitty resists the urge to hug her, aware that any comfort might make the whole event feel bigger.

"Hey," Sebastian says to Mitty, "I bought some fancy tobacco in Cuba last month." He nods his head toward the back door. "Join me?"

IN THE BACKYARD BENEATH THE GAZEBO, SEBASTIAN points a remote at a pit of white rocks and a fire blooms to life. They're surrounded by raised beds, congested with aloe and cacti, fat stems curling possessively around one another. Mitty sits at the opposite couch and watches the fire, stretching out her hand until the heat greets her palms, just to confirm it isn't holographic. Sebastian lays his bag of tobacco on the cushion next to him. A label printed in foreboding bold font, beneath a photo of black organs, warns something in Spanish about cancer.

"I hate these fucking pictures," he says when he catches her trying to read the bag. "They used to only have words. Which is why I preferred foreign tobacco." He takes a pinch and sprinkles it across the mouth of a Raw paper. "When it kills me, I can just say I didn't understand the language."

He rolls it to shape for a few turns, then swiftly folds and tucks it, licking the edge and laying it down to stick. He presents it proudly. "Not bad, eh?" Then he seals the bag and tosses it to Mitty.

She hopes she still knows how, she must. Occasionally, she and Bethel treat themselves to something loose and moist from the musky cigar shop down the road, where men watch news in the dark and talk about everything except their phallic addictions. *If you can French braid, you can roll a cigarette*, Bethel would say, with no explanation as to how the two are related.

"Lena can get a little neurotic," he says, "about cleaning and all that." The tobacco slips out the end of the paper and Mitty starts over. "I guess at least this neurosis is useful."

"What do you mean?" Mitty asks.

"Oh, she gets obsessive about all kinds of shit," he says. Mitty thinks of the fish bones, the cable car. "And she's nosy, too. Always wanting to know too much about things that aren't her business." He offsets his criticisms with a gentle laugh. "Seems like putting all that energy into cleaning yields better results."

Mitty is teeming with questions about Lena, but it feels wrong, sacrilegious somehow, to seek out the answers from Sebastian.

"You were in SF before this?" she asks instead.

"Some obnoxious, gentrified apartment, yeah." He chuckles. "I guess this isn't much different"—he motions toward the gleaming house—"but yeah, I was there since my early twenties. It was fun."

"And you and Lena moved here—why?"

"Crowds aren't really her thing. My friend mentioned Santa Cruz, how quiet it is, and after that she wouldn't let the idea go. So we took a road trip down and I liked the quiet, too. It's obviously a different world than San Francisco or Palo Alto, but I still keep running into my co-workers." He pauses to light the cigarette. "Weird to move away only to see everyone you know."

She finally wraps her cigarette into completion and holds it up. "Guess it wasn't such an original idea, then."

"There she goes," he says, teasing. He leans over the table and lights the tip for her. She exhales toward the sea.

"I've been meaning to say," Mitty says. "I'm really sorry about your friend. I heard you guys went to the funeral recently."

He pauses. His face grows stern. "Lena told you that?"

Mitty realizes that maybe she'd already said too much. "Oh, at the bonfire." She flattens her voice. "One of your friends brought up that it would be happening soon."

He nods, satisfied by this response. Mitty eases back into her chair.

"Well, thanks for the condolences. But it was bound to happen."

He smiles curtly, and Mitty remembers what Lena expressed about the funeral, Sebastian's general detachment. But still, the comment seems so ungracious, removed of any real mourning, even for a man like him.

"Bound to happen," she repeats quietly. "What do you mean by that?"

Sebastian shrugs. "Industry stuff."

Mitty can tell that the conversation should end here. But her head is light from booze and her body feels loose enough to keep talking.

"How did you two know each other?"

He rests his ankle on the opposing knee and studies something on the bare patch of skin beneath his pant leg. "We were working on a couple projects together," he says dully.

"So you work in AI, too?" She runs her hand along her calf, rough with stubble newly apparent in the frigid air.

He takes another long drag of his cigarette and squints his eyes to look at her.

"That's what any app on your phone is, you know," he says. "AI isn't just robots." His voice sounds suddenly callous.

"I wouldn't know," she says, forcing a harmless giggle.

He tilts his head, wrinkles his nose, as if to get a better look at her. "Well, what do you want to know?"

The question throws her for a moment. She breaks eye

contact to reseal the seam of her cigarette with her tongue. She dims her voice. "I guess I want to know what you think happened to him."

He smirks, as if he's almost relieved by the simplicity of her question. Then he leans forward, bracing his elbow against his thigh. The way men do when they're ready to explain something.

"Okay, so say one day, you come to work and they tell you that you've lost your job," he says. "You've been replaced by a machine. You'd be angry, right?"

Mitty nods. She'd considered the threat before. An eight-armed faceless contraption balancing dishes in each of its metal palms.

"Well, Pax was the one who built the machine."

She feels more confident now, aware that as long as she forgoes any real opinions, he'll remain open. "And who did that machine replace?"

"Plenty of people. Plenty of jobs. Those kids that killed him, they'd just been laid off because they were replaced by motorized trimmers on a weed farm."

He says it like it isn't a theory, but an inarguable fact. And it could be, Mitty thinks. If anyone would know, it would be Sebastian. But still, his certainty doesn't feel like the truth so much as it feels like the need to arrest Mitty from her own conclusions. "So they weren't put up to it," she says, carefully forming the question as though it's a quiet reflection only to herself, "because he was a whistleblower? That's what everyone keeps saying."

He bursts into laughter. "Is that what they're saying?"

Mitty nods. "All over town."

Sebastian shakes his head, still smiling. "That's silly," he says. "But I get why people believe it."

"Because it's possible?" she asks.

"No." He wrestles a piece of ash off of his tongue. "Because it's fun."

They go quiet. Sebastian spins the ice around the bottom of his glass. Mitty watches him, his bulky fingers making the tumbler look like a shot. She can understand why a girl like Lena, who seems so desperate to have everything explained to her, would end up with Sebastian, why his certainty would make her feel safe. And she understands why men like Sebastian, who believe they deserve to be trusted, would end up with a woman like Lena. Someone willing to abide by the strict constitution he's written about life and how to live it.

"Here she is," Sebastian says, jolting Mitty out of her thoughts. Lena approaches from behind to sit on the arm of the couch, then collapses back into Sebastian's lap. Somehow, Sebastian has managed to perfect the delicate balance of being both endearing and patronizing at once, always referring to women in third person. *Thatta girl. There she goes. Here she is.* Like they're sleek, muscled horses, racing around a dirt track, nimble and refined, sent to the kill shelter if they break a leg.

LENA WANTS TO GO SWIMMING. SHE IS LYING WITH HER head against Sebastian's thigh. She runs her fingers along his stubbled jawline.

"Mitty, will you come with me?"

"Let me go grab my suit," Mitty says, half hoping the trip will buy her enough time to invent a reason not to swim at all. If it were just the two of them, she tells herself, she would go in her underwear like an adult woman in the company of other adult women, free in their togetherness, released from the expectation of teenage insecurities and string-tied swim- wear. But with a man watching, the experience becomes in- herently competitive, a game she's bound to lose.

"You don't need a suit," Lena says. "We never wear suits." She mocks the word *suit*. Like clothing is a punch line.

"You should go," Sebastian says, his voice easy. "It's ca- thartic." Mitty notices that his eyes are barely open, his head tilting up toward the sky. "Just follow the farm girl," he says, his words blurring together. "She's not afraid of any- thing."

Mitty puts out her cigarette, careful not to bend it. Lena is already gone, heading through the backyard. But when Mitty lets herself out through the back gate, she hesitates. She realizes she can't see anything past the first pile of drift- wood. Behind her, Sebastian calls out something about how the ocean won't do anything in the dark that it wouldn't do during the day.

It isn't until she gets to the tide that she can see Lena, al- ready knee-deep in the water, hair whipping around her skull. There's a bizarre familiarity to it all—Lena naked, the ocean gaping out in front of her. But Mitty knows that as soon as she comes closer, the image will crack and she'll have to step inside it, become a part of something she had only ever witnessed from afar. Before she can say anything, Lena turns around, wet teeth glowing in the dark.

"Come," she yells over the water.

Mitty leans forward to tie the skirt of her dress around her upper thighs, but Lena has already started walking back toward her.

"It's better without clothes," she says, breathless. "It's the only way to get used to it."

Mitty's stomach surges and she forces herself not to hesitate, yanking the straps of her dress off her shoulders, shimmying it down around her waist. She tosses it as far as she can toward the sand, trying to forget about the possibility of a dress at all.

When Lena takes her hand, Mitty uses the opportunity to glance at Lena's body up close. She's seen it before. Bent over tables and couches, pressed against a railing at dawn. But in advertisements, too. On billboards. Always the after photos, never the before. Never anything but what she is now. Mitty knows Lena's body better than she knows her own—all that time she avoided looking in the mirror, she was looking at a woman like Lena instead.

"We can go slow," she says. "Just walk forward."

They take one step at a time, their legs gradually being devoured by the water. Steam is dissipating from Lena's skin, and Mitty's brain is gauzy, every drink she's had now floating into her head.

"Hey, are you okay?" Mitty asks. She hadn't even realized how long she'd been waiting to ask that question until it comes out. "What was that with the vacuum?"

Lena looks over her shoulder, clocking their distance from the house.

"Yeah," she says, lowering her voice. "I was trying to get you out of there."

"Out of where?"

"I don't know, that situation," Lena says. "Maybe it was weird."

It would be too humiliating to admit that she wanted to be there, that she liked the suspense of being touched by the both of them at once. And was Lena being honest? Mitty had assumed it was a benign encounter, one she'd only heightened with her own imagination. But maybe there was something she didn't see.

"It wasn't that weird," Mitty says coolly.

Lena is oblivious, clearly taking Mitty's comment as a forced but willing comfort. She squeezes Mitty's shoulder and smiles.

"Get on your back. I'll float you."

Mitty obeys. She releases her knees and lets her body fall backward into the water. Lena takes each of Mitty's hands and guides her arms outward and up toward her ears, then pulls her gently along the surface. She closes her eyes, allowing her physical self to go weightless amid the salt and Lena's control. All of her is exposed; she can feel the wind on her nipples, the water washing over her pubic hair. But somehow the thought of what she must look like is just that, a thought—not something she needs to obscure or enhance, but something she can easily picture and then let drift away.

With her body weightless, she imagines that she's pressed

to the window of a soundless, serpentine train, gunning through the dark geography of her brain's underground tunnels. Every few seconds, it slows to a stop at some station, a thought or memory, and she only has a few seconds to take it in before she's shuttled off to the next one.

She's thinking of the oven. She can't remember if it had been turned off before they left. What would usually send her into a panic dims just as easily, and she moves her mind to the windowsill in her bedroom, where there is a stockpile of dead flies, mummied with spiderwebs, that she's been meaning to clear off for days.

She thinks of her father. The time he caught a fly and put it in the freezer. When it had gone into a coma, he tied a piece of dental floss around its body, then let it thaw. *Flies don't die from being frozen,* he explained, *they just disappear for a while.* When it came back to life, now lassoed with string, he carried it around the house, making jokes about how he was taking his fly for a walk. It seemed terrifying to Mitty, disappearing into slumber and waking up to find yourself bound to a leash, a whole room of people laughing at your inability to move. But she always felt so oversensitive for struggling to laugh. She knew it was just a party trick, an opportunity for him to know something that other people didn't. His neck bursting pink as he laughed, while scanning his audience to make sure they were laughing, too. But even when she tried, she could never quite see it as anything other than plain torture.

And then, the last time she saw him, at a burger joint during a seventh-grade field trip. He was sitting in a booth, peeling soft pickles off a bun. Despite the fact that they hadn't seen each other in almost four years, he talked to her like a co-worker, cordial but slightly dreading the entire exchange. He'd gained weight in his neck and jowls, and his cheeks were cratered from acne scars, and she couldn't bring herself to say how obvious it was that he'd been drinking. She was thirteen, and even then, she knew. He was carrying a plastic water bottle that he refilled with root beer from the soda fountain and talked for ten minutes about how the Church of Scientology was invented by a science fiction writer. He showed her pictures of his job as the oldest PA on the set of a daytime television show called *Man Becomes Money*, hosted in the ballroom of a casino near Lake Tahoe. He didn't ask about her mother. Mitty told him about how she liked school, and he started to cry but swiftly interrupted himself with a coughing fit. Finally, when they left, she walked him to his car and saw that the back seat was a bed.

Inevitably, her mind will arrive at Esme. Sometimes, it's just simple chronology that takes her there. Other times, it's association. Here, it's the feeling of shame—the low and humming rot that lived inside her as she parted ways with her father, made her way through the parking lot behind her classmates, knowing that as soon as she climbed onto that bus, someone would inevitably ask her who that man she was talking to was. It's the same rot that appeared in the bathroom that day with Esme—Mitty watching her scratch away at her face in the mirror, skin eroding as she told Mitty that it was over.

The difference between Esme and every other memory is

that it feels impossible for Mitty to keep moving once she's arrived there. Something forces her to disembark, to walk through the sliding glass doors and meander around the musky station of her life back then. Take in every detail. Esme's voice, an echo, humming down some infinite hallway. Her scent, candied body butter and girl sweat. Her jewelry—dainty gold hoops and charm necklaces dripping with sentimental beads—dispersed across the third rail as though they'd been tossed in some cruel act of revenge. And when the announcement comes, alerting Mitty that she has only a few seconds before the train leaves without her, she rushes back through the doors. Safe again once they've closed behind her. Only when she's settled into her seat does she realize that she's carried Esme's smell with her.

She opens her eyes. The sky above her is poked full of stars. She feels the urge to confess something to it. She remembers the time that she and Esme were eating bowls of boxed macaroni on her bedroom floor. The orange mess of shell noodles, doused in black pepper. But Esme wasn't eating. She just kept drowning her spoon, turning over the food like she was shoveling sand. She had looked up at Mitty, aware that she was being watched. But instead of asking why, Mitty jerked her eyes away, toward the wall, the ceiling. It's one of the moments she regrets the most. How obvious it was that Esme wanted to tell her something, and Mitty couldn't bring herself to hear it.

She opens her mouth before any sound comes out. She knows once she speaks her voice will crack. And she's right. "I noticed you don't eat."

"What?" Lena's voice is loud. Mitty had forgotten how close they were. She begins to remember that her body is anchored by Lena's grip. Mitty's nipples are suddenly alerted, her breasts candied in goosebumps.

She hesitates. "Is it because he won't let you?" She tilts her head upward and sees Lena's face, upside down, studying her. She knows the water lapping against her armpits must be frigid, but she can't feel it. She knows the sandy floor must be nearby, all she would have to do is lift her head, sodden with salt water, and tip her body forward to stand. But she doesn't want to do that. She wants to stay here, in this frothy cradle, where it seems that anything she says out loud will be carried out to sea. But then Lena lets go and Mitty is forced upward.

"You know, you don't really know me well enough to say something like that."

Mitty submerges her shoulders, the outside air far colder than what's underneath. Lena is shivering, her arms wrapped around her chest. She looks, for the first time that Mitty has seen, angry.

"Sebastian pushed your hand down at dinner."

Lena's eyes turn glassy and she looks away. "He's weird about etiquette," she says. "Eating while talking."

Mitty thinks of all the moments he spoke with his mouth full, smacking his lips while he told his rambunctious stories, wiping his chin with the back of his hand. It's futile, she realizes, to go up against Lena when she's protecting him.

"I'm sorry," she says. "I didn't mean to jump to conclusions."

Lena lowers herself to Mitty's eyeline, her body relaxing into the water.

"Why are you always trying to figure me out?" Lena tightens her jaw. Mitty hadn't realized that she'd been so easy to read. The word *always* feels like a blunt rod, thrust into her chest. "It's not like you're open with me about anything."

Mitty can see that whatever thoughts are coursing through Lena's brain are now coalescing into something clear. Her throat closes. "Lena," she says, "I wasn't trying to get you to open up to me. I was just trying to understand."

"And what if I want you to open up to me?" She's almost yelling now. "You want to know why I don't eat, you want to know about my relationship and my past, but you're cagey about everything. You never talk about you and Bethel, not really. Or where you came from or why you ended up here. You don't seem to know anyone in this town. And if I asked, you wouldn't tell me."

"I would," Mitty says.

"Okay, then why did you come here?"

Mitty goes silent. Lena is staring into her.

"I had to get away."

"But why?"

She can see Lena's breath through her chest, rapidly expanding and deflating, rationed and sharp. The longer she's quiet, the angrier Lena becomes. "Why?" she repeats.

Mitty feels like an army of animals are clawing at the inside of her belly. Her face is numb. But the animals are getting louder, more frantic. She can feel the admission building, forming in her throat, her tongue becoming sappy with the threat of vomit.

"Because I think I killed her," she blurts out.

When it comes out of her mouth, whatever she was expecting—an explosion, a flock of sirens ignited and headed her way—doesn't happen. Instead, she feels lighter.

"Killed who?"

Mitty goes silent. The world around them, too. They must be in between wave sets, she thinks. A limbo of stillness that forces her to feel her own heartbeat, the rough chatter of her teeth.

"This girl I knew. Esme," she says. The sound of her own voice is foreign, and it's comforting. To briefly believe she is someone else. "We liked each other. We had a thing, and she ended it. I was angry."

Lena's face pales. "What do you mean, you *think* you killed her?"

Mitty feels tempted to leave it here. In this awful but simple truth. Let Lena imagine that what she had done was definitive. That Esme had already turned to dust.

But she can tell that Lena is growing angry. The color has already returned to her cheeks, the contours of her nostrils flaring in the moonlight.

"You can't just say something like that," Lena tells her. Mitty can hear Lena's throat closing. She knows far too well what it feels like to be looked at by a person who is afraid of you, and it's too painful not to keep talking.

"She was a dancer," Mitty begins. "And something she had told me before was that ballerinas always die twice. Once when they stop dancing, and once when they stop breathing." She can't stop. "If I'm the reason she stopped dancing, then that means I killed her."

"What did you do?" Lena's hands are gripping her forearms like tourniquets.

"I made the floors slippery so she would fall," Mitty says. She is surprised by the fact that she doesn't feel frantic. Just hollow. Emptied. "But I was hoping it would be, at worst, embarrassing. And instead, it ruined her."

"This was when you were young?" Lena asks.

"Eighteen."

Lena goes silent. She chews on a fingernail, seeking counsel from the black water. When she looks up at Mitty, the hard edges of her face have been buffed into a distinct softness.

"You were a child."

Mitty shakes her head. "I'm not asking for your forgiveness." Her eyes begin to well and Lena immediately grabs her hand. Mitty thinks for a moment that drowning wouldn't be such a bad way to go, the silent harmony of sinking. "What I did, it ruined her. Last I checked, she had moved back in with her parents. Has never even left Arizona."

"I don't know Esme," Lena says, firmly sticking to only the cold, hard facts. "But maybe, I just think it mattered what your intentions were." She pauses, clears her throat. "Do you want to tell me the whole story?" Mitty can feel her neck ballooning, the sting of tears in her eyes. "Or maybe you can just tell me what you remember."

That's part of the tragedy, Mitty wants to tell her. Just like Lena, she can't trust her own memories. They are silhouettes, in which the shape says nothing of the actual anatomy underneath, only what she wants to see. She wants to believe the shadowed architecture of a head and shoulders is looking at her from a window. But just as easily, it could be looking away.

"HOW WAS IT?" SEBASTIAN SAYS AS THEY LET THEMSELVES in through the gate. He holds up Mitty's half-smoked cigarette, offering it like a reward.

The wet cotton of Mitty's dress sticks to the backs of her legs, her hair slick against her shoulders. She watches Sebastian's face change when he takes them in, roused by the aftermath of something he wasn't a part of. "Everything okay?" He polishes off the rest of his cocktail. "You guys look like you just survived a shipwreck."

Mitty puts her hand to her mouth and exhales hot air into her fist.

"It's nice out there," Lena says, her voice tranquil, her skin glossy. As they lower themselves onto the cushions, Mitty can feel her posture wilt. She presses her knees tight against each other and slips her hands in between her thighs to warm them, the only comfort she can locate and control. When she looks up, Sebastian is scanning her face. She smiles, but he doesn't return it. On the table in front of them is the disassembled pie.

"I've been nibbling," he says. "It's fucking delicious."

Lena leans forward and inspects the dessert. She glances up at Mitty, a fleeting frustration on her face.

"Hey, I've got a question about Bethel," Sebastian says.

"Yeah?" Mitty struggles to relight her cigarette with a trembling hand.

"What's with her scars?"

It was impossible that Bethel had talked to him about the accident. She never brought it up to strangers, and the scars are practically invisible. It took Mitty years to spot them without Bethel pointing them out herself.

"An accident," Mitty says. "Did she mention it?"

Sebastian shakes his head. "I mean I could tell it was some kind of reconstructive surgery." He leans back into the couch. "They did an amazing job."

"I'm surprised you noticed them." Mitty takes a long drag. "I find them so subtle."

"She must have broken every bone in her face, no?" he asks.

"I didn't notice at all," Lena says. She seems suspicious of Sebastian's observation, her eyes darting between him and Mitty, as though they're sharing a secret.

"You've got a keen eye," Mitty says, careful not to divulge any more than Bethel would want. Sebastian shrugs, humbly.

As they continue to eat and smoke, the conversation

fades, Sebastian occasionally breaking the silence to compliment the crust or ask a clarifying question about the science of baking. Everything seems suddenly so polite. Like the more time they all spend together, the stranger they are to one another, their conversations only sending them backward into a deeper unfamiliarity.

AT ONE IN THE MORNING, SEBASTIAN STRETCHES HIS ARMS above his head and lets out a droning, forced yawn. Lena is quiet, nudging her pie around the plate, her eyes restless.

"Maybe I should get home," Mitty offers.

They make their way inside, where she heads straight toward the doorway. She slides on her shoes, not stopping to peel off her wet socks or fix the rumpled tongue against her foot. Lena trails behind, then eventually finds her way beneath Sebastian's arm.

"This was great." He sounds earnest.

"It was really, really nice," Lena echoes. Though her tone is less convincing. Her smile lingering for too long.

"Thanks so much for having us over," Mitty says, stepping onto the porch. "I guess I'll see you around?"

Something occurs to Lena, and her eyes light up. "Hold on," she says, and disappears into the living room. She returns with a crate of a dozen or so records and holds them out to Mitty. "We've been meaning to give you these."

"Figured you and Bethel might make use of them," Sebastian adds. "My collection is getting out of hand."

Mitty takes the box into her arms, scanning what she can of the stack. All she sees are a few obvious selections, albums Bethel probably already owns.

"Thank you," she says. "Bethel will love this."

Lena wraps her arms around Sebastian's waist, barely able to cover the circumference of his torso. Mitty catches his eyes, flickering beneath the porch light. She realizes then, watching the couple hold each other, sharing a life she has only briefly wandered into, that the story she told Lena about Esme will very likely make its way to Sebastian. Isn't that what you're agreeing to when you confess something to one half of a person? But somehow, the thought of him wrestling with her vague confession isn't scary. She had been listening to him explain away his various hypocrisies all night. Maybe it would be good for him to know, helpful to have a man who had probably been just as bad in his own ways, telling her it all makes sense.

AT HOME, BETHEL IS LISTENING TO THE RADIO, HAVING changed out of her party clothes and into her nightdress. Mitty sets down the crate of records and leans back onto the windowsill, droplets crawling down the length of her back.

"What's that?" Bethel asks, leaning forward in her chair.

"Some hand-me-down records." Mitty takes a half-smoked cigarette from the ashtray and lights it. "Probably not the best selection."

Bethel nods, quickly losing interest in the gift.

"I thought that was surprisingly easy." She pauses, squinting as she fills her mouth with smoke. "I always forget how charismatic those rich tech guys are."

"He's likable."

"And handsome." Bethel gestures vaguely in the direction of their home. "I get why Lena went for him."

Mitty pulls her dress up to her thighs and lets the hot breath of the heater hit her legs. "Do you think she's happy?"

"For now," Bethel says. "But I think she's got a lot more of the world to see."

The radio announcer begins to rattle off the sweepstakes, a solar-powered night-light for caller number twelve.

Bethel looks to Mitty. "Should we?"

It's a dance Mitty knows too well, a dance they rarely allow themselves to indulge in. But she's awake now, and the world is quiet. She considers the popularity of the station—relatively high—and the population of the town—relatively low—in addition to the time of day and how that might influence the number of people tuning in. She calculates the rough number in her head, waits fifteen seconds, then picks up the phone to dial.

The line rings four times before a receptionist picks up and breaks the news that they'd missed the call by one slot. Even though Patricia is far away, Mitty imagines that it must be her mother who'd elbowed her way to the front. Somehow, it is always Patricia on the line, claiming her prize. She imagines a scenario in which there's a glitch in the system that leads to them being on air simultaneously, the host asking for their names and what part of town they live in. But regardless of whatever lie her mother answers with, Mitty would recognize her voice. She knows it too well—that specific pitch of counterfeit excitement she takes on when she's won something, already thinking about how much it's worth and who she can convince it's the thing they've always needed.

One day, Mitty will tell Patricia how much she has missed her, the life they used to have. How much she resents that their relationship had been reduced to Mitty half listening to all of Patricia's little dramas. The awful fluorescent hallway lighting in her dentist office, or the ongoing problem of her boyfriend's kidney stones and how it hinders their sex life. One day, she will tell her about all of those ephemeral, unsung morsels of wisdom Patricia had passed on—how to wrap her hair in a cotton T-shirt to avoid frizz or using a spot of lipstick for blush—things she'd dismissed as a teenager but now clings to in private, tiny cardinal practices that still ferry the pulse of her life. She will tell her that every time she folds her blood-soaked pad into its adhesive, she remembers watching her mother do the same, while going on about cotton tampons growing mold inside the body. This was when Mitty was still young enough to sit on the toilet while her mother bathed, studying the way she reached deep into the corners of herself to wash out soap. One day, Mitty will tell her mother that she was always listening, even when she pretended she wasn't. She will remind Patricia of the time she said, *Mitty, all your beliefs about the world are based on everyone else's ideas,* how she criticized the way Mitty would mull over things that ended a long time ago. She will finally tell her mother she was wrong. Nothing ends. It's all there inside her somewhere, a looping supercut of people around her who always seem to be talking. But somehow, when Mitty thinks back, she feels like she never was. Somehow, no one is ever quoting her. Somehow, the only thing she can't remember is anything she's ever said.

BEFORE

Mitty confessed everything to her mother the evening of Esme's fall, still unable to stop seeing the image of Esme's bone sticking out of her leg. Patricia listened with a patience that Mitty could only later describe as godly. She said things like, *We will make this right* and *You didn't mean to hurt her.* But later, Mitty could hear her in her bedroom, crying quietly to herself, and she knew that her mother was shocked by her own daughter's anger, the brutal awareness that she had raised a child who could do something so terrible.

She was fired from the ballet studio immediately. It was the obvious outcome and, in many ways, felt less like she was being let go and more like she was being set free. She couldn't imagine having to step back into that building after what she'd done. She'd been so focused on thinking of it as liberating that it took her days to realize that she hadn't only stopped hearing from Esme, but from everyone else she knew, too. Those innocuous text messages she got from girls she'd known from school, chain texts warning against bad luck or invitations to pool parties, had stopped entirely. She reasoned that it was the summer after senior year—maybe that's just what happened when a chapter closed and people began looking toward their lives in other cities, focusing instead on building friendships with future dorm mates. But even as she gained the courage to reach out, the messages and phone calls went unanswered. Days passed, and her life was silent.

It was a blistering August and she had nowhere to go. The longer she stayed behind them, the more her bedroom walls seemed to pinch together like pleats on a skirt. She was waiting for the day when a team of police officers would show up on her front porch and take her away. Patricia wouldn't admit it, but she was, too. It was the first time since Mitty's father left that she had seen her mother at the front window again, looking out onto the street with sick anticipation.

But even if Esme hadn't reported her, she had surely warned everyone she knew that Mitty was a liability, a danger to the people around her. Mitty reasoned that there must be a handful of people who wouldn't believe it. What kind of girl does that to another girl? How could it be anything other than a tragic accident? But she couldn't imagine who those people would be, and she wasn't brave enough to leave her house to find out.

She distracted herself by helping her mother package the prizes she'd won to resell them on eBay. They rarely spoke while they worked, running the tongue of packing tape along the seam of a cardboard box. But occasionally Mitty would look up to find her mother staring at her, as though she no longer recognized her own daughter.

"I saw Esme today," Patricia said, finally puncturing the silence and burying her hands into a pile of Styrofoam peanuts. She repositioned whatever was beneath them. The sun split the room and Mitty became aware of how hot it was, her thighs itching beneath her denim.

"Where?" Mitty said, her voice already forceful and interrogating.

"At the post office," Patricia said. She seemed poised. "She was with her mother."

"Did they say anything?"

Patricia shook her head and folded down the wings of the box, then gestured for Mitty to hand her the tape.

"Why are you looking at me like that?" Mitty's voice sounded far away, like it had sunk into the depths of her skull.

"Am I not allowed to look at you?" Patricia asked. "I forgive you. You know that."

"What the fuck kind of answer is that?" Mitty spat.

"I'm saying that I will always forgive my daughter."

Mitty's body was shaking. Her blood simmering behind her eyes.

"Forgive me for *what*? I didn't do anything to you."

"For anything. For everything." Patricia paused. "It's not just you who's affected by this, Mitty. Esme saw me, you know. She looked like she was afraid of me."

Mitty wanted to explain to her mother that Esme carried fear with her everywhere she went. Mostly, it was the fear of her own body and the various ways it could betray her, the possibility that in the midst of her impossible contortion, one small fracture could keep her from the life she imagined for herself. But Mitty decided to keep this to herself. Because the more she thought about it, the more she realized that the only way she ever really saw Esme was in the context of their togetherness, just the two of them. And if all Mitty ever saw was the way Esme looked at her, maybe what Esme was actually afraid of was Mitty.

IN THE DAYS THAT FOLLOWED, MITTY COULDN'T BE ALONE. Despite her constant anger and fear, she wordlessly accompanied her mother on every sales trip and followed her from room to room while they were at home, napping on whatever cushion was nearest to where Patricia was working. In the brief periods she was on her own—which had been reduced to when she was bathing or using the bathroom—the image of Esme's bone, shooting out from her skin, replayed in her brain until she was dizzy and nauseous. Each time, she watched herself from the outside, bolting out the door. She went through alternative scenarios: One where she'd run over and helped, made a show of her own heroism. One where someone had unknowingly interrupted her in the utility closet, that small interference sobering enough to make her realize what she was doing. But she always had to return to reality, where nothing could be changed, and then she was left stumbling through the house to find her mother, sobbing until she fell asleep.

She could tell that Patricia was fearful of what Mitty might do if she left her to her own thoughts, and even when Mitty tried to reassure her that she was okay, her mother insisted that she take leave from her night shift, that Mitty join her on her errands throughout the day. Mitty wondered if, on some level, she cherished her daughter's newfound desire to spend time together. It had been so long since Mitty had climbed into her bed and curled into the curve of her mother's stomach while she slept. But Patricia must have known it wasn't because her daughter suddenly appreciated her. Her daughter needed her. And in a way, Mitty thought, wasn't that the same thing to a mother? Those small, tender moments of reliance were still a break from their arguments, which had become explosive, detonated by the smallest details.

But while Mitty's panic ended once she was lulled into sleep, she knew Patricia's only took on a new form. There were several nights that Mitty had woken up to find herself alone in bed. Her mother had clearly waited until Mitty's breath came in long, undisturbed strokes, her body still. Mitty would tiptoe toward the kitchen and, from the shadowed hallway, watch her mother smoking cigarettes in the dark. She wondered where she allowed her brain to wander at this hour, into all the places it didn't have time to go during the day. Maybe she was resentfully tracking all the money she'd lost over the last few weeks. Or imagining showing up on Esme's columned doorstep and outing Mitty as the attacker. Maybe she was letting herself be angry at Mitty, for the ways she let herself get swept up in her own desires. She must have imagined the many paths Mitty's life could take: community college and a new job, how she would go about finding friends now that she was no longer in school. She must have known that Mitty would be immovable to any suggestion that required her to step back into the world. To Mitty, this was the world. And it was a world that didn't want her to return. Somewhere inside her, Mitty knew that her mother was not immune to this feeling. Patricia had felt it in the post office and at Magnolia's Dresser, an entire universe in which she was no longer welcome.

The difference, one that would take years for Mitty to realize, was that Patricia had lived long enough to know that there is always somewhere else to go. That life, despite its brutal corners, is actually quite forgiving as long as you continue to move through it. But how could she expect her daughter, who had existed for less than two decades, who had only ever lived in the same small suburb, to know this? Mitty's perspective was, like her, small and bordered.

Mitty would come to theorize that it must have been at that kitchen window that her mother thought of Bethel. The woman who—in January 1994, when a then twenty-seven-year-old Patricia was seven months pregnant with a baby girl and driving down the coast with her boyfriend and their old Volvo had broken down in the parking lot at New Brighton State Beach—offered her pull-out couch to the young couple with sunburned cheeks. The woman who made them scalloped potatoes and creamed spinach for dinner, who tucked them in with flannel sheets. Who greeted them with hot coffee in the morning and took them for a walk on the beach. Who asked politely to place her hand on Patricia's stomach and waited for the baby to kick. Who drove them to the mechanic the next morning to retrieve their car and wrote her phone number down on the back of a receipt and handed it to Patricia. *If you're ever out this way and you need anything,* she said. *Or even if you're far away.* The woman who Patricia called almost a decade later, when the father of her child left too soon. To whom she mailed wallet-sized photos of her daughter's pimpled yearbook pictures, despite Mitty's insistence they be burned. And eventually, the woman who began to call Patricia for her own reasons, griping about her failed speed dating for seniors and then, after every earthquake, no matter the size, just to let Patricia know she was safe.

Mitty imagined that as soon as the idea struck her, that this was the person who could show her daughter that it's possible to start over, she couldn't stop herself from calling Bethel right then. It must have been past midnight, after Mitty had retired from her spying and gone to sleep, when Patricia explained what had happened as Bethel listened intently on the other end.

"Can she stay with you for a little bit?" Patricia must have asked, out of breath just from telling the story. "I think we need to get her out of here."

The plan was to only stay a month. During which Mitty would learn that there are people living entire lives in other places who have no idea who she is or what she did, who might not even care if they knew, or who would forgive her regardless. People who had done bad things themselves or had been accused of bad things that kept them up at night, wrestling with what was true. People who went on living despite this. Just like her.

She must have known Mitty would protest if she waited till morning to propose the idea. Which is why she began packing their bags that night, rousing Mitty before dawn, and loading them into the car. What Patricia couldn't have known, what neither of them could have known, was that exposing Mitty to a place in which she wasn't living in the threat of her past would also mean she might not come back.

Mitty always wondered, if someone had warned them of this, would they still have made that trip? Or if, in the end, no matter how much pain Mitty was in, Patricia would've chosen to keep her close? Mitty knew her mother resented the way she had moved on. That she hid that resentment for fear of seeming selfish. She must have resented it when she learned how little Mitty and Bethel fought. When she came to realize that Bethel didn't have to comb through every sentence in her mind before she spoke it aloud, just to circumvent Mitty's anger. She must have felt guilty when she relished in the times that they finally had a disagreement, no matter how small. But eventually, Mitty's absence became a fact of her mother's life just as much as it had become a fact of her own. And so another phase began.

After Mitty leaves, Lena is at the kitchen counter hunched over the keyboard of her laptop. The fluorescent glare of the screen splashes onto her face in the midst of the pitch-black living room. She tries to type quietly, careful not to wake Sebastian upstairs. She maintains a habit of glancing above her computer, half expecting that at any moment he might be standing right in front of her.

She is buried in a corner of the internet she's never taken an interest in until now. The graveyard of abandoned social media profiles and decade-old blog posts. People talking about themselves. But she has a reason this time. A focus. She is looking for someone specific. She is looking for Esme.

She searches all the details she remembers from their conversation in the water. She types in *Esme, Ballet, Paradise Valley, Injury.* The first article is a simple profile in a local paper about the dance studio's rendition of *Beauty and the Beast,* over a decade prior. She clicks on the page and scrolls down to find Esme's headshot—a pale, skinny girl with a coy smile, chin pushed down and gaze floating up toward the lens, like she and the cameraman were sharing a secret.

She returns to the main search page and keeps scrolling, clicking, scanning. In the same local paper, she reads how Esme retired from ballet at the age of eighteen, after a devastating fall. Mitty's name is not mentioned. According to several digital phone books and a slew of other sites, she once lived in Phoenix, where she owned a children's dance studio that boasted almost perfect reviews, before it closed down a couple of years ago. Now the only address listed that mentions her name is a home in Paradise Valley that belongs to her parents. Her life seems quaint and uncontroversial. It's unclear whether she's still dating the lawyer she's kissing beneath a waterfall in her Facebook profile picture, taken on a trip to the Dominican Republic three years ago.

The less Lena finds, the more guilty she feels for looking at all. What is she trying to confirm? Mitty had trusted her with so much already. She didn't deny what she had done. Based on her brief and shallow investigation, Mitty was being honest. So why does it feel disappointing? Maybe Lena wanted there to be a villain. It would make all of this simpler. The hurt and the person who caused it. But what if all of this pain has been caused not by a person, but by the things people won't say out loud to one another, all the assumptions we make to fill the silence, until it's too late? Lena thinks of everything she fails to say out loud, how so much of her life has unfolded because she was silent about what hurt. All the things Sebastian must have decided for her while she wasn't talking.

The next morning, Mitty wakes up parched. She inhales a glass of water on her nightstand in three gulps, then huffs back down onto the pillow. A sliver of stale yellow light leaks through a fold in the curtains. A streetlight hums. Her memory of the dinner party last night is soupy and comes in bursts. The baking tension of their three-person two-step. The echo in the empty bathroom as she opened and closed every cabinet. The bloody tweezers. Bethel's quiet observance, the knowing grin that remained on her face all evening. As she begins to recall her admission to Lena in the water, her body aches. The sheets suddenly feel too heavy, their fibers painful against her muscles. Why had it slipped out of her so easily? Was it a sign of her comfort with Lena or was it the conditions around them, the permission of weightlessness and the dark? She folds down the corner of her duvet and crawls out from under it. She moves toward the window and slips between the curtain and the glass, her body pressed against it, how she used to win a game of hide-and-seek as a child. Across the yard, the kitchen light in Lena's house is on and the room is exposed, every detail illuminated against a black sky.

And then Lena emerges, as if Mitty had called to her. She walks to the sink, facing Mitty head-on. She turns on the faucet, then lets her arms hang at her sides. She is watching the rope-thick stream of water empty into the sink. Mitty can't quite make out the expression on Lena's face, but she doesn't look distressed. She doesn't look focused or concerned or sleepy either. She looks like nothing at all. She looks like the beginning, before thoughts, a white hallway with no doors, a room so long your voice disappears before it can echo. Mitty becomes aware of every movement Lena makes, which to most people would be none at all. But to Mitty, she may as well be a swarm of locusts charging through a still field—the hair on her arms standing up, her eyes blinking every few seconds in perfect rhythm, her chest expanding and collapsing, her lips parted to let out something like breath.

Later that morning, it is Lena who is pressed against her bedroom window, watching. In the distance, Sebastian paddles along the horizon. From here, his body is no larger than the space between her first two knuckles. She likes imagining him this small. Small enough to pluck off the surface of the water and tuck into her pocket. Small enough to let him run along her bare torso, his tiny feet tickling her rib cage. Small enough to dangle him above the mouth of a spotted koi fish while he screams, begs for his life.

But Sebastian is big. That's one of the many characteristics that attracted her to him in the first place, isn't it? She liked the way he gripped his knife and fork in each hand before he ate, holding them upright on either side of his plate like a pair of columns. She liked how he shoveled food into his mouth like its only purpose was to fuel the demands of his body. In the beginning, just watching him eat made her want him. It meant he would only get stronger. She liked feeling as though the bed frame might crack beneath them when they fucked. She liked watching his hands braced against the back of the couch when he bent her over the cushions. She liked what animals they were, how comfortable it was to just lie there afterward, covered in sweat and cum.

But lately, after sex, she has found herself wanting to shower. She feels itchy if she leaves the scent of him on her skin for too long, desperate to get back to the version of herself that had been untouched. It is such a sudden instinct, one that arrived seemingly overnight, without reason. What is she trying to rid herself of beneath the water, she would ask herself as she burnished her thighs with a bamboo brush. What is she trying to forget?

Her theory is that people always fall out of love for the same reasons they fall into it. Everything exciting eventually becomes a nuisance. Recently, on a camping trip, Sebastian forgot to pack pillows and arranged their clothes into lumpy rectangles to cushion their heads. She stayed up all night, glaring at him, his heavy breath always inching toward a snore. But she used to gush over these small acts of innovation after first meeting him. Like when he secured a handle to the middle of her surfboard so she could carry it beneath her arm. Or built a step stool when he noticed she could barely reach the upper cabinets in his house. Now she feels annoyed by how much useless knowledge he seems to carry. That they can't go anywhere without him regurgitating trivia. At the coffee shop, he boasts to the barista about his expertise in siphon pots. At the dentist, he talks with a full mouth of metal tools about ancient methods of molar removal.

She has watched him begin to resent her, too. He used to be so taken by her curiosity when they went on walks and she kneeled down to inspect a beetle or peeked in through the windows of an abandoned house, enchanted and grinning. But now what he clearly used to see as a charming eagerness to know the world has evolved into words like *nosy, invasive, disrespectful*. She has watched his fondness distort into resentment and his responses to her stories tighten into sour nods. She has tried to change the things about herself he's started to hate, to breezily look the other direction when something catches her interest. But while she thought she could harness her questions until they learned to heel, all they do is yank at their chains, bloody and barking in her brain.

SEBASTIAN ALWAYS CLAIMS SALT WATER IS THE BEST HANG-over cure. And even though Lena didn't have anything to drink the night before, she still felt too groggy to leave the bed when he got up to surf. Pressure mounting behind her temples, her tongue slick with sour spit. Everything about the dinner the night prior still feels unfinished, and she is now consumed by a combination of exhaustion and restlessness. She gives up on watching Sebastian at the window and takes herself back to bed. But when she lays her head back down on the pillow and closes her eyes, her mind begins swimming with half-formed questions, a pressing countdown for when Sebastian will return home and her day will be swiftly possessed by his presence. She must have eventually fallen asleep, because when she wakes up, he has already left for work.

She feels a pressing need to see Mitty and Bethel before the memory of their night begins to dissipate. There are things she wants to remember, things she needs to ask. And since Mitty's confession in the water, she has also been prompted to consider her own secrets, what she might tell Mitty if she were weightless in her arms, with nothing to do but think.

Determined, she forces herself up and throws on a pair of cotton shorts and a T-shirt. She darts down the stairs, hardly pausing to slip her feet into sandals. Outside, the sun has started to punch through the clouds, a faint breeze is whispering along the grass, the earth warming beneath her. She runs across the yard and skips every other step up to Bethel's porch. She collects herself, taming her breath, then presses her forefinger against the small, glowing bell. Beyond the door, she can already hear the shuffling of footsteps growing closer. Soon, Mitty is standing in front of her wearing waffled long johns.

"Can I come in?" Lena's voice is still green from a full night's sleep. She runs her tongue along her lips, clears her throat. Mitty's eyes briefly narrow to gauge her demeanor.

"Of course," she says, stepping to the side.

The living room is buzzing with morning life. Bethel greets her from the balding recliner, her voice buried by the crisp sound of a newspaper page turning. The stream of the radio babbles in the corner. The coffee maker sputters and coughs. Lena kicks off her sandals and wiggles her toes into the wormy shag carpet. She wants so badly to fall asleep, to curl up beneath a plush blanket on that itchy couch and doze off to the chorus of another person's rituals. But instead, she leans against the wall across from them. When Mitty offers her a seat, she shakes her head.

"Did you have a nice time last night?" Lena asks, though the question feels like a placeholder.

"We did," Bethel says calmly. "You doing all right?"

Lena's face is drained of color, her foot tapping antsy against the floor.

"I'm okay," she says. Mitty's body suddenly feels sober and tense, watching Lena's eyes flick around the room. "I couldn't really sleep."

Bethel nods and takes a long, breathy sip of coffee. Mitty still hasn't managed to sit down. She tries to still her body from pacing by twisting a stray thread on her shirt around the tip of her finger until the skin goes blue.

After a beat of quiet, Lena stands up and leaves her mug on the sill behind her. "Can I talk to you upstairs, Mitty?"

Mitty has imagined this scenario before. The day she finally opens up to a person, and naïvely believing her confession would live and die in that moment, that they would both silently agree to leaving it alone in that liminal space of impulsive vulnerability. Only to be reminded that to tell someone a secret is an act of handing them the other end of a rope. That, in the end, they will always be able to tug you back toward them if you ever forget you're attached.

MITTY HOVERS BEHIND HER IN THE UPSTAIRS BATHROOM, waiting for a wary question, a painfully polite termination to their friendship. But Lena just stares at her reflection, occasionally lifting her hand to touch one of her own features.

"Do you imagine me when I'm not in front of you?" she asks.

Mitty pulls down the sleeves of her long johns so that they're covering her knuckles, gripping the fabric in her palms. She is already trying to figure out how this question will inevitably become about what she'd confessed the night prior. "You, as in people?" she says. "Yeah, sure."

"I mean me." Lena shifts her eyes to Mitty's. "Do you think about me when you can't see me?"

A pause. Mitty's throat swells.

"Sometimes."

"What do you think about?"

"Not concrete thoughts, as much." She struggles to keep her voice in a steady place of logic. Unmoved by her own fears. She focuses on solely answering the question in front of her. "But I have knowledge of you living next door. I'm aware of your presence."

"Okay, and if you touched me. Do I feel more or less real to you?"

"Lena," she says, "what are you asking?"

Lena returns her attention to her own eyes. Her brow is furrowed, her cheeks returning to their usual pink. "I'm always afraid that if someone can't see me, it means I'm not real."

"What do you mean not real?"

Lena searches for an answer, before taking Mitty's hand in hers, lifting only the forefinger from Mitty's clenched fist, and placing the tip on her own temple. All Mitty can think about is her own pulse, drumming through her finger against Lena's head.

"Close your eyes," Lena says.

She takes Mitty's hand and guides it to the top of her forehead, along her hairline and down toward her other temple, then lets go. Mitty pauses.

"No, keep going," Lena says. "Feel out the entirety of my face."

Mitty obeys. She runs her finger up and around Lena's neat ears, she traces the corners of her jawbone down to the oblique point of her chin then up the side where she began. She tries to embrace the tenderness of it all, ignore the confusion. She moves to Lena's brow, feeling each hair, all of them placed with what feels like the precision of embroidery, then the dip between her eyes, descending down her nose, landing on her Cupid's bow. When she gets to her lips, she feels Lena's mouth open and her finger falls into the gap, brushing against her tongue. Mitty jerks her hand back.

"I'm sorry," she says, wiping her finger on her T-shirt. "I didn't mean to do that."

Lena looks unconcerned and grabs Mitty's wrist, taking her hand back into her mouth. She pushes all four of Mitty's fingers against her tongue, past the second knuckle. Mitty shudders, attempting to pull back, but Lena is stronger, a wordless resolve glazing her face. Within seconds, she is swallowing the entirety of Mitty's hand.

Bile burns against the roof of Mitty's mouth as she watches Lena's lips close around her wrist. She knows she must be telling her to stop, but she can't find her own voice; it's hovering somewhere out of reach. She keeps expecting her fingers to fold against the back of Lena's throat, but they never do. They recline into what seems like a bottomless pit. Her hand floating in a dark, humid room. Lena's eyes are maniacal, still trying to shove Mitty's limb in deeper, gunning toward her elbow. But she isn't choking, she's vacant. Mitty is pleading in fragments now.

"You don't have to," Mitty says. "You don't have to do this." But Lena is silent, the only sound coming from her is a light gurgle purling from her windpipe, which is dammed by Mitty's forearm. "Please," Mitty says. "Lena, please stop."

When Lena doesn't respond, Mitty braces her free hand on the rim of the sink and pushes her foot against Lena's stomach, thrusting back. Like a snake surrendering a swallowed mouse, Lena's throat releases her arm, slicked with spit. Lena collapses onto her knees, back animated as she pants and coughs, a hand pressed against her clavicle. She looks up at Mitty, her face now streaked with tears.

"I just wanted you to feel my insides," Lena chokes. She

crawls to her feet and faces the mirror, looking at Mitty's reflection instead of her own. "I don't know if they're there."

Whatever empathy Mitty once had for Lena's paranoia is gone now. Everything is too foreign and terrifying, a bloodless air passing between them.

"I think he built me," Lena says. Her entire face is weighted, skin tugged toward the ground in a way Mitty hadn't even realized was possible for her. "And that's why I can't remember anything from before."

"Before what?"

"Before him."

Mitty stares at her. She knows Lena is waiting for a comforting response, something that will bring them both into a new, peaceful place. But Mitty doesn't feel wise. All she feels is an ache for a quiet afternoon in Bethel's bedroom. Smoke leaching from an incense stick, perched against the lip of a ceramic tray. The jaunty laughs of a daytime talk show, an interview with a C-list celebrity she and Bethel will fall briefly in love with. The piddling cove of their lives on those days, where all that's left to manage is their own minds.

But she is here. Across from the girl she has wanted to be across from all along.

"Yes, you can," she says, taming her voice until it sounds certain. "The farm. Up north. You told me all about it."

"But it feels like a script," Lena says. "I know they're the stories about my life I'm supposed to tell. But even imagining them, I don't know if it's because I've told them so many times or because I actually experienced them."

She grabs at her stomach, gathering the skin in her clenched fist.

"This doesn't feel like mine," she says. "I don't think it ever was."

Mitty examines Lena's face—her blinking, half-pipe eyelashes, her trembling mouth, the subtle collapse of her nostrils as she inhales. She places her finger on the bridge of Lena's nose.

"Someone gave you this, but it wasn't Sebastian." It comes out sounding like a lie. "You inherited it."

Lena slides her finger beneath Mitty's, running it up and down the steady incline.

"Right," she says, as if discovering it for the first time. "I think my dad's nose was like this."

Mitty nods, eager to acknowledge it as a truth, then pulls Lena's finger away from her nose, holding it up to their shared eyeline.

"And your nail beds, those came from somewhere, too. Not from Sebastian."

Lena studies her curved cuticles, then Mitty points to her foot.

"No one invented that." She's speaking louder now, like Lena is floating away.

Lena begins to shake her head, growing more furious the longer Mitty tries to convince her.

"No, no, no," she says. "You don't get it."

Mitty tries to keep her face blank, but she can feel herself getting angrier. "Well then, can you explain it to me?"

"Only in the water," Lena says. "Like you did."

"I don't want to go in the ocean right now, Lena," Mitty says firmly.

Lena turns and scans the bathroom, then points to the tub. "In there," she says. "I'll tell you about it in there."

MITTY EMPTIES A BAG OF EPSOM SALT INTO THE TUB. LENA is standing in the bedroom, staring expressionless out the window, the shadows of outside traveling across her face. When Mitty asks if she is hungry, she only shakes her head, picks at her cuticles.

"I need you to stay here with me," she says when Mitty shuts off the faucet. Mitty sits on the lid of the toilet seat, while Lena removes her clothes and lowers herself into the water. "No, I mean I need you to get in with me."

Mitty almost wants to laugh. There were so many versions of herself that had fantasized about this moment at various points in her life. The knot of envy she used to feel when she thought of girls and their friendships, their closeness, how little they seemed to care about whether or not they were in love. Because they were. But here, with Lena, isn't the moment she'd imagined. Her limbs warping beneath the water like sticks of gum, her eyes childish and pleading. And still, it feels impossible to say no.

Lena looks away, focused on something internal. Mitty strips and climbs into the tub, weaving her limbs across her chest and torso.

"You're lucky you have a past," Lena says.

Mitty leans her back against the faucet, submitting to the metal horn stabbing her spine. "You have one too, Lena."

"Not like you." Lena locks eyes with her, scowling.

"Well, thank goodness for that." Mitty forces a laugh, but Lena doesn't budge.

"Have you ever thought about going back?"

"To Arizona? Sometimes. But the idea kind of horrifies me."

Lena shakes her head, disappointed. "You're taking it for granted."

"I can't just go back, Lena. It's not like I left for college. I ran away."

Lena leans her head back and groans miserably toward the ceiling. "But it's why you're so unsure of everything. Because you're detached from the place you came from. I know, because I feel it, too. The difference is that I don't have any-where to go."

What a brat, Mitty thinks. She wants to point to Lena's giant, comfortable home, the boyfriend who bankrolls her riskless life. "You really can't remember anything?"

"Not in a normal way," Lena says firmly.

"Okay, then let's start with something more recent." Mitty readjusts, leaning forward to rest her elbows on her knees. "How did you meet him?"

"In San Francisco," Lena says, straining. "But I don't re-member anything before that."

"Had you ever dated anyone else?"

"I don't have any memory of anyone else." Lena lifts her

leg over Mitty's shoulder and turns on the faucet with her foot, sending the cold down Mitty's back. "It was like he found me and then I was born."

She picks up Mitty's ankle and examines the bottoms of her toes.

"Your body thinks you're a fish," she says, running her finger across the balls of Mitty's feet. "I read about the evolutionary purpose of the tips of phalanges getting wrinkled when they're submerged in water for long periods of time. It's because your body is reminded of when it had to grip on to slippery surfaces. Before you became a human."

Mitty inspects her shriveled fingers. "That sounds like one of those regurgitated ideas that became a fact just because so many people repeated it."

"I don't care," Lena says. "I think it's nice. The idea that something other than your brain has memories." She holds up her splayed hand, mooning Mitty with her palm. "Mine doesn't." And she's right. The tips of her fingers look almost polished, smooth and rounded like lightbulbs. "That was the first thing I noticed."

They slip into silence. The only sound is the occasional repositioning of a limb, the sloshing of milk-warm water. Lena fills her cupped hands and lets the water dribble over Mitty's knees. "Have you ever seen us through the windows?" Her tone is neutral, leaving Mitty with nothing to respond to except the actual question.

"I have." She avoids Lena's eyes. "Only once." She removes a floating hair from between them and swirls it against the tile. "I'm sorry."

Lena rests her elbow on the edge of the tub. "I'm not upset," she says. "I was just wondering." She lets out a faint exhale. "Did you notice anything"—she pauses—"strange?"

"Strange?" Mitty's insecurity is audible and sharp. "I don't know how to define *strange*."

Each time she studies Lena, it seems like she's eroding right there, in the tub. Like the more she acknowledges herself, the more she disappears.

"Well, you noticed that I don't eat," she says. "You knew that was strange."

"Yeah, and you got upset about it."

Lena sighs. Mitty's jaw tightens. She feels uneasy, sick, each time she catches herself trying to locate even the faintest blue vein at the bend of Lena's inner elbow. A blood vessel in the corner of her eye. Some dry riverbed snaking between her eyebrows. But it's all smooth and creaseless. A glass of heavy cream. She doesn't really know why she's looking. She doesn't know what she's trying to believe.

THE WATER COOLS. WHILE GETTING TOWELS, MITTY PAUSES outside Bethel's room. What would she gain from telling Bethel about Lena? There is already such a chasm between the two of them when it comes to deciphering who Lena is and what she needs. Everything they understand about the world, all the wisdom that their lives have offered, feels too far apart to come together now.

When she returns to the bathroom, the water is pink. Lena is watching it grow dark around her, a ripe, fuchsia stream snaking up from beneath her leg. She looks up, her eyes glassy.

"I've been working on it for a few days," she says, "trying to see what's underneath."

Almost immediately, the water has turned a deep red and Lena's typically glowing skin fades to the color of chalk. Mitty rushes over and pulls at her limp arm, urging her to stand.

"I'm fine," Lena says, shaking her off. "It just reopens when it's wet."

Lena lifts her leg and points to a wound, the size of a silver dollar, shining back at Mitty.

"Stand up," Mitty orders.

Lena grumbles and gathers herself. The bathwater plunges without her mass. She presents the back of her thigh. Up close, the hole is blistering and furious, a pulpy tunnel where something has burrowed toward the bone. Mitty instinctually puts her hand over it, like she's trying to shield herself against its heat. She remembers the tweezers, the blood inching up the arms.

"It doesn't hurt," Lena says, like she's irritated, like Mitty is fussing over a hangnail.

"It's fucking infected," Mitty says. She feels another glare of anger toward Lena, as she kneels beneath her in her blood. Like she's praying to a saint.

"Well, this isn't helping." Lena swats Mitty's hand away and twists her torso, trying to get a better look.

"I'll be right back," Mitty says, ignoring her. "I'm gonna go get something to clean it."

"I'm telling you; it doesn't hurt." Lena pauses between each word with a forced, patronizing clarity. "I just want to find the wires."

"Lena." Mitty collects herself, the fury in her chest only growing louder. "What are you talking about?"

"I know there are wires in there." She presses her finger into the hole and Mitty winces.

"There are no wires, Lena," Mitty says. "There's blood."

Lena's attention snaps away from her body to Mitty. Her face is twisted with an adolescent impatience, angry about something she'd already deemed obvious. "Yes, I know," she hisses. "Of course he would give me blood."

LENA SITS ON THE FLOOR HOLDING HER KNEES. SHE'S WEAR-ing a pair of Mitty's cutoffs and an old white T-shirt. She refused to put back on the clothes she'd arrived in, scowling at them like they'd gone bad.

"I'm not crazy," Lena says. She's speaking into her thighs, her voice muffled. "All that talk about AI—what I'm feeling isn't crazy."

"I don't think you're crazy," Mitty says. She's surprised by how certain she sounds. "I just want to make sure you're safe."

"What does that even mean?" Lena looks up at Mitty, her eyes narrowing into slits. "I'm safe. No one is going to hurt me. But that's not what I'm worried about."

"Then what are you worried about?"

Lena huffs. "I'm worried that I'm not real." When she says the word *real,* she juts out her chin and uses every muscle in her face to enunciate the syllables. "I can't remember the last time I had my own ideas," she says. "They're either his"—she motions to the room around her, the invisible galaxy of Sebastian's brain—"or someone else's."

It's the first thing Lena has said all day that Mitty really understands. She had spent so much of her life taking on the thoughts and opinions of the people around her. "Okay," she says, collecting herself. "Then let's give you an idea that feels like your own. Close your eyes and think." Lena obeys, her head tipping slightly, too heavy for her neck. "I need you to tell me exactly what you want to do right now."

Lena struggles to say it, her mouth parting, then closing again. Until finally, she speaks.

"I want to go home," she says. She looks at Mitty like her face is a tunnel, like she might try to climb inside it and crawl toward somewhere else.

MITTY GRIPS THE STEERING WHEEL, ONLY LOOKING AWAY from the road to check on Lena. She's in the passenger seat, her face close to the window, breath blooming against the glass. The adrenaline of everything else has started to fade and now there's a resounding silence. A relief, Mitty thinks, that they have settled on something together and all that's left to do is think.

They agreed that they wouldn't tell Bethel where they

were going. Instead, they shuffled out the door and Mitty muttered something about taking Lena to the pharmacy to get medicine. When they merge onto 17, Mitty is reminded of its nickname, Blood Alley. The forest closes in on them as the road becomes narrow enough for one car in each direction, even though it's split into four lanes. There is no median, just oncoming traffic separated by a snaking yellow line, a suggestion, barely wide enough for a briefly drifting mind.

Ten years ago, as Mitty and Patricia made their way toward Santa Cruz, Patricia started talking about her funeral. *Just don't turn me into a saint,* she said. *It's disrespectful.* Mitty hadn't considered before that grief was a selfish act, the fact that the people who've been left behind are really only mourning what was taken from them. It took her years to realize that her mother was probably also trying to teach her a lesson about losing Esme. Her mother didn't want her to romanticize a girl she'd only known for a few short months. But what Patricia also wanted—a lesson she couldn't teach but instead could only hope the seeds she planted would bloom naturally in Mitty's mind with time and space—was for Mitty to understand the importance of letting people go.

Patricia talked about how death is sometimes the easiest way to lose someone. It does the hard part for you. It removes all possibility, leaves behind the unexplained and frustrating artifacts of the person's private self, the things they hid from you, the things that made them human. At the time, Mitty had thought of what she left behind in Arizona, the things her mother would inevitably find when she turned her childhood bedroom into a gym. The gas station pizza wrappers stuffed against the bottom of her trash bin, a miniature heap of plucked bikini hairs forgotten by the sink, the underwear with a bleached crotch left in the hamper. She thought of her mother's death, everything she would inherit, all of those impersonal belongings Patricia had won in various sweepstakes, how they might suddenly take on a sentimentality she couldn't bring herself to get rid of. When she said this to her mother, Patricia laughed, loud and forgiving. *No, no,* she said. *Those should be a reminder of all the things you didn't like about me.* She looked to Mitty in the passenger seat. *Everyone has something you won't miss,* she said.

Now she thinks of what there could be to uncover about Lena, if her body ever putters to stillness. What truth would be revealed? If her house is any sign of what she would leave behind, then the answer is nothing. She wonders about the pathologist assigned to split Lena's torso open for an autopsy. She imagines them finding a hoard of wires, the black ribbon of a cassette tape tangled around her organs, the glittering city of a Kelly-green microchip.

Mitty doesn't realize she's holding her breath until the car is spit out onto a wider, multilane highway, punctuated with signs for San Jose. She lets out an audible gasp. She notices Lena look forward for the first time. Mitty can't tell if she's even aware they just survived something. But she knows Lena sees it, she must—the world in front of them, expanding.

When Lena thinks about the life she could've had, she imagines an apartment with ceilings that are freckled with hooks, hanging pots with leggy plants climbing over their edges. She imagines candles precariously left unattended as the wax bleeds onto the coffee table, and the bed unmade, blankets tousled with the memory of a body. The shower running until the windows in the living room are murky from steam. A crowded bookshelf organized in an order only she understands. She longs for everything in excess, like at Bethel's house, the world around her overflowing. It's the opposite of her life now, which has been yanked into a polished efficiency, as taut as the strings on a corset.

But now she wonders if that other life was ever even an option. If Sebastian had, in fact, built her, then it would mean she wasn't like other, real people, whose lives unfolded based on a series of decisions, every second of every day dictated by choice. If Lena's fear about her own existence is right, it would mean that all of those minuscule moments in which she thought she'd chosen one particular route over the other—the decision to sleep in rather than go out paddleboarding or the decision to wash her body before her hair— were actually predetermined. It would mean that she was merely selecting one of two options that had been curated for her by someone else. It would mean that nothing in her life happened by chance. She reaches around to the back of her thigh and presses her finger against the soft wound. This, she feels, is the thing she can control. When she touches it, she feels like she's holding on to her glazed and bloody heart.

What if even her departure is part of some larger plan, she wonders. What if Sebastian is just testing her? Trying to see where she goes when she starts yearning for a home that doesn't exist?

But when she met Mitty and Bethel, she reminds herself, she did begin to imagine that maybe something could happen to her without Sebastian's involvement. Surely he wouldn't choose to let her meet these two women, whose lives were storied and messy. Women with pasts: memories, secrets, mistakes they hadn't yet learned from. Only when she stepped into that house did she realize what she'd been missing. A life. An entire life. There's no way Sebastian would have planned for that epiphany. Because as soon as she had it, she felt the urge to run.

Mitty is sitting on the hood of the car, hot metal seeping through the ass of her denim shorts, the rugged purr of the engine beneath her. Her feet are propped up on the front bumper, the sun beating against her forehead. Next to her, Lena shields her eyes and peers out at a field of tall grass fringed by trees.

"Anything?" Mitty asks. Lena shakes her head.

"You are supposed to feel something when you go back to your childhood home, right?" She looks to Mitty for confirmation.

Mitty shrugs. "I wouldn't know."

"It looks familiar," Lena says. "But it doesn't feel familiar."

"Maybe it's just been too long." Mitty scans the property, trying to make out any semblance of tire tracks, but there's nothing. The land is bushy and alive. She points to a boarded-up farmhouse in the distance.

Lena stands and takes a few steps forward. From here, she looks like a little girl, cotton T-shirt billowing up past her rib cage, legs too skinny for Mitty's shorts. It had been so difficult to imagine Lena as any other age, but now Mitty can see it perfectly—a nine-year-old Lena making mud cakes in Dixie cups and hunting for lizards, not blinking twice when her bare foot sinks into a mound of cow shit. She can imagine the people who raised her, a mother with a soft belly beneath a shapeless linen dress, ringing the bell on the porch. A father with an axe wound along his shin.

"Okay," Lena says, taking a breath. "I'm going to start walking."

She turns back toward Mitty and comes to stand in between her legs, cupping her palms over Mitty's kneecaps.

"I never really saw myself in anyone until I met you," Lena says. "Did you know that?"

Mitty's throat swells into itself, her eyes begin to well. She wants to resist this being a goodbye, but she's too familiar with the way people speak when they know it's the end. The tragic kindness of it all.

"Where will you go?" she asks.

Lena lifts Mitty's wrist to study her watch. "I'm just going to walk until he shuts me off." She grins, but a glimpse of fear, so small it's almost unrecognizable, flashes across her face. "But I need you to promise me something. You're not going to follow me, or come looking for me. I don't want you to remember me that way, as a dead girl in a field."

Mitty begins to cry, helplessly. "He's not going to shut you off, Lena." But still, she can't help but imagine what that would look like. Lena, somewhere in the grass, curled into a fetal position. She feels selfish for wanting to beg her to stop, to insist they turn around and go back to Santa Cruz before Sebastian can notice they were gone.

"Whatever happens," she continues, "I want you to get in that car and I want you to drive home. Okay?"

"What am I supposed to tell Bethel when I get home?" Mitty says, through fractured sobs.

"I'm not talking about Bethel's house, Mitty." Lena holds Mitty's cheek in her palm. "I'm talking about Arizona." Now the roles have switched. Lena no longer seems like a child, but instead an all-knowing mother, who can grasp the future in a way this little girl, weeping in front of her, can't.

"Why?"

"Because that's the only way you're going to realize who you are," she says. "You're not a bad person, Mitty. You just have to go see that for yourself."

"And if he doesn't shut you off?"

"Then I'll keep walking." Her face is serene in a way that feels new to Mitty. She has always seen Lena as composed, but now, as she relaxes into the possibility of her own freedom, Mitty realizes that she's been wound tight all along, her features laced into a suffocating politeness.

"Okay." Mitty looks down at her knees.

Lena bends down to meet Mitty's eyes again. "You promise?"

"Yes," Mitty says. "I promise."

Lena pauses, internally debating something. Then she leans forward slowly and presses her lips against Mitty's. It's the first time Mitty has been kissed by anyone since Esme, and it happens so quickly that she hardly has time to move her lips at all. She just allows herself to accept it. Feels the current surging through her body as Lena's warm breath sneaks into her open mouth. Tongue grazing against her teeth. How she missed this distinct comfort. How she regrets waiting so long to seek it out.

When Lena pulls away, Mitty hesitates to open her eyes. She doesn't want to see the look of regret. But when she does, Lena is only smiling, admiring Mitty with distinct tenderness, as though she'd just been watching her sleep.

Lena turns to face the field. She kicks her canvas sneakers off her feet. A breeze cuts through the grass, the spiny stalks bowing to the left. She takes a single breath and starts walking. Soon, her lower half is obscured by the weeds, and all that's visible is her bobbing head, her chestnut hair, flailing in the wind. Mitty realizes she would do anything to hear the sound of Lena's feet padding through the dirt, the rhythm of her panting, her breath like a second hand counting down to zero. But then a howl sails up into the sky; Lena has started to run, lifting her hands above her head, still gunning forward. She's laughing, which causes Mitty to laugh, too, sharp, guttural thrusts of joy that feel so close to sobs she can't quite tell the difference.

Lena runs until she shoots out from the other end of the field, her laughter diluting in the air the farther away she gets. When she reaches the mouth of the forest, she stops and turns around. Even from here, Mitty can see her beaming. Next to a redwood tree, she's tiny. But her wide, toothy mouth says it all. She's never felt bigger. She lifts her hand and waves. Mitty waves back, trying to smile big enough so that Lena can see. She glances at her watch, still keenly aware of how much time has passed. And when she looks up, Lena is gone.

Mitty jumps to her feet on the hood of the car. It dips beneath her weight. She can only see the jagged pathway that Lena's body had sliced through the tangled farmland. She wants so badly to imagine that Lena will land at the front door of the farmhouse and knock, where her mother— skin spotted from age—will answer. And before she can lunge forward to hug her daughter, she will call out for her husband, who is silently tinkering with his reading glasses in another room. Together, they will take Lena into their arms, tell her that there's food on the stove, her bedroom has been preserved exactly as it was when she left, her childhood quilt still tucked cleanly beneath the mattress, the magazine cutouts she worshipped still collaging the walls. Or maybe the house will be empty. And Lena will keep running to the neighboring town, cozy up in the booth of some shitty diner, and order a bowl of soup. She will spend her days alone, falling asleep beneath the starched comforter of a motel bed, lit by the static glow of the soundless television. Then she'll rent a car and drive to a city with museums and trains and wild parks with hidden trails.

But what if Lena is right about Sebastian? Beneath the cloudless sky, the air as brisk as chewing gum, mountains looming on either side, the faint wisp of cars winding along Highway 17. What if these are her final moments? And all that's left is Lena's body. Lena's perfect body, obsolete.

M itty knows her cheeks must be patchy from crying, her eyelids swollen like pink slugs. By the time she enters the house, it's early evening. She moves slowly and in silence, careful not to alert Bethel, who is somewhere upstairs. She splashes her face with cold water at the kitchen sink, pausing to let her head hang, allowing herself a few deep inhales. She can hear Bethel's television, a documentary about ancient Egypt. She climbs the steps with light feet and goes straight to her own bedroom. She lets herself out onto the balcony and this time doesn't grapple with whether or not to study Lena's house. Her curiosity feels warranted now, all of her previous investigations suddenly forgiven.

The world seems quieter than usual—the beach is free of dog walkers, the breeze docile. She scans the rooms of the dollhouse, half expecting to see Sebastian frantically running through the house, shouting his girlfriend's name. But there's an eerie nothingness, the only evidence of him a wetsuit hanging from the railing. She considers that he might've already left, looking for Lena. Would he come to Bethel's? Would he demand an answer she couldn't give? And what would it be like to stand in front of him now, imagine the ways he might have played with his girlfriend's body, molded her brain into something remarkable?

She wonders if sometime in the next decade, when the ethics of the whole ordeal will have been buried by time, a glowing profile will be written about his work, referring to Lena only as a project that came and went, whose life span was predetermined. Her technology by then will be archaic, laughable to children raised on the lab-made breast milk of their robot nannies, children who have never held a pencil long enough to earn a callus on their finger, who can hardly imagine why they would ever willingly take on the challenge of loving a person when they could just build a person who loves them.

But then Sebastian appears in the living room, on the phone, talking with his hands. She tries to make out his expression, whether or not he seems panicked. He starts laughing, tossing back his head, nodding vigorously. Maybe all of it was in Lena's head, she thinks. And only when a few hours pass will he begin to wonder where she is, like any good partner. But there's another, nagging possibility. That his ease comes from knowing that she can't get away. That no matter how far away she gets, he will always know where she is, he will always be able to press a single button and make her stop.

MITTY PACKS A BAG. ONLY THE NECESSITIES—ENOUGH PAIRS of socks and underwear, a couple of T-shirts, the hundred-dollar bill she keeps beneath her mattress. She hasn't gone on a trip in so long, she can hardly think of what it is she needs to survive, what she would even miss. She scans her scant bedroom, hardly decorated. To a stranger, it would be a room that belongs to no one, not unlike Lena's. She has never tried to make a home of her own here, not really. She was always just satisfied with disappearing into Bethel's belongings.

She walks to Bethel's room, leaving the bag in the hallway. Bethel is perched on her bed, surrounded by papers, glasses balanced on the tip of her nose. When she sees Mitty in the doorway, she looks up from whatever puzzle she's trying to solve and smiles.

"Did you get her what she needed?" It takes Mitty a moment to register what she's talking about, to remember the lie about the pharmacy. "You were gone all day."

"She just needed Monistat," Mitty says. "But we grabbed food and walked around Capitola, too."

Bethel chuckles. "See?" she says. "Even women like that get yeast infections."

Mitty offers up an unconvincing laugh.

Bethel removes her glasses and studies her. "Everything okay?"

Mitty nods. She had never considered how honest their relationship had been until now, when she realizes how difficult it is, the act of hiding something.

"What time is it?" Bethel asks, leaning to check her bedside clock. She seems surprised by the time—just past six—closing her eyes and massaging her temples. "I'm exhausted."

"Me too," Mitty says. She takes in the room. The emerald paisley drapes. The collection of expired lotions displayed on the oak dresser. Tweezers and extractors and cuticle clippers, all those tools for removal. She feels porous, trying to absorb it all exactly as it is. "Can I tuck you in?" she asks. She doesn't wait for Bethel to respond before she begins to help clear the papers off the bed. Bethel lets her, folding down the duvet to climb beneath it, tossing the throw pillows onto the floor. She exhales with relief as she sinks onto her back.

"You know I won't give up on this fucking crossword if someone doesn't force me."

Mitty sits at the edge of the mattress and moves Bethel's silver hair away from her cheeks, tucking it behind her ears. Bethel's eyes are already heavy. Mitty has always been envious of the ease with which Bethel can fall asleep, something she claims comes with age, the body getting more comfortable with the practice of plunging toward death.

"In the morning, I'll make a big bowl of egg salad," she mutters, her words already blurry.

"I love you, Bethel," Mitty says. She had only ever said it twice before. Once, by accident a few years back, a stock goodbye as she left for work. They'd both burst into laughter, bemused by the touching mishap. And another time, on Bethel's most recent birthday, when Mitty was hit with the fact of Bethel's mortality and it seemed only right to make sure she said it at least once on purpose, to tell her before it was too late.

Bethel reaches forward and pats Mitty on the back of the hand.

"My Mitty," she says. Her fingernails are long and yellowed. "I love you, too."

When Mitty is certain that Bethel is asleep, she takes one last look at the room. She doesn't know how long she'll be gone. Any time away from Bethel is significant. Her eyes land on an ashtray, congested with bent filters. She rummages through it and selects one, the end of which is dipped with coral lipstick. Occasionally, Bethel wears makeup but hides it, even from Mitty. She only knows because Bethel would come downstairs in the morning and she could see the small ridges of her lips that she'd missed while trying to wipe it off with tissue, her face wrecked with a child's guilt. Mitty tucks the filter into her pocket and leans down to kiss Bethel on the forehead. She inhales the smell of her scalp—balmy and ripe, cut with old smoke. Somewhere, the faint snap of tea tree oil, from the last time she'd washed her hair.

BY THE TIME MITTY REACHES SALINAS, THE SUN IS LOW. THE farmland flanking the highway is licked in gold, light splitting through grids of produce. Warty heads of kale, fat spinach blooming in obedient rows. The air is hot in a way she immediately recognizes from a decade ago—the ground peeling back into the horizon, the sky choked with smog. Only when she pulls up to a gas station and turns off the car does she realize she's been driving in complete silence, her brain too occupied with chanting the cities to need another sound.

Her odometer has just tipped above two hundred and fifty thousand miles. How much of that has been spent run-

ning, she thinks, hurrying from one place to the next, trying to remain unnoticed? She buys a canned coffee from the
mini-mart and fills her tank. At the neighboring pump, a
girl is perched in the passenger seat of a raised pickup, sucking on the tip of an e-cigarette. Her feet are bare, resting
on the dashboard, toes pressed into the windshield. She
can't be older than twenty, pretty in the way her peers
must clamor over, dishwater-blond hair wrestled into a bun
with a pretend thoughtlessness, eyebrows drawn dark, cut-
off shorts slinking up past her ass. Sometimes, Mitty feels
like she never really got to be that age. Lawless and project-
ing love onto a gaunt boy who fancies himself an adult.
Was she lucky, having avoided the pregnancy scares and
constant yearning for some invented romance? Or had she
missed out on some crucial phase that would have made
her more discerning and less afraid of the people who might
hurt her? What was lost, she wonders, from being so protected?

SHE ARRIVES IN PALM SPRINGS AROUND TWO IN THE MORN-
ing and checks into a dingbat motel. The heat is just as ripe
and heavy at night. In the courtyard, the pool is lit fuchsia
and wreathed in lawn chairs. Pie-eyed guests, drunk off the
heels of a party, are scattered across the deck. Her room is in
a far corner, the window barely shielded by the large flaps of
a banana tree. As she sets her things on the made bed, she
remembers her mother in their hotel room a decade ago.

How calm she tried to seem while enforcing three different locks. The click of the dead bolt, sliding the chain into its groove, and then, as one final precaution, folding a piece of paper until it was thick enough to wedge tightly beneath the gap of the door. *You never know,* Patricia had said, when she noticed Mitty watching. *It's true,* Mitty remembers thinking. *I never know. I never seem to know.*

She stands still in the shower beneath the scalding water, any concern for wasting resources now the responsibility of someone else. She climbs into bed naked, feels her body pinned beneath the tightly tucked sheets. Her sleep is as heavy as death. For four hours, she has no dreams, just the padlock of some other, dark dimension.

In the morning, she fumbles with the cheap plastic coffee maker. Fills a cup with soured roast. The parking lot is silent, the streets beyond it empty. For now, her anxiety has dissipated, and she tries to welcome the calm. All of her movements feel steady, calculated. When she gets back into the car, she listens to local news radio until she gets far enough out of town that the station fuzzies into something else— Spanish pop, Christian sermons.

She skirts Joshua Tree, the desert gradually becoming more familiar as she drives. She's comforted by the consistency of the world around her. Miles of flat, taupe ground in each direction, specked with shrubs. Cellphone towers linked like vertebrae along the mountain range. The occasional rusted car, dumped on the side of the road, tireless.

But at a rest stop, she sees the sign for Blythe—the last on her list of cities that she'd grown so used to simply chanting, she'd almost forgotten it was real—and the sickness returns. She looks at her phone. Thirteen missed calls from Bethel and six from her mother. Before Mitty can think twice, she presses the call button, and the line begins to ring.

Bethel picks up faster than usual.

"Hello?"

"Hi," Mitty says. "It's me."

"Where are you?" She sounds irritated. As if Mitty's unexplained absence is an annoyance more than anything.

"I'm about to be in Blythe."

There's quiet on the other end of the phone.

"I can't tell if you're kidding," Bethel says, her voice cautious. Mitty hears the lighter, the sharp inhale.

"I'm not." She busies herself by wiping away the dust on her dashboard. "I'm going to Arizona for a few days."

"You didn't tell me you were leaving." Bethels reserves her vulnerability, pulling her voice in toward herself.

"I wasn't sure if I was going or not." She leans forward in her seat and lets the sweat cool against her lower back. "And by the time I decided, you were asleep."

Bethel takes another drag. "What prompted this?" Now the worry that Mitty knew must be buried somewhere inside Bethel is beginning to surface.

"I think it will be good for me."

Another bout of quiet. Bethel's steady breath.

"Well, will you let me know when you get in safely?" she says.

Mitty nods, before remembering that Bethel can't see her. "Yes."

"Does your mom know you're coming?"

"No," Mitty says flatly. "I'm sorry for not telling you sooner. I wanted to start driving before I started doubting myself."

"That's all right," Bethel says, resigning. They stay on the phone in silence for a few more seconds.

"I'll be back," Mitty says.

"I know." Bethel cuts herself off to cough, then takes a brief pause, catching her breath. "I know."

MITTY DRIVES SLOW OUT OF THE REST STOP AND MERGES back onto the highway. She stays below the speed limit, letting the cars careen past her. The closer she gets to the Arizona welcome sign—yellow and red rays shooting from an orange star, that awful flag announcing her arrival—the more absurd the notion of a border becomes. She expects something to happen, a subtle but apparent shift, as she crosses over that invisible line. Like an astronaut returning from space, only to realize her body has stretched by two inches. But when her car is on the other side, now in the state she had escaped all those years ago, the state whose area code still jolts her body whenever she sees it pop up on her phone, the state whose name she has tried her best never to say out loud, the state whose shape she could draw without reference— a square with a jagged left side, almost perfect, like a Club cracker broken in half—she feels nothing. All that time spent being afraid of a place, when really it's just the same land she's been living on for the last ten years, stretched like a goat hide across the frame of a drum.

ANOTHER THREE HOURS, AND SHE BEGINS TO SEE GREEN. Golf courses and vast, rectangular lawns. She knows she will end up at her mother's eventually, but first there are places she needs to visit on her own.

As she passes the strips of boutiques, all designed to look like Southwestern saloons, she realizes how little of the town she actually knows. She'd grown far more familiar with Santa Cruz. The breakfast spot on Portola Drive that pairs ramekins of corn salsa with every dish, the abandoned nunnery that every realtor is too nervous to take on, the scalloped roofs of pastel Victorians downtown, and the clock tower where people gather to protest fracking sites and student debt. She has become protective of Santa Cruz in a way she never was with Paradise Valley, a town that had been invented, not a town that had bloomed from its own history. Even its name was aspirational, a self-proclaimed oasis for people like her mother who think happiness is contagious, who believe that if you place yourself in the center of luxury, it will start to rub off.

She drives slow past the site of the ballet studio. She'd heard from Patricia that it had been shut down last winter, a Wells Fargo now in its place. But seeing it here, she remembers those glossy floors even more clearly, now being trod by loafers rather than pointe shoes, the mirrors replaced with stock photographs of an Arizona sunset. It suddenly seems so silly to feel anything about a building. A thing that can so easily be demolished or reimagined as something entirely new. Even her childhood home, where her mother must be deciding which furniture to leave on the street, packing the tchotchkes that have never been moved from their fateful locations on the windowsill, perhaps noticing how large the house could've felt had she only done this sooner. She thinks of who will come after, a new family brimming with optimism, who will paint over the pencil marks in the doorway that marked Mitty's steady growth, replace her notches with the borders of their own children's heads.

She turns off the main road and drives through the hills, which are adorned with sandy monochromatic homes. She hovers at each stop sign, knowing exactly which direction she'll turn but bracing herself before she does. She avoids the eyes of every dog walker. Every woman jogging, wrists and ankles bangled with weights. She takes in the glimmers of life at each house. A small pink bicycle with white wheels, lying on its side in a stone driveway. A boat obscured by a white tarp. Thick spools of sod, ready to be yawned across a dirt yard.

She remembers the first time she'd met Lena, how clear she'd made it that their glass house was not her choice. Mitty feels angry at herself for not having asked more questions, pried more into what she wanted instead. It has been almost twenty-four hours since Lena disappeared into the woods. By now, if she hasn't yet been shut off by Sebastian, her body shuttled back to the dollhouse, she might be in an entirely different city. The only image that brings Mitty comfort is of Lena in a bed and breakfast somewhere else, drifting into an afternoon nap, hardly aware of the wound on her thigh as it rests against the soft cotton sheets.

She turns left at the NO OUTLET sign, driving slowly into a cul-de-sac. She parks and turns off the car. She resists checking her face in the flap mirror, ignores the fact that her shirt is drenched in sweat. Instead, she just opens the door and climbs out.

The house in front of her is smaller than she remembered. All those details she used to revere—the mahogany two-car garage, the soft rock exterior, a gurgling three-tiered fountain—are meaningless to her now. The winding pathway she used to follow, careful not to make any sudden movements, lest her dirty shoes scuff the sandstone. The dapper lawn that made her wish she could do a cartwheel, feel the clean blades of grass against her open palms. Suddenly, she can see it for exactly what it is. A facade. A meticulous signal guiding the hand of an onlooker as they desperately attempt to write the story of who must live inside.

Mitty makes her way toward the massive doors, watching her feet. This is what Lena must have seen, she thinks, the ground beneath her blurring as she moved forward. In a way, they have the same destination. A return to an elsewhere that risks confirming all the reasons they'd escaped it in the first place. A place that is now something new entirely, a place they aren't remembered. A place that has existed as merely a concept in their minds for years and now is right there, real and only a few feet away.

She climbs the steps, curling her hand into a fist. But just as she looks up, ready to knock, the door opens. The gap is too slim to see who is standing on the other side, the room beyond it cloaked dark with heavy curtains. It is only wide enough to release a gust of frigid wind onto Mitty's face. She considers saying hello, considers smiling and introducing herself. But instead, she just waits for whatever comes next. Whatever she deserves. She lets the cold air of another world coil around her body. She lets it take her in.

ACKNOWLEDGMENTS

There are three people who will never read this book but whose stories are woven throughout it. My grandmother—Janette Florence Blaesi—a woman who abandoned her hopes of finding fame in Hollywood to become a librarian in Santa Cruz, whom I hardly knew but whose photographs I clung to as the portrait of beauty. Kay (Katherine Mary Kreiner), who taught me the importance of liberating oneself from the obedience that beauty requires, an ethos that greatly informed the character of Bethel. And finally, Niko Dellios, who brought me to Santa Cruz and, ultimately, to Mitty. Oh, how I miss you. Oh, how I wish I could see you again.

Infinite thanks to my editors—Clio Seraphim, Whitney Frick, and Charlotte Cray—for helping me turn this story over and over in my hands until finally it revealed itself. To my agent, Mackenzie Brady Watson, thank you for being my compass as I worked my way through the last four years. And my team in Los Angeles—Priya, Albert, and Berni—thank you for imagining with me the many lives this book can have beyond the page.

I am endlessly grateful to have a circle of friends who were willing to lend their minds and time to reading the many drafts of this book: Sam Rush, Joe Talbot, Melissa Lozada-Oliva, Shelby Condon, Gemma Doll-Grossman, Fritzi Adelman, Camille Peri, and Jeremy Radin.

Thank you to my community in Northern California, whose insight and accompaniment greatly informed the setting of this novel: Julia Dunn, Neighbor Shanj, Myles Morgan, Andreas Marcotty, Rob Bolduc, and Colton Chorpenning.

This story could not take place anywhere other than the strange, magical town of Santa Cruz. I want to thank the following locations and businesses, where I spent hours writing or contemplating this book: Privates Beach, Bookshop Santa Cruz, Sharks, Jack's, Cowell's Beach, Cat & Cloud, Paula's, Lulu Carpenter's, Portola Drive, Aptos St. Barbecue, and Sunny Cove.

Lastly, to my parents, thank you for encouraging me to believe that there's something out there worth figuring out, and that my findings are worth saying aloud.

ABOUT THE AUTHOR

OLIVIA GATWOOD is a screenwriter and the author of two poetry collections, *New American Best Friend* and *Life of the Party.* She has received international recognition for her poetry, writing workshops, and work as a Title IX–compliant educator in sexual assault prevention and recovery. Her performances have been featured on HBO, MTV, VH1, BBC, and more. Her poems have appeared in *Poetry* magazine, *The Lambda Literary Review,* and *The Missouri Review,* among others. Originally from Albuquerque, New Mexico, she now lives in California. *Whoever You Are, Honey* is her first novel.

oliviagatwood.com
Instagram: @oliviagatwood

ABOUT THE TYPE

This book was set in Aurelia, a typeface designed by Hermann Zapf in 1985 based on the forms of Jenson, an Old Style typeface developed by Nicolas Jenson in 1470 that still influences type design today. Zapf gave Aurelia a bit of his own personal style and adapted it to the demands of modern technology. Aurelia is a robust and classic font, suitable for both text and headlines. The family of typefaces was originally designed for use with the typesetting machines produced by the German company Dr.-Ing Rudolf Hell GmbH. The name Aurelia is a nod to the Roman emperor Aurelianus (214–275), who built the Via Aurelia in Italy.

*The Dial Press, an imprint of Random House,
publishes books driven by the heart.*

Follow us on Instagram:
@THEDIALPRESS

Discover other Dial Press books and sign up for our e-newsletter:

thedialpress.com